H
LA

KERRY WATTS

HEARTLANDS

Bookouture

Published by Bookouture in 2019

An imprint of StoryFire Ltd.

Carmelite House
50 Victoria Embankment
London EC4Y 0DZ

www.bookouture.com

ISBN: 978-1-78681-792-1
eBook ISBN: 978-1-78681-791-4

This book is dedicated to my wonderful mum and dad, Allan and Catherine Melloy.

Dad, because I know you are proud and support me every step of the way. Mum, because I wish you were here to share my success. Miss you. Thank you both. X

14 AUGUST 1681

'I curse you all to hell and all of those you hold dear,' Morag McIvor spat as the vibrant orange flames crackled and licked around her ankles. 'Mark my words, from this day forward a blight will rain down on you and yours with the fury of Satan himself. My death will be avenged. Maybe not today. Maybe not tomorrow, but one day soon you will all, each and every one of you, rue this day.'

PROLOGUE

1996

Jack MacKay was genuinely surprised by the amount of blood and, if he was honest, this discovery wasn't unwelcome. He had punched her once, and only then to stop her screaming. The noise invaded his brain and he couldn't think. Her cries affected him in a way he hadn't anticipated. It wasn't like this in his imagination. He hadn't factored in Sophie's feelings. He had to stop the noise so he could focus on what to do next. He had lost control and needed to get it back.

His best mate, Dan, had been easy to persuade. Boredom made him a willing partner in crime. The fantasy had burned inside Jack for months, and Sophie was perfect. It was an open secret that she'd had a major crush on him since the start of last term, twirling her hair and giggling when he spoke. Glancing away when he caught her watching, a subtle pink flush rising on her cheeks.

He had envisioned what doing that to her would feel like. It had become an obsession that filled his every waking hour. It became like a drug he craved. If he hadn't done this, he feared his brain might have exploded. Everywhere Jack looked he could see himself with her, forcing her, hurting her. It was exhilarating and holding Sophie's lifeless body was just as thrilling as it was in his dream; all those nights alone with his fantasies. Images of the women on screen filled his mind until he had to see for himself, feel the pleasure for himself.

*

Daniel Simpson couldn't speak. His words remained in a jumbled mess inside his throat. His DNA would be all over her body. He was only fifteen, he couldn't go to jail.

Something about Jack's reaction scared him. His friend seemed happy with what they had done to Sophie; excited by it, even. Apart from the blood trickling from her nose, she looked like she was just sleeping.

Daniel shuffled back from her body and dropped his head into his hands. His heart thundered in his chest and threatened to burst free from his ribcage. A rush of nausea gripped him.

'Come on, help me get her up.' Jack's words tore into the silence.

Daniel stared blankly as his shoulders rose and his gut tightened until Jack loomed over him, his eyes menacing. Fear of what he might do to him snapped Daniel sharply back into focus. Jack squeezed his shoulder.

'Come on.' He paused. 'Wait a minute.'

Jack jogged to the back of the cattle shed and yanked a feed bag from inside an abandoned food storage container. Mr Forbes wasn't the tidiest of farmers, and for that Jack was grateful. It appeared that all those hours hidden there smoking and drinking meant he knew the layout of the shed perfectly. If Robbie Forbes knew the boys hung out there, he didn't let on. Perhaps it reminded him of his own misspent youth. A feed bag would be more than big enough for Sophie's small frame. He laid it flat next to Sophie's body.

'Grab her legs,' he hissed.

His voice was now unfamiliar to Daniel. Jack had morphed into someone Daniel didn't know at all as they shifted Sophie outside.

'Start digging. We can be out of here before anyone realises she's missing, if we hurry.'

Daniel was on autopilot. Sophie's long blonde hair wasn't completely covered by the tarpaulin and when the soil hit it, it caused his stomach to lurch. He turned his head to vomit, forcing his lunch onto the ground at speed. Jack laughed. Daniel dropped to his knees and sobbed. The kind of tears that your body ejects uncontrollably, ripping your gut apart with the pain. He struggled to control the trembling that had started in his legs then travelled up his body, and now even his fingers shook.

'Get up, I can't do this on my own!' Jack spat through gritted teeth, fearful of discovery. It wouldn't be long before Mr Forbes would be back. 'Look, nothing is going to bring her back. It was an accident. I'm sorry, OK? I just lost it. I snapped. I didn't plan any of this. Please, mate, help me out here.'

Jack's coldness stunned Daniel out of his stupor.

'What's done is fucking done? Is that all you can say?'

Daniel leapt to his feet and pushed Jack to the ground with force, adrenalin providing his strength. He drew his hand back to punch him, only to see Jack laugh again. Daniel shoved him away in disgust. He sniffed and rubbed his eyes, then picked up his spade to fill Sophie's grave. Jack was right. What's done is done and, if they wanted to avoid getting caught, she had to be buried properly. He was as guilty as Jack. He knew Sophie didn't want to have sex with either of them but, with Jack's encouragement, he got carried away. Kidnap and rape was bad enough, but now she was dead. Nothing would ever be the same again.

Daniel stared down at the patch of disturbed earth while Jack checked the shed for signs they had all been there. Everything had changed irreversibly. Daniel's childhood was over. Part of him wished he was buried in the ground with Sophie.

The loud hum of a motorbike drifted towards them.

'Shit!' Jack grabbed at Daniel's arm. 'Come on. Let's get the fuck out of here.'

Daniel snatched his arm back and ran after him. The teenagers moved quickly through the trees without looking back, away from Sophie's shallow grave. The gentle breeze blew the loose soil across the top of the disturbed earth and the sun peeked out from behind the trees in stark contrast to the dark, threatening clouds in the distance.

CHAPTER ONE

Present day

Jessie Blake wiped the sweat from her face and throat, then tossed away the damp pillowcase. She'd been wrong to assume tonight might be different to any other night of the past four years. At least she was waking up from these nightmares.

'Smokey, what a fright you gave me!' she chastised her Russian blue as he leapt onto the bed. A gift from her ex-husband Dan, he had been in her life through it all; the highs and the lows. People often call the Russian blue the archangel cat, and an angel he certainly was.

Jessie peeled off her pyjama top and flung it towards the laundry hamper. It might be put inside in the morning, it might not. Jessie still revelled in these little decisions. Her bedroom had never been in such chaos since she was a teenager, and for that Jessie was grateful. She downed a glass of water. Maybe she would give her counsellor a call, she pondered.

The roar of her upstairs neighbour's motorbike revving made Jessie jump again and Smokey arched his back before expelling a long, loud hiss; the kind that meant business. She hated that bike. She hated all motorbikes. The way they smelt. The way they sounded. Jessie particularly hated the sound of an approaching motorbike, then it stopping. But that wasn't Dave her neighbour's fault. Dave was a lovely guy, and had always been friendly and generous. When Smokey disappeared for three days after Jessie first moved into the flat, Dave was there for her.

She wandered barefoot across the bedroom floor and glanced out of the window at the driving rain that battered the ground outside, wishing she had brought her little bit of washing in from the line before she had settled down for the evening. That chilled glass of Chardonnay had called her name louder. It had been such a long day yesterday and, despite having spotted the dark, threatening clouds on her short drive home from the station at eight o'clock, she couldn't be bothered with going back into the driving rain to fetch it.

The distraction of the text hadn't helped. She knew Carol meant well, but it came as a gut-punching shock all the same. It had been so long since she'd heard from Carol that she was excited to see her name. Carol was her best friend throughout the darkness of her time in London. She had been there when Jessie was at her lowest. That excitement soon evaporated. It wasn't like Jessie didn't know it would happen one day, but still, she wasn't prepared. She would call when she was ready, but not yet. Smokey curled his slender body around Jessie's legs and purred as she refilled her glass and guzzled the refreshing chilled water from the fridge. She wiped the drips from her mouth, then lifted him into her arms and snuggled her face next to his.

'It's not breakfast time yet, you silly wee man.' She tried not to release the tears that were slowly building. Sometimes the memories crept up on her when she least expected. As if he could sense her feelings, Smokey licked Jessie's ears the way he had done so many times before, purring softly with every pause. The warm, bristly sensation grounded Jessie. She was safe, and Smokey wanted her to remember that.

Jessie headed back to her room with Smokey snuggled in her arms and rested her head on the pillow, then glanced at her alarm clock, which read 3.15. She sighed, knowing she wouldn't get back to sleep. She reached for her phone and tapped on the Twitter app. It was surprising how many friends she had that would also be awake at this time. That was the thing about social media. You could make friends with people from all over the world. People who didn't know you or your secret. People who wouldn't judge you on your past. They only knew Jessie Blake in the now.

There was another text from Carol, but Jessie couldn't bring herself to read it. She already knew what it would say, and she wasn't prepared to think about that right now.

CHAPTER TWO

Rob Taylor held his new wife close. Their bodies swayed to the gentle rhythm of the band in the garden of the exclusive Atholl Lodge Hotel. Ben Lochty was the stunning backdrop to their special day. Its imposing snow-topped peak was the goal of many of the tourists who flocked to the area every year. Wildlife tourism was big business here; the attractions ranged from the elusive pine marten to the growing population of beavers. The sun peered out from behind the thick cloud as if in acknowledgement of their big day. As if Mother Nature gave her blessing to the union.

Rob and Cassie's guests were seated exactly as Cassie planned. The dozen white doves were released on schedule and flew in formation the way Hector, their wedding planner, promised. Cassie and Hector had been thick as thieves for months, and Rob wondered sometimes if he was even invited to this wedding. Rob didn't have much by way of family, but he was fine with whoever Cassie wanted to share their big day. He'd helped her that rainy day after her carrier bag split, spewing its contents all over the pavement, her oranges rolling away at speed. She called him her knight in shining armour when he jogged over to help, and insisted on taking him for coffee as a thank you when she realised that he was Rob Taylor her favourite science fiction author. Rob found her funny and smart. She was the breath of fresh air that blew into his serious existence.

'I love you,' Rob whispered as Cassie's parents joined them on the dance floor.

Cassie shut her eyes and smiled contentedly. Yes, this was exactly what she had imagined. She reached her hand down and stroked her stomach. Rob was not only going to be the perfect husband, but also a wonderful father to their baby. A baby arriving so early in their marriage wasn't planned, but Cassie knew it was right. He was kind and gentle, strong and protective. The kind of husband she had always wanted. Her soft blue eyes drifted up to meet his. That smile of his did things to her that no man had ever come close to before. When Rob's eyes fixed on her, she felt like the only other person in the world. He pressed his lips against hers and the longing that only his touch created enveloped her.

'This is the happiest day of my life,' Cassie whispered as she nestled her face into Rob's muscular chest.

Louise Ross glanced over at the happy couple and caught Rob's eye. When he realised she was looking at him, he offered a half-smile and turned away. She mustn't look.

Louise had thought she was prepared for today, and she had been fine until that moment. She couldn't take her eyes off Rob as he twirled Cassie before pulling her close again. They looked so happy. Jason's kiss woke Louise from her trance.

'Do you remember our first dance?' he asked.

Louise smiled. 'Of course, but we had Dougie's disco, not a six-piece country band in the grounds of a five star hotel, for ours.'

Jason's laugh comforted her. Everything about Jason was comfortable. He worked hard for his family, and she and Shannon wanted for nothing. He had supported her through the two miscarriages, just as Cassie had, that had broken her heart. Cassie was her best friend. Rob was Jason's best mate. Of course Louise wished them all the happiness in the world.

Jason took Louise's hand and invited her to dance with him, which made her smile. He had made a huge effort for Rob and

Cassie's wedding; he'd even had his hair cut. He did look handsome in his suit. Jason was the only man Louise had ever been with when they married at twenty. She had followed him to Germany with the army and waited anxiously when his regiment was deployed to Iraq. It wasn't long after their wedding that Shannon arrived to complete the family. Louise glanced past Jason's shoulder. Rob's eyes met hers. This time, she turned away.

Shannon shuddered at the sight of her parents' public display of affection. Jason had promised her he wouldn't embarrass her by dancing today. Surely they were too old for that shit now. Shannon offered Rob a brief smile, then blushed and turned away. Eric grinned at her reaction.

'What?' She frowned. 'What are you staring at?'

'Put your tongue back in.' Eric laughed. 'Mind you, Rob does fit that suit well, doesn't he?'

Eric Baldwin had been Shannon's best friend since nursery. He loved the same things as Shannon even then, and as their nursery had a huge dressing-up box, they never had to argue over the princess dresses – or the dolls, for that matter. Shannon and Eric were forward-thinking in that in their game the children always had two mummies. Mummies who wore pretty dresses and had great big handbags. Eric could be himself with Shannon. Admitting he was gay to her was easier than admitting it to himself. Shannon had hugged him and that had been enough. He understood exactly why Shannon's cheeks flushed the way they did when she looked at Rob Taylor.

Shannon watched her mum's expression when she glanced over at Rob dancing with Cassie. Louise struggled to take her eyes off him and Shannon didn't like that. She didn't like that one bit.

'Come on, let's hit the dance floor.' Eric dragged Shannon by the arm. 'This is a party, let's show these oldies how it's done!'

Shannon couldn't help but laugh as the tempo increased and Eric waved his hands high with his hips swinging in time to the music. Rob grinned at him, then glanced at Shannon, who blushed and smiled awkwardly then grabbed Eric's hand.

CHAPTER THREE

Eric stared unashamedly at his drama teacher. *The* Calum Bailey, from the now off-air television series he'd enjoyed when he was ten. A child actor, Calum Bailey had become disheartened by the business and retrained as a teacher, which was what he had wanted to do as a boy. So here he was, Head of Drama at Inverlochty High. Although being head of a two-man drama department wasn't exactly his ambition, it was less hectic than his previous life. He loved the enthusiasm of the teenagers; well, most of them, but this class had two particularly keen members, and he liked that.

'Take a script and pass them back. This is a short piece I wrote myself when I was at drama school…'

The short eruption of sniggers made Calum smile. He would have done the same thing when he was at school. Eric caught his gaze and he was sure he saw his teacher blush.

'Yes, yes, very funny. Shannon, are you OK with your part?' Calum Bailey asked.

'Of course, I like a challenge,' she replied.

'Good girl, I knew I could rely on you.' Calum Bailey winked as he grinned.

This time it was Shannon's turn to blush.

'That's a rare heat you've got glowing there,' Eric teased with his hands close to her cheeks.

Shannon frowned and stuffed her script and pens into her bag.

'Shut up,' she muttered under her breath. 'Listen, I'll catch you up.'

Eric laughed and stole a glance in Calum Bailey's direction, then blinked flirtatiously and looked away. He hated himself for it, but he knew exactly which one of them would win Mr Bailey's heart. Eric waited in the corridor while Shannon talked to Calum.

'Shannon, I really don't think I can,' Calum Bailey whispered, and glanced towards the classroom door. 'This isn't a good idea. We could both get into trouble, you know that.'

Shannon moved closer and whispered something in his ear. Calum stepped back and rubbed his hands up and down his cheeks.

'Just think about what I said,' she told him before turning to walk out.

Eric quickly removed his ear from the door where he was straining to hear what was being said.

'Come on, let's get out of here.' Shannon grinned.

'What was all that about?' Eric asked, unnerved by Shannon's behaviour.

Shannon shrugged, then linked her arm with his. 'It's nothing, don't worry about it.'

'Do you fancy going to the cafe before you head home?' Eric asked, when it was clear Shannon's secret would remain just that. He would have to find out another way.

Shannon hugged her folder close to her chest with her lips pursed.

'I'm buying,' Eric added playfully, tapping his back pocket.

'Go on then. You've twisted my arm.'

Shannon did really fancy a strawberry thick shake before going home to face her German essay. It was easy for Eric. Having a German mum was surely cheating, and she was knackered. She hadn't told Eric about the project she was working on which was keeping her up late, but when she'd stumbled on the information she had to see where it might lead.

'Shit, look.' Eric pointed. 'Ben and his crew of merry dickheads are getting their kicks as usual.'

'Hold that.' Shannon's folder slammed into Eric's chest and her bag drooped from her shoulder before dropping to the ground at his feet.

'Shannon, don't get involved!' Eric shouted after her, knowing his words were futile. He sighed and rolled his eyes.

'Ben, cut it out!' Shannon boomed as she jogged over to them. 'Give him back his keys.'

'Or what? What are you going to do?' Ben growled.

Shannon twisted her head back to Eric. 'I'll catch you up. Get me a thick shake.'

Andrew Foster sat perched on his front step covering his ears with his hands. 'It's too loud. Stop it. It's too loud.'

Eric knew better than to argue the point. Shannon had a soft spot for Andrew Foster, and Ben bullying him irked her. Andrew had been Louise's best friend when they were both young. Since the death of Andrew's mum, Shannon did what she could to support him. Eric watched the argument between Shannon and Ben play out. It was hard to believe the two of them were related; they were so different. It was also hard to believe he was actually Shannon's uncle, with the two-year age gap.

'Are you happy now, Ben?' Shannon's five foot two frame was dwarfed by Ben at a whisker shy of six foot. What Shannon lacked in stature, though, she more than made up for in determination. 'Just give me the damn keys and I won't have to tell Mum you've been bunking off and drinking again.'

Ben Randall was the complete opposite of his younger niece. Where Shannon was kind, friendly and generous, Ben was sullen, bitter and angry. Louise made allowances for her baby brother all the time, and explained away his behaviour as a reaction to his troubled past. Clashes with a variety of unsuitable stepfathers had turned the cute blue-eyed boy into an angry young man. When Jason explained to Shannon that Louise hadn't had the best of starts either, she shrugged and walked away.

'Come and get them, short-arse.' Ben dangled Andrew Foster's house keys in front of her, snatching them back at the last minute before she had a chance to grab them, much to the amusement of his friends. Shannon shot them a steely glare. Anger rose in her belly as she smashed her shoulder into Ben's chest, grabbing the keys from him before he fell to the ground at her feet.

'Come on.' Shannon placed her hand on Andrew's shoulder and smiled. 'I'll make us a cup of tea.' She threw one last angry glare in Ben's direction before heading inside with Andrew.

Ben Randall's pride wasn't the only part of him that Shannon hurt when he landed on the ground. She would regret making a fool of him.

CHAPTER FOUR

'I cannae believe this is book five already.' Maggie Malcolm held her copy of Rob's new book close to her face and patted the cover. 'And I cannae wait to find out what happens. Please dinnae tell me you've killed anyone in this one.'

Rob's laughter was genuine. He was fond of Maggie. She had served behind the bar of The Black Witch the whole time he had lived in Inverlochty. Maggie loved telling Rob the legend of old Morag McIvor. She even suggested Morag make an appearance in one of Rob's books. Maggie had explained that if he was ever to venture alone into the wood, he should remember always to nod a greeting to Morag. Show her respect, so she didn't curse you and yours. Something Rob never forgot. Not that he was superstitious. It was just such a quaint story. Maggie was always first in the queue to have her book signed. He supposed, in some ways, that she was motherly in the way she spoke to him. Rob liked that. That was something he missed.

'I don't want to spoil the surprise, but be sure to leave a review as always,' he teased.

Rob still had to pinch himself some days. Signing his name on book five was just as exciting as it had been on book one of the series, which had begun as a simple thought that had evolved into an idea then a plan and eventually into a bestseller. He hoped Fantasy had saved other people from reality the way it had him.

'Can I get a picture?'

'No!' Rob immediately put his hand up in front of her phone. 'No photos.' He offered an awkward smile when it was obvious his outburst had startled her. 'I'm sorry.'

'Thanks, honey.' He sipped, then licked the froth from his top lip.

Rob was gasping for his coffee. Talking to people, even if they were all locals, was exhausting. Groups of more than four people dragged Rob out of his comfort zone.

Cassie's arm draped round the back of Rob's shoulders and she dropped a soft kiss on his head. 'Maggie said she would be here.'

He grinned. 'Of course. Bless her. My superfan.' Rob sank the last of his coffee to the scraping of chair legs on wooden floor.

'Thanks, Bill,' he shouted through to the back of the post office-come-general store-come library. His publisher had persuaded him to do book signings at the larger book stores in Glasgow and Edinburgh, but Rob hated them. Inverlochty was where he was comfortable. The quietness of the place helped him relax His years in his Glasgow flat within earshot of Buchanan Street railway station had created a yearning for peace; solitude even, some days.

'Are you ready for home?' Cassie's hand dropped easily into his. 'We can pick up fish and chips on the way.'

'That's sounds perfect.' Rob kissed her hand and smiled in agreement. He liked the sound of that.

The feel of Rob's hand in hers made Cassie feel safe, protected.

'Whoa, watch where you're going!' Rob yanked Cassie back from someone thundering past; head down, hood tucked tightly over his head. Ben Randall. He did mutter something inaudible which might have been sorry, Rob wasn't sure.

Cassie's eyes narrowed. 'Ben Randall has one mood these days, and it's not pretty. I wouldn't be a teenager again if you paid me. Poor Louise, he's doing her head in with his nonsense. She's had the school on the phone twice this week about his attendance.

If he's not careful he's going to end up getting chucked out, and then what's he going to do with himself? There are no jobs here, unless there's something going at the hotel or with Maggie in The Black Witch.'

Rob wrapped his arms round her and pulled her close to kiss her lips.

'That's me away to make a start on this.' Maggie Malcolm's words startled the couple. She held aloft her copy of Rob's book and shuffled past.

'Goodnight, Maggie,' Cassie shouted after her and cuddled close to Rob.

In the half-light they saw Ben sat alone on the bench at the gates of the ancient Inverlochty churchyard that was a common shortcut through to Back Street or the Dark Walk, as it was known for as long as anyone could remember. Some said it was connected to a time when the witches were burned in the town. Not that it was actually dark these days, with the lights of the adjacent houses glowing along its length. Before they could catch up to him, Cassie's phone buzzed in her pocket.

'Hang on.' Cassie's phone lit up while she scrolled. 'That's weird.' She frowned.

'What's up?'

'Louise has cancelled tomorrow night. We were going to have a girls' night. Just the two of us. I thought maybe she wanted to talk about something.'

'Again?' Rob raised an eyebrow.

'Yes, that's the third time she's cancelled on me. Is everything OK with her and Jason?'

Rob shrugged. 'I think so, but I can ask him.'

'Would you?' Cassie suddenly clasped her hand to her mouth. 'It's not the baby, is it?'

A small tear gathered at the corner of her eye.

'Honey, no, they're both happy for us.' Rob hugged her.

'I know, but...' She sniffed. 'After the miscarriages, maybe she resents me.'

Rob's hands moved to Cassie's cheeks and he bent to press his lips against hers.

'Of course she doesn't resent you. She's your best friend. I'll talk to Jason,' he whispered.

Cassie's smile was evidence that she was satisfied with his answer for now.

Shannon knocked once, then slowly pushed the door open with one finger.

'Andrew, it's just me.'

Shannon closed the front door behind her and covered her nose with her hand against the smell of stale food. The kind of smell that builds in a poorly ventilated house and sticks to curtains and carpets. She walked through the hallway to the kitchen, past newspapers piled high on either side. A delusion based on messages written in newsprint made it difficult for Andrew to throw papers away. He had to be alert for the signs, he said. The stench of dust stuck in her throat and she coughed. Then the sight that greeted Shannon froze her to the spot.

'Andrew, what have you done?'

Her bag slid through her fingers and onto the floor.

'Andrew?'

CHAPTER FIVE

1996

Journalist Blair Crawford considered himself to be a strong man, but the sight of Laura and Ray Nicoll sat in that courtroom, day after day, nearly broke his heart. It was bad enough for him to hear the details of Sophie's murder, but the agony her parents faced must have been horrific. The boys were not in court to hear the evidence, and their plea of not guilty to murder divided the country. There were those who described Daniel Simpson as a victim, incapable of understanding the enormity of what he had done. Both boys were described as vulnerable to the influence of violent movies and the widespread availability of extreme pornography. Jack MacKay was a spoilt brat who should know right from wrong. The other side wanted them locked away for life without the chance of parole – and they were the more liberal. Bringing back the death penalty became a hot topic of conversation, and for a lot of people it didn't matter that they were juveniles. Death should be punishable by death.

Seventeen-year-old Tom Nicoll was struggling to come to terms with his loss. The constant nightmares were making schoolwork impossible. The woman from Victim Support tried her best, but Tom wasn't ready to say it yet. He had not yet uttered the words 'Sophie is dead'. If he didn't say it, then it couldn't be true. He couldn't accept that his little sister was gone, particularly in such a brutal way. The fact that he knew her killers was torture. He had spoken to them in the school cafeteria. He had sat close to them on the bus. He knew Daniel well from football. Tom was struggling to make sense of it all. It was impossible to comprehend why they would do that to her. Jack had a reputation as a bit of a troublemaker, sure, but murder?

Judge James Blackman took his seat for the last time and stared into Laura Nicoll's eyes as he sat. The overwhelming evidence made a guilty verdict inevitable. A plea of manslaughter on the grounds of diminished responsibility was not accepted. Semen belonging to both boys was found on Sophie's body and skin cells from Jack MacKay were scraped from under her fingernails. Daniel Simpson's version of the events of that day were very different to Jack's. Jack claimed that Sophie was the one who had instigated the sexual encounter, and that she had a reputation as being sexually promiscuous. As expected, his accusation caused uproar from Sophie's family and friends, who were forced to defend her honour.

Jack sparked outrage when he suggested that Sophie was responsible for his actions and that her advances drove him over the edge. Daniel, on the other hand, broke down under police questioning when they were arrested and told how they had raped and murdered Sophie. He sobbed that he was sorry, and Judge Blackman truly believed the teenager, but was bound by law to punish him. Their being juveniles limited the judge's sentencing options. When the sentence of five years was handed down it sparked a frenzy countrywide. Ian and Susan MacKay had to flee their home in the middle of the night after a petrol bomb was thrown through their kitchen window. Death threats were issued against Daniel and Jack daily.

Blair Crawford peered in through the filthy window at the chaotic mess inside the living room. He was surprised that she'd agreed to talk to him. The press had been scathing about her during the trial. Rita Simpson was portrayed as a drug-addicted, alcoholic single mother who neglected Daniel from a young age. Abuse at the hands of a variety of boyfriends was also alleged. A figure sprawled over a chair in the far corner caught Blair's attention.

'Shit!' He hammered his fist on the front door, flecks of paint chipping off and falling to the ground. 'Rita Simpson, it's Blair Crawford, open the door.'

He grabbed the door handle and dialled 999, but it was too late. The needle was still in Rita Simpson's arm as she slipped away; escaping, in the eyes of the world, her responsibilities again. Her neglect had created the monster that stole Sophie's future.

'Are you a relative?' PC Alex Duncan asked when he arrived at the scene.

Blair Crawford was appalled at the prospect that he thought he was related to her. He reached into his jacket pocket and thrust his business card at the officer. Alex Duncan raised his eyebrows.

'You lot can go now. There's nothing left for you here.' Alex pointed his finger at Blair. 'The stuff you lot wrote about little Sophie was disgusting. You should be ashamed of yourselves. Go on, get away from here before I find a reason to arrest you.'

Blair Crawford didn't quit that easily.

'It wasn't my newspaper that did that. I agree with you, it was awful. My editor refused to stoop that low. Listen, if Mr and Mrs Nicoll want to talk about Sophie then I will be more than happy to write her story. Sophie's story.'

Blair directed his words directly into Alex's eyes, with his card tucked into his outstretched hand. He didn't have to wait long for the officer's response.

'OK, I'm going.' He yanked his arm back from the officer's grip. 'At least give them my card. Give them a chance to think about it.'

The fact that PC Duncan stuffed Blair's card into his pocket gave him a glimmer of hope that he might scoop an exclusive after all.

CHAPTER SIX

'You put your money away, Rob Taylor. This one's on me,' Maggie Malcolm insisted as she placed the two pints on the bar. Jason gulped almost half of his down before Rob had a chance to thank her. He frowned at Jason.

'Thanks, Maggie.' Rob winked and nodded, then stuffed the ten-pound note back into his pocket.

Maggie wiped her cloth across the bar top and tutted in Jason's direction.

'What? I'm thirsty!' He laughed.

Rob shook his head and smiled. 'Get him another, Maggie.'

'Aye, well, this ain't free, Jason Ross, so get yer hand in yer pocket.'

Maggie winked at Rob's grinning face.

'Spoilsport,' Jason teased, and sank the last of his first pint, then belched loudly.

Rob grimaced and wondered, as he often did, what Louise saw in him.

'Is Louise OK?' Rob sipped at his pint. 'She's cancelled on Cassie again and that's the third time now.'

'She's fine. I don't know why she cancelled.' He hesitated. 'Actually, she didn't go to that book club of hers either this week. Don't know why she bothers with that. She never reads the damn things anyway.' Jason frowned, then returned to his pint. 'So, how's the missus? Still enjoying the honeymoon period, I bet.' He winked.

Jason was Rob's best friend. He was like a brother to him, but sometimes he could be so crass.

'Yes, everything is good. I've never been happier.' Rob looked away then and down at his shoes when he spoke. 'Cassie's getting her bag ready for the hospital.'

'What? She won't need that for a while.'

'You know Cass, she likes to be organised.'

Rob raised his glass and caught Maggie's eye. 'Same again.'

Jason smirked. 'Well, she's in for a bloody big shock when the wee one gets here.' He nudged Rob's arm. 'Lots of things change when a bairn comes along, I can assure you. Enjoy each other now because, when that bairn's here—'

'All right, mate, I get the picture.' Rob dropped his change into his pocket. 'What's new with you, anyway?'

'You see it all, buddy; work, sleep, repeat. That's me at the minute.' Jason caught Maggie's attention. 'I'll take a whisky chaser when you're ready.'

Rob sank the last of his pint. 'Bugger it, mate. I'll have one an' all.'

'Good lad!' Jason gripped Rob's shoulder and shook it.

Both men lifted their whisky glasses high.

'Sláinte!' Jason announced for them both before they sank their nips in one.

'Argh.' Rob screwed up his face and gave a shiver. 'Yes! Hit me again, Maggie.'

Jason beamed and his hand reached for Rob's shoulder again before squeezing it hard.

'Won't Cassie be sending out the search party for you?'

Rob glanced at his watch. Another pint wouldn't make much difference. She would probably be fast asleep now, anyway.

'Are you still celebrating the book launch then?' Maggie laid another two nips on the bar.

'Of course he is.' Jason reached for a ten-pound note and slammed it down.

'Does that mean you've read books one to four then, Jason Ross?' Maggie pursed her lips and winked at Rob again.

Rob punched Jason's arm lightly. 'Ha! Roasted, buddy!'

Maggie threw Jason a narrow-eyed glare and scooped up their empty glasses.

'She totally fancies you.'

'Shut up. She's old enough to be my mum.'

Rob Taylor was handsome. He was aware of the attention he attracted, but avoided it whenever he could. Being a muscular six foot three made staying in the shadows hard for anyone, but when you factored in the huge, piercing hazel eyes and blond hair, Rob Taylor stood out from the crowd. Jason wasn't exactly short on admirers either. At six foot one, with the blackest hair to accompany his hypnotic, dark green eyes, Jason could certainly give Rob a run for his money in a beauty contest.

'Seriously though, mate, well-bloody-done. I don't know what you're still doing in Inverlochty. Surely you can afford somewhere better after five books.'

'I think you're overestimating my success a bit.'

Although Rob could easily afford to move, he wanted to stay where everything was familiar, and that place was right there in Inverlochty.

Jason stood up quickly from his stool. 'Louise?'

Rob turned to see Louise approach the bar with worry etched on her face.

'Hey, babes, what's up?'

Louise allowed her eyes to meet Rob's, but only briefly.

'Have either of you seen Shannon?'

It was obvious from her face that she was worried. Jason took her hands in his.

'Have you tried Eric?' he asked.

Louise snatched her hands back. 'Of course I've tried Eric. He hasn't seen her since this afternoon. She was supposed to meet him for a shake, but she didn't turn up.'

'Is she not at your—'

'No, if she was at my mum's I wouldn't be here now, would I?'

Rob pushed his pint glass away. 'Come on, Jason. We'll check the park. You go home, Lou. Just in case she's there.'

Louise avoided Rob's gaze as she bit her bottom lip.

'Call me as soon as you find her. It's ten o'clock. She's usually home by now.'

A loud commotion drew them outside.

'Andrew,' Louise shrieked and raced forward towards the stumbling figure coming towards her. 'Someone call an ambulance!'

She tied her cardigan around his wrists to stem the flow of blood that was dripping from his arms and puddling on the ground at his feet.

'Hurry!' she screamed at Jason, just as Andrew collapsed. Before slipping into unconsciousness, Andrew whispered something inaudible in Louise's ear.

'Ssh, it's OK, Andrew. Hang in there, help's coming.'

CHAPTER SEVEN

1996

'Sit down, Daniel.' Social worker Camilla Walsh hung her cardigan over the back of her chair.

'I'm fine standing,' he answered without turning round.

Daniel Simpson enjoyed the view from that window. Before ending up in Carseview young offenders' unit, Daniel hadn't spent much time in the countryside. He did recall one holiday with his mum and one of her boyfriends when he was ten, although most aspects of that week were best forgotten. He remembered the smell. Daniel never forgot the smell from the nearby farm close to their rental cottage. When the window was open in the dining room at Carseview that exact same smell wafted inside, and Daniel liked it. It was bizarrely hypnotic and comforting; uplifting even.

'I'd really like you to come and sit down.' Cam shook her head at the officer who moved forward to force Daniel into a seat. 'Daniel, I have something I need to tell you.'

Cam moved across to join him at the window. At five foot two she was dwarfed by the teenager, who stood almost a foot taller than her. She gently rested her hand on his arm.

'Daniel, sweetheart, I have some bad news.'

'Do you suppose he slaughters the lambs himself?' Daniel scratched his chin and remained fixed on the field. 'You know, gets really hands-on from start to finish?'

Cam raised her eyebrows at his question.

'Your mum has died, Daniel.' She had no choice. He had to be told.

Daniel's eyes shifted for the first time. They drifted as far as the clock above the serving hatch. 'It's curry day. I fucking love curry day.'

Cam drew her hand to her face before she sighed and patted his arm. 'I'll come back tomorrow.' She gathered her cardigan again and left the dining room after nodding to the officer.

Daniel's heart raced, and he struggled for breath. He screwed his eyes tight shut and concentrated on his breathing; in and out, in and out until he regained control. He craved control. Without control, he couldn't cope. He had to find a way out. He always needed an exit. He took one last look at the farm, then turned to the officer.

'Can I go back to my room now?'

Daniel followed him out of the dining room into the hallway and sniffed. He was shocked by the feelings that were building, washing through him. He recognised the irony of the years he'd wished her dead, but the reality didn't feel anything like the way he thought it would when the day finally arrived, which could have been any time in the past fifteen years, given Rita Simpson's lifestyle. There were days she disgusted him so much he could have choked the pathetic life out of her himself, and others when she gave him a glimpse of the love a mother should always show her children. The unconditional self-sacrifice they deserve.

Daniel envied Jack. It angered him, the way he spoke about his mother. She nagged him non-stop, Jack told him; trying to control every aspect of his life, especially when his dad was away on the rigs. Jack became even more reckless during those weeks. *Perhaps if he hadn't been away*, Daniel pondered.

CHAPTER EIGHT

'His name is Andrew Foster.' Louise stood back, biting at her nails. 'He suffers from schizophrenia. Has done, for years.'

A handful of curious tourists stopped to stare before shuffling on, maps in hand.

'Thanks.' Paramedic Dougal MacLeod knelt close to Andrew. 'Andrew, my name's Dougal. Can you hear me, buddy?' He leaned his ear close to Andrew's face. 'He's breathing, let's get him to the ambulance. Well done, you probably saved his life.'

Andrew Foster had been in Louise's class at primary school. She remembered him as a dreamer with a huge talent for art and writing. He was writing poetry at ten while the other boys were still playing tag. It was Andrew who introduced Louise to watercolours. Sitting under the trees on the riverbank, sketching the finger-like branches dangling down to the water's edge with a pad of paper had once been where she wanted to be. Listening, with her eyes closed, to the rush of the current pouring past the two of them.

Louise loved the river. She was in awe of her raw power. The power to choose, it seemed. Some days the water would meander and twist gently through town, barely noticeable as the rest of the world carried on its business. But there were days her presence was undeniable as she thrashed and hugged the riverbank on her race towards the sea at Dundee. The tropical scent of coconut drifting from the broom on the hillside was another memory Louise loved. Long days chilling in the breeze with Andrew, blethering about everything and nothing, watching peacock butterflies busy themselves with the task of gathering nectar.

She loved going to Andrew's for tea, too. In a lot of ways Louise recognised her friendship with Andrew in Shannon and Eric. She kept the sketch Andrew did of her. One of the many he drew of her. It wasn't something Louise felt she could part with, even if it was a source of argument early in her relationship with Jason. Louise regretted losing touch with Andrew at secondary school, but her life moved on. As far as she knew, he had been accepted into Glasgow School of Art and it was there that schizophrenia first gripped him. Mary Foster did everything in her power to support her son until her death a year ago. Community psychiatric services in rural areas are under such pressure, and the shortage of acute care beds was a disaster waiting to happen for Andrew.

Louise grabbed her phone. 'Hello, Mum, no, she's not back yet. I'll call you when she gets home.'

Rob glanced at the stress painted on her face. 'You go home. Me and Jason will head out and see if she's at the park. We saw Ben heading there earlier. Shannon's probably with him.' Louise managed a small nod before ducking through the lane to go and wait for Shannon at home.

'Who's that?' Calum Bailey handed his guest a glass of wine then licked a dribble off his thumb.

'Thanks.' Eric took the glass and slid his phone onto the coffee table. 'It's nothing, don't worry about it.'

Eric sipped slowly. Wine wasn't exactly his tipple, but he wanted to impress Calum.

'Are you sure? You looked very serious when you read that text.'

Eric didn't want anything to interrupt his night, but he was worried. It wasn't like Shannon to be out this late, especially without him. He was her usual partner in crime. The second text from her mum asking if she was with him made him very uneasy.

'It's Shannon – she's kind of missing. Well, she's not home yet, and her mum wondered if she was with me, that's all.'

'Does Shannon know about us?' Calum's fingers gently brushed Eric's shoulder from behind him.

'Of course not.' Eric's words were soft and low. 'What we've got is between us, and anyway, we haven't done anything wrong.'

Eric's comment produced the sexy grin on Calum's face that he loved. Eric wouldn't do anything to jeopardise their friendship. Coming out had been harder for Eric than he made out. Calum's support was important to him.

'Have you tried calling Shannon's number? Maybe she doesn't want to speak to her mum for some reason. She might answer if she sees it's you.'

Eric reached for his phone and dialled, shook his head. 'It's going straight to voicemail again.'

His frown told Calum there might well be something to worry about. 'Look, maybe you should go.'

Eric was disappointed, but Calum was right.

'Shannon, is that you?'

The front door clicked shut and Louise raced into the hall in the hope of her daughter's return. The sombre faces of Rob and Jason sent shivers tearing through her. Her gut tightened not to see Shannon's smiling face standing next to them. It wouldn't matter where she had been or why. The gathering darkness grew inside her. Something wasn't right.

'Tell her what you told me.' Jason pushed Ben forward.

Louise hadn't even noticed her little brother behind them.

'Shannon got pissed about me talking to that psycho freak. She went into his house with him.'

'What were you talking to Andrew about? I warned you to leave him alone!' Louise shouted. Louise despaired of her baby brother, because to her that was what he was. It didn't matter that they didn't have the same father. They were brother and sister. The huge age gap made her feel more like his mother than his big sister. Ben's father arrived on the scene long after Louise's left. She was about ready to leave home by the time Ben was born. Those few years with Ben's father had been hard on both of them. She felt responsible for him, and she was responsible now that clashing with another stepdad made living with their mother impossible for Ben.

'Whatever.' Ben stormed past, slamming his shoulder into Louise.

'Ow, you little shit!' She rubbed the ache and scowled after him.

'Do you want me to stay, mate?' Rob could see the worry etched on Jason's face, but Louise quickly answered for them both.

'No thanks, we'll be fine,' she spoke directly to Jason. 'I'm calling the police.'

Rob closed his eyes to the sound of arguing as he shut the door behind him with a sickening feeling in the pit of his stomach.

'Hey, Rob.' Eric's arrival startled him through the darkness.

'Is Shannon not with you?' he asked.

Eric shook his head.

'Probably be better to leave them.' Rob pointed to Shannon's front door. 'The police will be on their way.'

The enormity of Shannon's disappearance hit Eric like a train. He clasped his hand to his mouth.

'Jesus, I should never have left her.'

Rob wrapped his arm round the teenager's shoulder. 'It's not your fault.'

The pair walked further into the darkness fragmented only by the flecks of blue flashing lights. Rob looked back once, desperate to stay and comfort Louise, but he couldn't. It would be wrong to lie to them.

CHAPTER NINE

Detective Inspector Jessie Blake hung up her phone and shuddered. She hated missing kid cases. She felt bad about it but, nine times out of ten, her first instinct was that someone close to home was responsible. She read the text with the address and hit Dylan's number. She was irritated when it went straight to voicemail.

'Call me,' she boomed. 'Immediately.'

The thought of the hour-long drive didn't fill her with joy. Highland Perthshire was stunning at this time of year, with the leaves evolving into a glorious spectrum of autumnal colour, but she didn't look forward to driving the A9 in the dark. Coming back to Perth was the best decision Jessie Blake had made for a very long time. Still, she would have moved anywhere in the world to escape the memories. She pinned her shoulder-length black hair into a messy bun and checked her lipstick.

Her phone rang. At last.

'Where have you been?' she growled to DC Dylan Logan, then puckered her lips. She applied lipstick and chucked it and the mirror back amidst the debris at the bottom of her bag.

'Sorry, Jess, Mum had another fall. A bad one. Might be a bit more than just bruising this time. They don't know yet. My phone was in my car, sorry.'

Jessie felt guilty for booming at him now. Why did she always bark first and ask questions later? 'Is she OK?'

'What? Yes, well, not really, but she will be, I'm sure. The girls are great with Mum. I'll come now.'

'Scratch that. I'll pick you up. You still at the home?' she asked. Rivendell care home was on the way. It would be silly for Dylan to drive down, then back up and past it again.

'Aye. What's going on?'

'Missing teenager up in Inverlochty. Hasn't been seen since half three this afternoon. See you in ten minutes.'

Jessie hung up before making her way down the three flights of stairs in the old Perth police station building. Dylan teased her about her aversion to lifts, but she did it because it kept her fit – or so she told him.

'Come on,' Jessie tutted at the stop sign for the roadworks on the outskirts of Perth. 'Is there any part of this road you haven't dug up yet?'

It was as if the contractors knew her route some days and hotfooted it to dig up her path.

Dylan waved as Jessie pulled into the nursing home car park.

'Hey, boss.' He tugged at the seat belt of her Ford Fiesta. 'Inverlochty, eh? I don't think I've been up there in ten years.'

Jessie grinned. 'It probably hasn't changed much. Do you remember the wee caravan park just outside there?'

Dylan's face lit up. 'Do I remember it? I loved that place as a lad. My granny and grandad had a caravan there. I used to go there every summer and October holiday. Grandad took me fishing. Aye, good times, they were.'

Jessie laughed at his enthusiasm. Why couldn't all men be as lovely and sweet as Dylan Logan? Shelly Logan was a lucky woman to have such a great husband.

'Whoa!' Jessie slammed on her brakes to allow the driver of the oncoming Ford Escort, who appeared out of the darkness, to get past on the wrong side of the road.

'I'll call in the reg to Traffic.' Dylan grabbed his phone as Jessie exhaled sharply.

'Bloody A9!' she exclaimed. 'My damn heart's pounding now.'

That was exactly the reason Jessie hated this road at night. The long stretch of single carriageway comes quickly after a short patch of dual, leading drivers to lose concentration and overtake when they shouldn't. A dark autumn night doesn't make the situation any better.

'They're going to look out for them when they hit Perth,' Dylan told her. 'Are you OK?'

'Aye, I will be, but it's just taken twenty years off me.'

'Aye, and you're no spring chicken as it is.' Dylan boomed with laughter.

'Very funny. You're a funny guy.' Jessie mimicked his laughter, indicated and slowed before turning into the outskirts of Inverlochty, past the caravan park on the left. 'It's still there, then.' She chuckled.

Ben Lochty loomed large on the horizon as they turned onto the main street of the small Highland Perthshire town.

'That is quite something, isn't it?' Dylan pointed up at the moon shining down close to the summit.

'If you like that kind of thing,' Jessie answered, and nodded towards the police car parked outside the address she was given. 'Come on, we're here.'

PC Molly Wilde, community police officer, greeted them at the door.

'Ma'am.' She nodded to Jessie, then shot a glance in Dylan's direction and blushed. 'I'll leave you to it.'

Molly pulled the door shut behind her.

'What's the story there?' Jessie narrowed her eyes at Dylan.

Dylan raised his hands in the air and shrugged. 'No idea.'

All of Jessie's senses were heightened. Her skin bristled. Even the hairs on the back of her neck stood up. The first interaction with the parents was so important.

CHAPTER TEN

1996

Dr Julia Hudson pushed her large yellow glasses over her nose while she waited in her office. They were Jasper Conran this time; a little treat to herself, she thought. She smiled when the door opened behind her.

'Hello, Daniel, how are you today?'

Daniel walked straight to the consulting room window. 'I'm fine, thanks. How are you, Dr Hudson?' he asked, without breaking eye contact.

'I'm great, thank you for asking.'

Julia observed the growth in his physique since her last visit. He was obviously enjoying the recreational sports therapy she'd prescribed. His height had even increased by at least an inch, probably due to the decent nutrition he now had access to.

'Come and join me, will you? So we can talk.'

Daniel remained silent, his gaze fixed on the open fields on the horizon as far as the eye could see. Daniel Simpson's stare had unnerved Julia when they first met. He seemed to stare without blinking for long periods.

'When will I be able to go outside again?'

Julia considered her answer carefully. The boys in Carseview needed positive behaviour modification, but they also needed honesty.

'Not for a while yet, Daniel.'

'When, then?' His question betrayed the frustration he was feeling.

'Not yet,' she repeated gently.

Daniel cracked his knuckles loudly, then leaned right back in his chair.

'Cam Walsh tells me she gave you some bad news about your mother. How did that make you feel?'

Daniel smiled and scratched his closely cropped hair.

'She says you don't want to go to her funeral. Is that right?'

When Daniel didn't respond, Julia didn't push the point. Instead she changed the subject.

'I hear you enjoy spending time in the gym.'

Daniel nodded with enthusiasm. 'It's got some great equipment. Look at these bad boys.'

He lifted his arms to flex his growing biceps.

'I'm glad you like it.' Julia shuffled papers on the table and pushed a form across at him. 'There's an opening in the library coming up, and I thought of you. If you fancy it then fill this in and I'll sort it out for you.'

Daniel was a bright boy. Julia wanted to keep him occupied.

'OK.' He stuffed the form in his pocket. 'I'll think about it.'

A brief pause was punctuated by Daniel's unexpected question: 'Does Jack ever ask about me?'

'You know I can't discuss Jack with you.'

Daniel sighed. 'I know, I was just curious about whether he talks about me...' He hesitated. 'About what we did.'

'Do you miss Jack?'

Daniel immediately scoffed. 'Fuck off, I wasn't his boyfriend.'

'There are many kinds of love in relationships. Caring for a best friend is perfectly natural. You and Jack shared an extremely personal, intense experience. I'm not surprised you think about him.'

Daniel frowned. 'I'm not thinking about him. I just wondered, that's all.'

'Do you ever think about Sophie?'

Daniel's eyes darted left then right as he sniffed, and he shook his head. He apparently didn't dare say what he thought.

'No,' he whispered.

'Would you like to talk about Sophie?'

Daniel closed his eyes and shook his head.

'OK then, we won't. Not yet, but when you're ready, let me know.'

Daniel's eyes remained closed. 'How's Tom?'

Julia inhaled a deep breath. 'I'm not going to lie to you. I'm not going to say he forgives you, if that's what you're looking for. Losing his little sister has broken his heart.'

She didn't have to wait long for his response. His aggressive outburst wasn't a surprise. It was more of a disappointment. The complex nature of Daniel's personality meant that there would be many more setbacks to come.

Julia looked on from the small window in the dining room door. The two officers had a job on their hands bringing him under control. Daniel's mix of anger and grief was a recipe that created in him the strength of a bull and the speed of a cheetah. There was good reason that the dining room furniture was bolted to the floor. There was nothing loose for him to throw. The most damage Daniel could do was to himself. His knuckles bled from hammering into the wall again and again until he was subdued, after much struggling. Today was not the right time to tell him that Jack MacKay was found hanged in his room three days ago.

Blair Crawford couldn't believe how nervous this interview made him feel. It had been good of PC Duncan to give them his card, if somewhat surprising. The fact was, Laura Nicoll's late-night phone call brought Blair to Sophie Nicoll's home. Blair listened to the footsteps on the wooden floor as they moved towards the front door.

'Mum, that reporter is here,' Tom Nicoll shouted before Blair had a chance to introduce himself. His offer of a handshake was ignored as Tom brushed past him dressed in his school uniform. 'She says go through.'

Blair nodded and closed the front door behind him. He spotted the vast array of family photos immediately. The hall table was filled with photos of Tom and Sophie at various stages. They looked like such normal kids. Missing teeth. Dreadful haircuts. The same as everybody else. But their little family was different. One member was missing. Stolen from them in the most brutal way.

The wall that followed the staircase was adorned with the more professional family portraits. They were a beautiful-looking family, Blair thought. Sophie had inherited her honey-blonde hair from her mother, who was more like her sister than a mother. A lump stuck in Blair's throat at the sight of her smiling face staring back at him.

'Mr Crawford, please come through.' Laura Nicoll smiled a greeting.

'Call me Blair, please.' He reached out his hand to shake hers. 'Tom's back at school, I noticed. How is he?'

How is he? What a ridiculous question, Blair chastised himself. His sister was murdered, you idiot.

'He's OK,' Laura shrugged. 'Well, I don't know, to be honest. He doesn't say much.' She opened the kitchen door. 'We'll talk in here. Come on through.'

More photos, Blair noticed. Pictures and certificates adorned every surface.

'You have a lovely home, Laura.'

'Thank you. Can I get you a tea or coffee?' she asked. 'I think there's bit of sponge left over, too.'

Blair didn't think he could ever be as brave as the woman in front of him.

'I would love a cup of tea.' He rummaged in his bag and pulled out a notebook and pen. 'I hope you don't mind if I take a few notes.'

'Of course, no problem.' She laid a coaster in front of him. 'There you go. Help yourself to milk and sugar.'

Blair added two heaped spoonfuls of sugar and a splash of milk to his mug.

'I'm very grateful you've allowed me to meet with you like this.'

Laura smiled and sipped her tea. 'I need to do this. I want people to know the real story. The real Sophie was an amazing, witty, kind, generous—' Laura's words fizzled into tears. 'Sorry.' She sniffed. 'I miss her so much.'

'I understand it must be so hard for you all.'

Laura exhaled slowly. 'OK, where do you want me to start?'

'Tell me about her. What did Sophie like to do? What made her smile?' Blair clicked his pen on.

Laura grinned at the memory that popped into her head. 'Horses. Sophie loved horses. Like a lot of teenage girls, I suppose, but it wasn't the cute ponies she was fascinated by.'

'No? What, then?'

'Racehorses. Sophie loved horse racing, just like her dad. Ray has a share in one, or a leg, I should say. Stupid term. Sophie loved going to meetings with him. His horse was no Grand National contender, don't get me wrong. More of an always the bridesmaid, never the bride type.'

Blair laughed a little at her analogy. 'My dad loved the horses too.'

'He and Sophie would have got on then.'

'Perhaps. Dad was more a gambler, though.' Blair sank the last of his tea.

'Can I get you a refill? I'm having a fresh one.'

He clicked his pen off again. 'That would be lovely, thanks.'

'I'll cut the sponge this time, too.' Laura smiled.

CHAPTER ELEVEN

'I'll make us some tea.'

'Tea, Jason! Nobody wants bloody tea.'

Dylan shot Jessie a glance.

'Hey.' Jessie moved forward. 'Come on, Louise, let's have a wee seat and you can tell me what's happened. Jason, Dylan can help you get a brew on.' She nodded at Dylan to follow Jason into the kitchen.

Louise paced to and from the window to peer out through the blinds. 'Where the hell is she?' she exclaimed. 'It's not like her to be out this late.'

Jessie scanned the living room. The pine sideboard was adorned with photos of Shannon as well as a selection of candles and ornaments. The tall bookcase in the corner was filled with a variety of fiction, mainly crime, and a few biographies. The place was clean; a little untidy at worst. A chair in the far corner was hidden by a large pile of clean washing, which made Jessie smile. Everybody had such a chair, it seemed. Although Jessie's was in her bedroom and not the living room. A family photo of the three of them sat next to a single school photo of an older boy, which Jessie thought strange. Why wasn't he in the family shot?

Jessie joined Louise at the window.

'When did you last see your daughter, Louise? It's OK to call you Louise, isn't it?'

Louise nodded. 'Of course. Um, this morning when she left for school. I asked her if she had enough money for lunch.' She put her hands over her face. 'Oh God, where is she?'

'OK, OK, let's sit down and you can tell me a bit more.' Jessie guided Louise towards the sofa.

Louise sighed and flopped down as Jessie perched on the edge of the sofa, pulling her notebook from her jacket pocket. She glanced down at her ringing phone and pressed End Call with a frown.

'OK. Louise, have you any idea where Shannon might have gone? Who are her friends?'

Louise shot straight back up. 'You don't think I've done that already? I've called Eric. He says she was supposed to meet him for a thick shake but she didn't turn up. He thought she'd changed her mind and come home.'

'Now, I know this is hard, but I need you to calm down.'

'Here we go,' Dylan nudged his shoulder against the door as he carried mugs of tea in on a tray.

'Thank you,' Louise whispered as she took a mug from him.

Jason stood back from the rest of them. Jessie thought that strange.

'Jason, when did you last see Shannon?' she asked.

'I was up and out early, so it would have been last night, I suppose. When I said goodnight to her. I start at six, so I was in bed by ten last night. Shannon was still up. She was on her laptop when I popped my head in.'

'Could we possibly have a look at Shannon's room?' She put her mug down.

'What? Yes, of course.' Louise told her. 'It's the last door after the top of the stairs. It's got a huge picture of a horse on the door.'

Jessie stood up. Dylan took one last sip and followed her out. She turned left at the top of the stairs and peered in at the open door of what must have been Louise and Jason's room. Again, it looked untidy but clean. A bit like herself these days, she thought. The door between that room and Shannon's had a hole in it; about shoulder height to Jessie. It wasn't quite right through the wood but close as damn it. The only thing that causes a dent of that depth and shape was a punch – and a hard punch at that. The kind of punch only a man can produce. An angry man.

She turned away from that door to Shannon's. She stole a glance at Dylan before pushing it open. The contrast was immediately obvious. The bed was immaculately made. The dresser was organised with various sprays and brushes. Her make-up bag was closed and tucked back against her jewellery box. Her bedside table held a radio alarm clock and an empty glass next to a notebook, which appeared to be used as a diary with the pen neatly tucked into the wire spine. A laptop sat on her desk next to the window, which offered stunning views across town towards Ben Lochty. Jessie pulled on a pair of gloves, then lifted the laptop and dropped it into an evidence bag. Dylan tugged at his gloves in an attempt to make them more comfortable.

'They make these things so damn small,' he moaned as he lifted the notebook and scanned the pages.

'Dylan, the gloves are normal-sized. You're just a giant.'

Dylan laughed sarcastically. 'Very good. I'm only six foot one. Look at David Lyndhurst. How the hell does he manage? He must go to Monsters 'R' Us for his supplies.' Forensic pathologist David Lyndhurst was a man mountain at six foot six.

'I'll tell him you said that, shall I?'

Dylan tucked Shannon's notebook diary into another evidence bag, pulled back the duvet and lifted the pillow.

'If she was hiding under there I think we would have found her by now,' Ben murmured from the doorway.

Jessie spun round to see his sombre expression. 'Hello. I'm DI Blake and this is DC Logan. And you are?'

'I'm Ben, Shannon is my niece. Louise is my big sister.'

'You live here with your sister and her family?'

'Yes, I do,' Ben muttered.

Jessie narrowed her eyes at him. 'That's a right mess you made in your door there.'

The fact that he merely blushed and walked away answered her question. Perhaps this picture of contented family life wasn't quite all it seemed.

'We're going to take her laptop and this notebook. I hope that's OK,' Jessie said once they were all back in the living room. Then she noticed Jason wasn't there. 'Where's Jason?'

'He's gone outside for a smoke.'

'Excuse me,' Dylan muttered, then made his way out of the back door.

'Does Shannon use social media, you know, Facebook, Twitter, Instagram? Could she have arranged to meet someone from one of those sites?'

'Of course not! My daughter isn't stupid, detective. Could you just get out there and find her!' Louise shouted, right in Jessie's face. Then she started sobbing; that awful, uncontrolled sobbing.

Jessie felt terrible for her. She really did. Her pain looked real. It looked raw. But she knew very well that sometimes things aren't quite as they first appear.

CHAPTER TWELVE

Jason offered Dylan a cigarette. Dylan took one. He hadn't smoked since his son Jack was born six months ago. For some reason it seemed like a good idea tonight. Their garden was very dark, Dylan noticed, what with the house being at the end of the road. The streetlights didn't quite light up this end.

'Have you spoken to Ben?' Jason asked between draws. 'He says he saw Shannon going into Andrew Foster's.'

Dylan frowned. This was news to him. He shook his head, then pulled his notebook from his pocket. 'Andrew Foster. What's the address?'

Dylan waved to Jessie to join him outside in the hall.

'Hang on a minute.' Jessie patted Louise's shoulder before she exited the room. 'What's up?'

'Shannon was last seen by Ben going into an Andrew Foster's house.'

'What? Why weren't we told this straight away?'

Dylan shrugged before Jessie opened the living room door again.

'Andrew Foster. Who is he and where can we find him?'

Louise clasped her hand to her mouth. 'The blood! What if some of the blood was Shannon's?' Louise was clearly struggling to speak. It obviously hadn't even entered her head that this Andrew could do anything to Shannon. 'He's, erm, I mean, he's—'

'Andrew was rushed to hospital, detective,' said Jason. 'We found him barely conscious. He'd cut his wrists and he was bleeding all over the place. He was rushed to hospital by ambulance a couple of hours ago.'

'Where did they take him?' Jessie asked as she rummaged in her pocket for her car keys. 'Dylan, I want you to go and search this Andrew Foster's place.'

The drive back down the A9 didn't feel quite as long, and Jessie was relieved the ambulance had taken Foster to Perth and not Dundee, which would have added an extra thirty minutes at least to the journey. She slotted into the last space in the car park – much to the annoyance of the BMW driver who pulled into the hospital car park just after her. Small victories. Jessie held her ID up for the woman on Reception in the bustling A&E department.

'I'm looking for Andrew Foster.'

The woman glanced over at a row of chairs on the far wall.

'Have a seat and I'll get someone to come and talk to you.'

Jessie dropped down onto one of the cold, hard chairs next to a woman with a toddler on one knee snuggling close to her chest and a pram with a sleeping baby bundled up in a blanket. Her heart ached unexpectedly when she stared into the pram. She exhaled sharply, then stood to browse the assortment of leaflets in the wire rack. She hadn't anticipated that. It had been a while. A slight pain tugged at her belly; it was psychological, she knew that.

The smiling, thin, tired-looking doctor greeted her. 'Detective Inspector, sorry to keep you waiting. I hear you're looking for Andrew Foster. Andrew has just come out of surgery.'

'Surgery!' Jessie chirped. 'What's happened? I know he cut his wrists, but they required surgery?'

'That's the least of his problems. Andrew won't be fit to talk to the police for a while. Not until his acute psychosis is brought under control.'

CHAPTER THIRTEEN

Louise spat the remaining toothpaste into the sink and rinsed the residue away. She stared at Shannon's toothbrush and a gut-wrenching sickness slammed into her stomach. She turned and vomited violently into the toilet next to the sink. She retched until all that was ejected was the putrid bile that comes with an empty stomach. Louise didn't know when she'd last eaten. They certainly hadn't had anything for tea. It was going to be a chippy tea which she'd picked up after work but, with no sign of Shannon when she got in, she'd decided to wait and eat with her daughter. The part-time hours in the second-hand bookshop still suited the family, even now that Shannon was a teenager.

The thought that Andrew might have hurt Shannon was impossible for Louise to comprehend. Andrew was ill. He wasn't a bad man. He couldn't have hurt her, but the memory of all that blood swam round and round in her mind. She sat back and leaned her head against the bathroom door to catch her breath. As she tried to get to her knees, she was overcome with dizziness. She reached for the last of the toilet roll and spat into the toilet bowl.

'Louise, you OK in there, hon?'

Jason's voice tore into Louise's thoughts as she spat out the last of the vomit-streaked saliva, coughing to clear her throat.

'Yes, I'm fine,' she called back, her throat sore from retching.

'Do you want a cup of tea?'

Louise closed her eyes and sighed.

'More bloody tea,' she muttered to herself. 'No, I'm fine. I'll be out in a minute.'

'OK.'

Louise heard his footsteps move away from the bathroom door.

She took a long, slow breath, then exhaled while staring at her sickly, pallid reflection in the bathroom cabinet mirror. Her ashen colour reflected the fear she felt increasing inside her. Shannon never stayed out like this without telling them. She bent over the sink and splashed cold water over her face. She grabbed the towel on the rail and shivered at its dampness, then tossed it into the laundry basket next to the bath. She picked up the towel Jason had used for his shower that morning and wondered how he managed to miss a basket that size every time. Damp towels disgusted Louise. She raced into the bedroom at the sound of her mobile ringing to find Jason talking to her mum.

'That was your mum.'

'I gathered that,' Louise snapped. 'Give me my phone.'

Jason silently handed it over, then flopped down on their bed.

'Lou,' he called after her as he watched her leave their bedroom then heard her feet on the first step that creaked just a little.

'Go to bed, Jason,' she yelled back up the stairs as she dialled the number and waited for the answer.

'It's me, can you talk?'

CHAPTER FOURTEEN

2004 – Paderborn, Germany

'I think you've had enough, J.' Magda Leverkusen attempted to pull the beer glass away from Jason. 'Time you were heading back.'

Jason Ross gripped the glass in his fingers then lifted his head and tried to focus on her face.

'Jus' one more, then I'll go,' he slurred, then belched and tried to stand, swaying slightly before leaning on the bar top to steady himself. 'I'm fine, I'm going for a slash. Please, just one last pint.'

'Go home, Jason,' Magda repeated and kissed his cheek as she passed him on her way to collect empty glasses. 'I will see you tomorrow.'

'I think I might just love you, Magda.' Jason waved and staggered away. As he did so, he bumped into a man shorter and stockier than him on his way out of the NAAFI. 'Sorry, mate.'

'Watch where you're going!' the man yelled into Jason's face in a Cockney accent. 'Private Ross, I should have known. Get back to barracks and sober up. You're a bloody disgrace, man.'

Staff Sergeant Liam Bundy wiped lager from his shirt and trousers. Jason stared without saying a word, then – before he realised what he was doing – Liam Bundy, his commanding officer, was on the floor, punches raining down on him thick and fast. Again and again Jason pounded into him, months of frustration fuelling his outburst.

'Jason!' Magda shrieked. She called for help and, thankfully for Liam Bundy, the redcaps were on Jason in minutes, dragging him off and away from the bar.

'Ger off me!' Jason screamed, and kicked the police van door as they tried to restrain him. 'You should've let me kill the bastard.'

Magda sobbed from the door of the bar as she watched them take Jason away. Iraq affected the squaddies in different ways.

She'd known there was something troubling Jason. He'd just said he couldn't tell her what it was.

'Lucky for you, Staff Sergeant Bundy is going to be OK,' Jason's solicitor told him. 'He's not pressing charges, but they're offering you a medical discharge, which is an offer they don't expect you to refuse.'

Jason smirked. 'That's convenient, isn't it? One less person here to remind him, eh?'

'I think this is the best outcome under the circumstances, Private Ross.'

Jason scoffed. 'Best for who, exactly?'

'I think you'll agree that your drinking has become a problem. Perhaps a new start will give you time to reflect on your future.'

Jason signed the paper and, if he was honest with himself, this probably was for the best. Seeing the same faces around him. The reminders of that night were killing him. Her face never left his nightmares. The blood. The scream. The thud, and then the silence. The silence was the worst. He would have given anything to hear her scream again instead of the thick, deafening silence before the pitiful whimpers of the squaddie who was driving the Land Rover.

CHAPTER FIFTEEN

Cassie was fast asleep as Rob closed the bedroom door. The pregnancy was taking its toll and her energy levels were so low that, some days, it scared him. The sofa was comfortable enough for tonight. He didn't want to bother Cassie with Jason and Louise's fears. She would only worry and want to go straight over there.

He could probably get a bit of book promotion in too before he turned in. His US readers were up, and the Australians were likely just starting their day. Maggie Malcolm was right. Even Rob couldn't believe book five was here already. The isolation of the writer's life suited Rob. Having Cassie move in was difficult, but he was adjusting, slowly. He clicked on his laptop and checked his emails.

'Come to bed, honey.' Cassie's voice tore through the silence.

'I'm sorry, did I wake you?'

Cassie sounded weary as Rob stood to hug her.

'No, I needed to pee as usual.' She patted her stomach.

'You go back to bed. I'll be through in a bit.'

'Don't be long,' she answered, and reached up to kiss him before turning back towards the bedroom.

Rob couldn't concentrate. He grabbed his trainers from the utility room and pulled a sweater on. He needed to clear his head. He closed the back door quietly. He liked running when it was dark. It seemed to enhance the sense of isolation he craved. The back road between the main town and the small village of Weem was five miles there and back. Rob could run it in just under an hour.

All Rob heard was the sound of his own breathing along with the rhythmic slap of his trainers on the wet ground, until the hum of an engine approaching from behind made him tuck into the grass verge. He waved to Bob Massie as he sped past in his Land Rover.

He took the opportunity to catch his breath as he stared across at the outline of Ben Lochty, illuminated only by the moonlight, its imposing stature impossible to ignore. For thousands of years the mountain had stood proudly watching over the increasing expansion of Inverlochty, from small township of a few hundred to a rural town of over ten thousand. To the mountain both life and death passed in the blink of an eye.

Having the house on top of Scroggie Hill meant Rob could look out and watch the world turn without being trapped in the middle of the chaos. Some days the only sound was the call of the collared doves nesting in the mixed woodland that his house backed on to. The silence, mixed with the warm sunshine in the garden, had been bliss that first summer. It was like a dream after his previous place. Sitting writing, staring out at the snowdrop carpet after a long, harsh Highland Perthshire winter was unbeatable.

Before heading for a shower, the blue lights drew his attention and he shifted the blind to see exactly where it was headed. He wondered what the police would want with Andrew Foster now, and anyway, they'd be out of luck because Rob figured Andrew was still in hospital, the state he was in. His wounds were deep and would definitely have required stitching. He winced when he thought of how painful they must have been, and the sight of all that blood had made him retch.

'What's going on down there?' Cassie yawned and cuddled into him.

'Never mind that. You go back to bed.' He kissed the top of her head.

'Yes, boss.' She smiled and joined him at the window, then frowned. 'What's going on?'

'Don't know, you get back to bed, missus.' He tapped her bottom as she offered him a playful salute on her way out of the living room.

Rob smiled until she was out of sight, then resumed his observation. It looked like the officers were inside and, just as he prepared to move away, a van arrived with a canine officer. Rob ran his hand over his chin and pushed the blind back quickly.

'DC Logan,' PC Molly Wilde called out.

Dylan jogged into Andrew Foster's kitchen. He ran his fingers across the back of his head and exhaled a huge breath.

'Is it hers?'

'It's got Shannon's photos on it.'

Dylan clasped his hands at the back of his head and wondered how to tell Louise and Jason. Loud barking tore into his thoughts and he moved upstairs two at a time.

'Get the dog out of here. I'll get SOCOs in here asap.'

The sight of blood on the bathroom floor sent chills through him. Andrew Foster's home was now a crime scene.

CHAPTER SIXTEEN

1996

Daniel's eyes burst open. He inhaled a huge breath and grabbed hold of his T-shirt. That dream again. It was like a horror movie playing over and over in his mind. He feared closing his eyes. He saw her everywhere, behind every corner. And not just in his dreams. He wondered if Jack went through the same nightmares. Was it the nightmares that pushed Jack over the edge? When Cam told him that Jack was dead it was so much worse than losing his mum. Jack was more like family to Daniel. He ran a hand across his wet brow and rubbed at his damp neck. He turned his pillow in the hope of finding a dry spot to sleep on. Not that he would sleep much now.

Dr Julia Hudson was disappointed but not surprised to hear about the escalation in Daniel's violent outbursts over the past week. For a boy with serious anger issues to lose both his mother and his best friend in little over two weeks, it was always possible he would react like that. It was his last explosion that caused his social worker, Cam Walsh, to ask for the emergency consultation. The hospital said there were no broken bones, but the two young offenders he'd got into a fight with would be badly bruised and sore for a couple of weeks. The prison officer who intervened was treated for concussion but should be back at work sometime next week. Daniel was escorted by two officers and greeted Julia with a quick raising of his eyebrows before taking a seat opposite her.

Julia smiled a warm greeting. 'Hello, Daniel.'

'Hello,' he answered, his tone sombre.

'I hear there's been a bit of an incident since we last spoke.'

Daniel kept his eyes on his feet and shrugged. Julia began to read from Cam's letter.

'You've had your television and Sega Mega Drive taken away, is that right?'

He shrugged for a second time.

'Losing Mum and Jack has been hard on you.'

Julia allowed the words to hang in the silence, unanswered. It was important for him to acknowledge their passing. Daniel slouched low in the chair and nibbled on a thumbnail, but still Julia waited.

'I suppose,' he eventually muttered without looking at her.

'It helps to talk about people we've lost,' Julia encouraged him.

'Wait a minute.' Daniel snapped his head up. 'I was told that part of our sentence was that me and Jack were to be separated. Talking about him now, it's daft, don't you think?'

'Not when you consider the pivotal role Jack played in your crime.'

Daniel stared coldly, unblinking. 'I don't know.'

'Would Jack have done it without you?'

Julia knew the answer to that already, but she wondered what Daniel believed.

Daniel shrugged. That day Jack changed. Daniel didn't know anything about him any more. He was like a stranger to him after that. The days following what they did, Jack acted as if nothing had happened. In fact, if anything, he was the most relaxed Daniel had seen him for a long time. As if a weight had been lifted rather than sitting heavily on his mind.

'Why do you think he did it?'

His answer was given by way of a shrug this time.

'Do you ever think about what you and Jack did?'

'I guess so,' Daniel muttered, then scratched his nose and sniffed.

'How do you feel about it now that you have had time to reflect?' Julia probed.

Six weeks after his conviction, Julia was keen to hear his thoughts. It came to light in Daniel's statement to the police that Jack invited Sophie Nicoll to meet him that afternoon. He knew she fancied him and would be flattered by his invitation. Daniel claimed he had no idea what was about to unfold, and Jack's full motivation was still unclear.

'What we did wasn't right. I know that.' He resumed biting his nails. 'No, it's not that it wasn't right. It was so wrong. We should never have done that.'

'That's good to hear you say that. It's important to acknowledge what we've done. Taking ownership, you might call it.'

Daniel closed his eyes and nodded. 'I suppose.'

'Did you want Sophie to be your girlfriend?'

'No,' Daniel immediately scoffed, then frowned.

'You're very sure about that?'

'Very sure,' he insisted.

'Did Jack want her to be his girlfriend?'

'I doubt it.' Daniel shrugged.

'So what you're saying, then, is that the two of you only wanted to have sex with Sophie.'

'That's right.' He stared directly into her eyes until she was forced to look away first. 'Yes.'

'Are you sure?' Julia pushed harder. 'Did you need any encouragement?'

Daniel tilted back his head and smiled inappropriately.

'Did you encourage Jack in any way?' she asked again.

'Stop, Daniel, don't do this,' Sophie begged. 'Stop, please. You don't have to do this.'

Jack watched Daniel rape Sophie just like he had ten minutes before, exhilarated by their actions. When Daniel was finished, Sophie lay frozen in fear. He stood to fasten his trousers.

'Shit, man.' Jack laughed and patted Daniel's shoulder.

'Get off.' Daniel felt sick.

'What's wrong with you?' Jack questioned him.

Sophie rolled over and started to stand until Jack grabbed a fistful of her hair.

'Jack!' Daniel shouted. 'Leave her. Let her go. She's had enough.'

Sophie whimpered until Jack rolled her onto her back and started to undo his trousers. Sophie screamed in horror that her ordeal wasn't yet over. He had his hands around her throat as the memory faded.

'Daniel, did you hear what I said?'

He nodded. 'I suppose we encouraged each other.'

'Was Jack your best friend?'

Daniel shrugged. 'I guess he was.'

'Do you miss him?'

'Yes, I probably do a bit. He was a laugh.'

Julia smiled. 'You did lots of things together, then?'

Daniel grinned and held her gaze once more. 'When his parents let us.'

'How did you get on with Mr and Mrs MacKay?'

'They were actually really nice. Jack was always bitching about them. Like they were really strict and stuff. He even said once that he was jealous of me, can you believe that? Because Mum let...' He stopped to correct himself. 'Let me stay out as late as I wanted.'

'Do you think he did what he did with you that day because he knew his parents would disapprove?'

Daniel's mood darkened, and he withdrew slightly from the conversation. Julia allowed him some space and wondered if it was a good time to end their session, which she felt had gone incredibly well.

'OK, I think that's enough for today.'

Daniel interrupted her by unexpectedly reaching out for her arm, which startled Julia a little.

'How did Jack die?'

His question took her by surprise and she sighed.

'Jack hanged himself, Daniel. I'm sorry.'

She allowed the information to sink in.

'Thank you for being honest with me, Dr Hudson.'

Again, his eyes held hers the whole time as he stood up from his chair.

'You're welcome,' she answered with a smile.

CHAPTER SEVENTEEN

Rob and Cassie walked up the path hand in hand, knocked once, then walked into the house. The look on Cassie's face when he told her about Shannon was horrible. He hated telling her something so awful. Of course she had wanted to go straight over there, but Rob managed to persuade her that there was nothing she could do at that time of night. Jason greeted them when he reached the bottom of the stairs, his expression dazed and confused with a large dose of exhaustion. It was clear that Jason had slept very little and hadn't shaved that morning. Rob had seen Jason in some states, most of which involved copious amounts of lager, but he'd never seen anything like this. He looked broken; defeated. Jason shook his head in response to Rob's question about an update. Cassie moved forward and hugged Jason tightly. She saw Louise emerge from her bedroom at the top of the stairs and immediately released her grip on him to go to her friend.

'Louise,' Cassie whispered, and rubbed her hand up and down Louise's arm. 'Shall I make us all some coffee?'

'I need a cigarette.' Jason moved past Rob and out the front door. Cassie urged Rob to follow him with a nod of her head, which he did without question.

'Do you want one?' Jason held out the cigarette packet.

'No thanks.' Rob leaned back against the wall, unsure what was the right thing to say.

Jason inhaled and blew the smoke out close to Rob's face.

'They found her phone at Andrew Foster's house.'

'Shit, mate, I'm sorry.'

Jason stubbed out one cigarette with his foot as he lit another. Rob gently covered Jason's hand with his.

'Come on, let's get some coffee.'

DC Dylan Logan opened the garden gate before they could get back inside.

'Have you found her?' Jason rubbed his eyes with his fingers to wake himself up a bit.

Dylan's answer was a slight shake of his head. 'Let's go inside. Come on.'

Louise leapt from her chair at the sound of Dylan's voice and spilled her coffee all over the pine kitchen table. It dribbled down onto the vinyl floor.

'Shit.' She grabbed a cloth.

'Leave it.' Cassie tugged the cloth out of her hand. 'I'll get that.'

'What's happening?' Louise asked, her eyes searching for good news.

Jason reached for his cigarettes as Dylan explained: 'We're sending a team up Ben Lochty and another to search Inver Wood, just to be sure she's not got lost and fallen somewhere. The dogs are going to need something of Shannon's so that they can focus on her scent. Something from her laundry basket would be best.'

Louise didn't speak. She left the room.

'What are you not telling us?' Jason asked. 'Why would Shannon be in either of those places? Shannon wouldn't wander like that. She certainly wouldn't head into Inver Wood by herself.'

'Jason, sit down and let him do his job.' Cassie's voice was firm and unwavering as she stared up at him.

'Thank you. I'll be in touch as soon as I have any news.'

Jason grabbed his cigarettes and charged past Dylan to get out the back door.

*

Being in Shannon's room was torture. Louise could smell her as if she'd just stepped outside for a minute. On top of Shannon's pillow Louise found the pyjamas she had taken off that morning. She held them close to her face and inhaled every molecule of her scent. She rubbed the cotton top over her cheek while tears ran down her face.

By the time Rob got outside, Jason was stubbing out one cigarette and starting on the next. Rob wasn't ready for what happened next. Jason dropped to his knees and cried. He wailed like an animal and his words were completely inaudible. Rob's first instinct was to run, but he couldn't. He crouched down and put his hand on his friend's shoulder. Jason clung to Rob. 'Where is she? Where is she?'

Jessie stared at Andrew Foster as he lay curled up in the foetal position on the bed, his shock of brown curls pointing in several different directions. She noticed the length of his nails and wondered when they were last trimmed, or cleaned for that matter. Having the door locked loudly behind her unnerved her. The nurse who let Jessie in had warned her that Andrew probably couldn't be very helpful just yet. As soon as his wounds were stitched, Andrew had been transferred to the secure psychiatric ward for his own safety, and it was clear that his schizophrenia was acutely out of control. The nurse told Jessie that Andrew might have stopped taking his meds; something he did regularly after the loss of his mother. Some doses were missed down to genuine forgetfulness.

'Hello, Andrew, my name is Jessie Blake.' She pulled her ID badge out and held it close to him but he didn't even look at it. 'Can I have a quick word, if you don't mind?'

Andrew moved only to cover his ears with his hands and muttered something under his breath that Jessie couldn't make out. She knew she was out of her depth here, and she was aware of the nurse watching her. The nurse moved forward and knelt next to Andrew's face.

'The detective needs to talk to you, Andrew.'

Her words were firm but kind and created a frown of acknowledgement from Andrew. It was as if he'd just realised Jessie was there. She mouthed the words thank you as the nurse moved back from them. Andrew Foster looked up at Jessie for the first time.

'Hello, Andrew.' Jessie smiled.

'Hello,' Andrew's words were slurred, and he wiped a drop of saliva from his lips.

'I need to ask you a couple of questions, OK?'

Andrew nodded, and it was then that Jessie noticed the emptiness in his eyes. They were devoid of emotion.

'Did you see Shannon Ross yesterday?'

Her question got no response. Jessie undid her hair and retied it into a messy bun. She scratched her cheek and waited.

'Andrew,' she tried again. 'Did you see Shannon yesterday? Her mum and dad are looking for her. She didn't come home last night.'

Andrew sat bolt upright, startling Jessie.

'She's a good girl, Shannon. She helps me, especially when they try to get me. They try to steal my thoughts, you know. They didn't know that I knew until I told them. They thought they were so smart, but the signs were all there, you see,' Foster said, his finger extended close to Jessie's chest.

'When who tries to get you?'

Andrew started laughing, then pressed his finger to his lips.

'Why was Shannon's phone in your house?'

Jessie now knew this was futile. The buzz from her phone scared Andrew, who retreated back into a tight ball with his hands over his ears.

'DI Blake,' she answered, then listened before a sickening thump landed in the pit of her stomach. This was not the news she wanted to hear.

CHAPTER EIGHTEEN

Eric Baldwin put down his Xbox controller and grabbed his phone when it vibrated in his jeans pocket. Shannon had been on his mind all night. It wasn't like her not to answer his texts, and he hoped this one was finally from her. When the sender ID was C, he was torn between disappointment and excitement.

> *Any news yet? I've seen all the police activity.*
> *I still haven't heard from her.*
> *Want to talk?*
> *Can I come over?*
> *Of course. I'll see you in ten.*

Eric smiled and switched off his game. He slipped his feet into Nike trainers and grabbed a warm sweater. Agatha Baldwin intercepted him in the hallway.

'Don't be late home, *mein Liebling*.'

Eric kissed her cheek. 'I won't. I've got my phone with me.' He slammed the door shut behind him.

Eric had never seen so many police officers in Inverlochty. As he passed Shannon's door he saw a sharply dressed man waiting for the door to be answered. Eric's eyes met with Rob Taylor's before Rob closed the door behind him.

*

Andrew Foster emerged from his room in the mental health assessment unit. He pinched his fingers together in sequence, counting to ten then down from ten in a continuous pattern, his stained red T-shirt on inside out, before repeating Shannon's name over and over.

'Shannon's gone, Shannon's gone. We've got to find Shannon.' He crouched quickly and peeped his head round the dining room door. 'She's hurt. I've got to get to her. Her face. The blood.' He clasped his hand over his mouth and listened with narrowed eyes. 'No I didn't, I couldn't have done that.' He slammed his hands over his ears. 'Lies. That's all lies, isn't it?'

'Andrew, what's happening, buddy?' asked a nurse as he crouched low beside him. 'Can I help at all?'

Andrew eyed him suspiciously, then lifted his finger to his lips.

'Shh, they'll hear you. They say they saw me do it, but I didn't. I didn't do it, did I?' Andrew shook his head and gripped his ears, tugging them hard before slapping his own head. 'No, I wouldn't. Shut up. You're lying.'

'Hey, come on, let's get you something to make you feel a bit better.' The nurse laid a gentle hand on Andrew's arm to encourage him off the floor.

'No,' Andrew screamed in his face. 'I know what you're all trying to do. I would never do that. Never. Shannon is my friend.'

Jessie felt deflated after her attempt to interview Andrew Foster. She had no idea how long it was going to take before he was lucid enough to help her but, until then, that was all she had. She looked around the basic room at the rear of the small, rural station she had been given as an incident room, and tried to get used to the smell. She couldn't put her finger on it, but if she had to guess, it was burning dust.

She was lucky Inverlochty still had a station. Police Scotland cuts meant these places were an endangered species. This room was usually empty, so there had been no point having the radiators on until now. She laid Shannon's photo in front of her and tried to imagine herself in the shoes of a fifteen-year-old girl. Shannon had just helped Andrew Foster but hadn't turned up to meet Eric as she'd planned. The distance between the two places was no more than two hundred yards. She had asked the few uniformed officers based in Inverlochty to do a door-to-door interview with every house between the two and nobody had seen her. It was as if she went into Andrew Foster's home, then vanished.

CHAPTER NINETEEN

Jessie had been on the road for an hour before the first signpost for Inverlochty appeared. Highland Perthshire was stunning at this time of year. The metamorphosis in the leaves was spectacular. She understood exactly why thousands of tourists flocked here every autumn. The seasonal colours glowed despite the darkness that had descended on the small town. When the super suggested Jessie should stay at the heart of the investigation, she didn't realise that he meant she should literally move in while the investigation took place, but it made sense. Travelling to the rural station every morning wasn't practical.

'Hi, I'm Jessie Blake. You have a room for me,' she said as she walked up to the desk in the only hotel in town.

Maggie Malcolm, who was a whisker shy of five foot two, slung the tea towel over her shoulder, skimming her greying black hair, and gave Jessie a sombre smile as she handed her the key. 'Aye, there you go. Horrid business, all the same.'

'Thank you.'

Ten minutes later, DI Jessie Blake was booked into her room above The Black Witch pub. The room was basic but clean, and she pulled back the duvet to inspect the sheet. She did this out of habit – a reminder of her time living with Dan, where any kind of dirt or mess would have put him in a terrible mood and she would have paid for it. She was relieved to see that the crisp, tightly fitted white sheet was immaculate. The mini-kettle next to a wicker basket of individually wrapped tea bags and tiny tubs of UHT milk produced a wry smile. The twin pack of shortbread was the finishing touch to the traditional rural bed and breakfast. Jessie grabbed her keys and headed straight for the police station.

Louise woke suddenly from sleep. She had gone into Shannon's room to feel close to her. She had only laid her head on Shannon's One Direction pillow for a moment, but exhaustion consumed her and, two hours later, she was still there. For one brief, wonderful heartbeat Shannon wasn't gone, her daughter wasn't missing and she would be there any minute, angrily wondering why her mother was sleeping on her bed. Louise felt her shoulders rise with the pain of uncertainty tightening her gut. Two short taps on the bedroom door broke the silence.

'Jason's wondering if you want some tea,' Rob whispered.

Louise ignored his question and closed her eyes.

'Lou.' He closed the bedroom door and moved closer. He crouched low beside the bed and ran his fingers through her hair. 'Lou,' he said again.

His touch felt the way it always had, and Louise missed it. They hadn't planned on what had happened between them; it just happened. She turned to face him, then sat up on the edge of Shannon's bed, tears streaming. Neither of them said a word until Rob leaned forward and pressed his lips firmly on hers. Louise wanted him so badly she ached. She craved the comfort she knew Rob could give, but she pushed him away.

'No,' her voice quivered. 'It's over between us, and this isn't the time anyway.'

She stood up and walked to the door. Rob sighed. She was right.

'There you are.' Cassie almost banged right into Louise in the hallway.

'Here I am.' Louise's words oozed defeat.

Cassie was surprised to find Rob walking out of Shannon's room. They both watched Louise move slowly downstairs as Rob draped an arm round Cassie's shoulder before planting a soft kiss on her cheek.

'Do you think we should go?' she asked.

Rob sighed. 'I don't think we're much help here, are we?'

Ben startled them as he crept from his room. He scowled silently at the couple, then passed them on his way downstairs.

'Poor Ben, everyone is so wrapped up in their own worries I think we've all forgotten he's just a kid. He was the last one to see her, too. He must be missing her.'

'Come on, we should go. Jason will call if he needs us,' Rob added.

'You're right, but I wish there was something we could do.'

Tears moistened Cassie's eyes, but the doorbell rang before Rob could respond. Jason jogged in from the kitchen to answer it.

'Come in, detective, come in.'

Rob and Cassie slipped away, unnoticed by either Jason or Louise.

'Thank you.' Jessie wiped her feet before stepping inside.

'Have you found her yet?'

'No. We are doing everything we can to find your daughter, I can assure you.'

'"Everything" clearly isn't very much, is it? Why haven't you found her yet?' Louise's eyes misted over.

'I'm doing everything in my power to get Shannon back to you.'

Her words hung in the air and Louise nodded.

'Have you spoken to Andrew Foster yet?' asked Jason.

'He's not fit to be officially interviewed, but as soon as he is, I intend to speak to him, don't worry.'

Jessie turned to face Louise. 'Can you think of anyone that Shannon could have gone to see that you haven't considered before? Does she have any friends in Dundee or Glasgow or Edinburgh?

Are you positive she's not been chatting to someone online? Could she have a boyfriend that you don't know about?'

'No, of course not. I told you, Shannon isn't stupid. My daughter wouldn't go and meet a stranger she met on the internet.'

'I'm sorry if I've upset you, but under the circumstances, I do have to ask difficult questions.' Jessie glanced at Shannon's school photo on the sideboard and smiled. 'She looks like you, Jason, a blonde version of you, obviously, I mean.' Jessie hoped her words would defuse the increasing tension.

Jason grinned. 'Aye, she has the Ross eyes.'

'Look, I'm not going to lie to you—' Jessie's phone halted her mid-sentence. 'Excuse me a minute.'

She grabbed her phone and walked out of the living room. She snapped her eyes tight shut while she listened to Dylan's words. She exhaled loudly and pushed her phone back into her pocket. Her heart thudded when the living room door swung open.

'What is it?' The fear in Jason's voice was palpable.

'The drops of blood in Andrew Foster's home are Shannon's.' Jessie spoke in hushed tones. 'But let's not jump to conclusions.'

'I'll kill him, I'm going to fucking kill him!'

He pushed past Jessie before she could stop him and slammed the front door shut. She gave chase, but he sped out of the driveway before she could stop him.

'Dylan, get to the hospital!' Jessie shouted into her phone. 'Jason is on his way there. He knows about the blood.'

Louise watched, motionless, through the living room blinds as Jessie stared back at her.

CHAPTER TWENTY

Jason's Audi skidded to a halt, flicking up stones outside the hospital entrance. His heart pounded thunderously in his chest. The rage consumed him. Foster was going to answer his questions even if Jason had to beat the information out of him. Dylan Logan arrived seconds after to see Jason flee his vehicle, leaving the driver's door wide open and engine running, and enter the building.

'Shit,' Dylan muttered as he locked his car. 'Jason, stop!'

Dylan pursued him through the hospital, scaling the stairs two at a time. Sweat poured from his forehead as Jason seemed to get further away from him with every stride. When Jason arrived at the Psychiatric Intensive Treatment ward and found it locked, he screamed, 'Open this door!' He thrust his entire weight into the locked steel door, ignoring the searing pain that shot through his shoulder. 'What have you done to my daughter, you freak!' He hammered his fist on the door until the skin broke and bled, then he tried to peer in at the small shatterproof glass window at the top of the door.

'Jason.' Dylan finally caught up with him and raised his hand out in front of him. 'Just calm down. You know you can't go in there. Come with me.'

Jason spun to face him and spat, his eyes fixed and staring. He slammed his palm on the glass. 'Open that door!'

'You know I can't do that. Come on. Let's go somewhere we can talk about this.'

'Talk?' Jason screamed and hammered again. 'Talking won't help anyone. He knows where Shannon is. Let me in so I can get it out of him.'

'No, Jason,' Dylan repeated. This time he lowered his voice in the hope it would help neutralise some of Jason's venom.

'I said, open that damn door!' Jason roared at the top of his lungs.

'Jason.' Louise's voice was barely audible over the banging.

She grabbed hold of his shirt and pulled him backward. Jason's eyes softened but neither of them spoke. They just stared, Jason's pulsing anger seeming to decrease slowly.

'Do you want me to arrest him?' Dylan asked Jessie, who had rushed Louise there to see if she could calm Jason down.

Jessie shook her head. The last thing Louise needed was to be alone tonight.

CHAPTER TWENTY-ONE

1997

Dr Julia Hudson removed her cardigan and draped it across the back of her chair. Review day was always a long day and not always a satisfying one. Dealing with frustrating setbacks was part of the job. She rubbed her arms against the chill and resisted putting her cardigan back on, knowing the heat would soon build in the meeting room. It always did, although at times the cause of the heat was the content of the meetings.

'Good morning, Camilla.'

Cam Walsh poured them both coffee and took her seat at the table.

The two women were soon joined by Pat Murphy, a forty-five-year-old Irishman with the blackest hair and bluest eyes Julia Hudson had ever seen.

'Good morning, Pat.' Julia smiled and pointed to the table under the window. 'Camilla's got the coffee going already, you'll be pleased to hear.'

'Grand, I'm in need of something to heat me up. I can't get warmed at all this morning.'

The snow had been falling for days. Staff were having to do double shifts to cover for colleagues who couldn't get through the drifts. Julia had considered several times already that morning whether she should turn back and, by the look of the weather outside, she wished she had. She took one small sip from the piping-hot coffee before she began.

'Right, we'll start with Daniel Simpson.' She lifted Daniel's file off the top of her pile. 'Pat, what have you got for us?'

'Daniel is doing incredibly well. I for one am impressed with his progress.' Pat reached for his reading glasses. 'He's settled well into the library job. He's keen to work and is helpful, he even takes the trolley now. That one hiccup at the start came to nothing, just as I hoped,' Pat continued.

That one hiccup had been Daniel's impulsive response to being called a queer boy for working in the library. Since lashing out that one time, he had managed to find a way to control his temper, thanks to anger management sessions. Sessions he had balked at in the beginning.

'He is proving to be a hard worker.' Pat removed his glasses. 'The lad is incredibly intelligent. His academic progress has been astonishing.'

Cam Walsh beamed. She had spotted Daniel's potential early on and encouraged his studies. She could see that all he lacked was confidence and focus. His chaotic family background had destroyed his early chances at success, but Cam was able to spot the tiny flicker of hope and built on it. She encouraged his love of reading and pushed for him to study hard for his English qualification. He had a flair for maths, and even showed promise in art.

Pat put his glasses back on. 'Mr Solomon, his English teacher, is delighted with Daniel's progress, and has no doubt he will achieve several academic qualifications. His social interaction is a work in progress, however. While his anger is under much better control, my main concern is that he chooses to avoid interaction altogether whenever he can.'

Julia glanced at Cam, then frowned. 'Do you think he's becoming withdrawn?'

Cam shook her head. 'On the contrary, I think he's choosing his company wisely and that's no bad thing. He enjoys intelligent conversation, if you get my drift.'

Pat tilted his head back and laughed.

'What's funny about that?' Julia grinned.

'What she's trying to say is Daniel's too clever to be hanging about with some of the lads in here. I mean, he's the only one who's ever borrowed a George Orwell from the library.'

A wry smile crept across Cam's face.

'I'm afraid I can't do anything about the intellectual standard of his peers.' Julia answered.

After a rocky start, Daniel Simpson settled well into life at Carseview young offenders' unit. Intensive counselling to cope with his confused feelings about the loss of his mum and Jack helped. Coming to terms with the impact of his crime took longer, and he was still working hard on that.

Daniel Simpson sat on his bed. Spending his sixteenth birthday behind bars was not how he had seen his life panning out. Although he had no idea what he would have been doing if he wasn't locked away where he was. He couldn't imagine his mum would have been able to celebrate properly with him. Jack would have been cool about it. Despite everything, he still missed Jack. He was a good mate.

'Come on, hurry up, they're waiting for you.'

The hammer of the officer's fist on his door interrupted Daniel's daydreams.

'Sorry, I'm just coming.'

Daniel was escorted to the meeting room to join the team for his review. A commotion interrupted them when his escort had to intervene in a potentially inflammatory disagreement between two inmates. Daniel stood back from the argument and watched the teenagers lash out angrily at each other. Once upon a time Daniel would have been one of them.

*

'Hello, Daniel.' Julia welcomed him with a warm smile.

He reciprocated her welcome with a nervous smile.

Cam spotted his anxiety immediately. 'Have a seat.'

Daniel lowered himself into the chair in front of them and rubbed the palms of his hands across his legs, then coughed to clear his throat. Pat leaned back and pushed his coffee cup onto the table behind him.

'We've got nothing but positive things to say about you, Daniel. School is going well, I hear. Your library work is going well. You're staying away from confrontation.'

Daniel glanced up once from staring at the floor to nod his acknowledgement. He wasn't used to praise. He didn't know how to react to her encouraging words. It wasn't that Rita Simpson had been actively cruel to her son. She was a child herself when Daniel was born. At sixteen she wasn't emotionally capable of motherhood. Life as a single mother was a struggle and the escape offered by alcohol and drugs too powerful to resist. Her neglect led her intelligent son into thrill-seeking to ease his feelings of loneliness. Although he avoided alcohol and drugs because he didn't want to end up a zombie like his mum, Daniel Simpson developed a taste for extreme horror. As he got older it evolved into hardcore pornography. It was that freedom he had been given to watch harmful images that contributed to the murder of Sophie, the judge had decided.

'You should be very proud of your progress. I've been telling Dr Hudson about your academic achievement,' Pat added. 'We're all really very pleased with you.'

Daniel struggled to maintain eye contact, and Cam scribbled a note in her pad to remind her to spend time with him to work on his self-confidence. It was early days, but a little extra input wouldn't hurt.

'Is there anything you would like to talk to us about, Daniel?' Julia asked.

Daniel chewed his bottom lip and shook his head. Cam frowned at the contradiction of his body language.

'Are you sure?'

'Can I have a notebook and one of those pens with the four colours?' He lifted his eyes to Cam.

'I'm sure Pat can sort you out with that,' Julia told him.

Pat nodded. 'You know we have to read any letters you want to send, don't you, Daniel?'

Daniel shrugged. 'I know. I've got nothing left to hide.'

CHAPTER TWENTY-TWO

Blair Crawford dropped the handle of his small suitcase and raised his chin to attract the barmaid's attention, then rubbed his arms against the cold. He'd figured Scotland in October would be chilly, but he hadn't anticipated being able to see his breath in the air this soon in the year. But the drive up there had been spectacular. Scotland in autumn really was amazing, but it also reminded him of the past; his first case as a rookie. He didn't want this story to end the same way, especially when he was so close to retiring. Earning a living as a journalist was wearing thin. Now he was hitting fifty and had been diagnosed with Type 2 diabetes, it was time to make changes. His nest egg would keep him going while he wrote the novel he'd dreamt of doing for many years. Let's face it, he'd seen enough evil to fill a crime novel many times over in his career.

He thought perhaps a series with a retired private investigator as lead character would be good. A maverick not afraid to push the boundaries. A man who trod a fine line between legal and not so legal. He might even make him a fifty-something, slightly overweight, balding man. Blair knew how a man like that would think, let's face it. The temptation to make him luckier with the ladies would be hard to resist. Hell, it's fiction, after all.

'What can I get ye?' Maggie Malcolm draped her tea towel over her shoulder and walked over to serve him.

'I have a room booked in the name of Crawford.'

Maggie put a tick next to his reservation.

'Aye, you're in room two. Through the door, up the stairs. It's at the end of the hallway. I can do you breakfast at eight, if that suits.'

She handed over the key, which made Blair smile because it had been a long time since any place he had stayed used real keys. A credit-card-sized key card was more the norm these days, and Blair knew that better than most. Just over twenty years as a crime correspondent had taken Blair Crawford to hundreds of places to cover all sorts. Shannon's disappearance gave him the chills. It was an echo of the Sophie Nicoll case from twenty years ago. Teenage girl. Didn't come home from school. Not been seen or heard from since. Blonde hair. Blue eyes. Something about this case made Blair very uncomfortable.

'I'll take a pint before I go up,' Blair said while Maggie went back to drying the glasses.

'Aye, nae problem.' Maggie held the glass under the tap. 'You're no' from round these parts.'

Blair pulled a five-pound note from his jacket pocket and slid it across the bar with a smile.

'You'll be a journalist then,' she added.

'Is it that obvious?' Blair grinned.

'Aye, it's the 666 tattooed on your head that gives it away,' she chuckled.

Blair almost choked on his pint. 'That's a good one. I've never heard that before.'

Maggie wiped the top of the bar. 'Don't you go bothering her family now, you hear? They've got enough to worry aboot.'

'I'm one of the good guys, don't worry. I know they're going through hell right now.'

Blair sipped from his glass, then wiped his mouth with the back of his hand.

'Shannon is their only child?' he asked.

'Aye, that's right.' Maggie stared at Blair in a bid to size up his intentions and made her decision; his eyes were kind. 'Of course, they wanted more but Louise's last two pregnancies ended in heartbreak, and now this. They dinnae deserve this. Jason and Louise are such a nice young couple. I hate to think that—' Maggie abruptly stopped talking and began to wipe down the bar again. She sniffed back a tear. 'If you need anything else, just ask.'

With a sharp flick of her tea towel Maggie disappeared through to the back of the pub.

Blair made himself comfortable on the bar stool to finish his pint. A large framed oil painting at the end of the bar caught his eye. He screwed up his face to try to read the inscription underneath it until he was forced to pull out his glasses. It read:

> Morag McIver burned as a witch on this day of 14th
> August 1681. To this day the Black Witch wanders the
> Inver Wood in search of retribution.

The painting depicted a shadowy figure, long grey hair flowing behind her, running between thick rows of trees. The Black Witch pub was said to be built on the spot where witches were burned at the stake.

He sank the last of his pint and slid his empty glass across the bar. He picked up the room key. 'Thank you.' He raised his hand to Maggie, who smiled and nodded in return.

As he turned to walk away, Blair nudged shoulders with a well-dressed, pretty woman whom his radar immediately identified as a detective.

'I'm sorry, that was my fault. I wasn't looking where I was going.' He smiled an apology but kept his questions for later. Blair needed a freshen-up and perhaps even a shower after his long drive.

Jessie smiled and accepted the apology. She glanced down at her watch. She intended to spend the morning studying Shannon's diary and laptop. The mountain rescue team was heading back up Ben Lochty later that morning with the dogs. A group of volunteers had joined the officers and the search of Inver Wood had begun at first light, which was a monumental task given the vast acreage it covered. It was perfectly possible for someone to fall in the middle and not be found for days. She hoped that was what had happened to Shannon, but at this point, nothing could be ruled out.

She waved a greeting at Maggie, who raised an eyebrow in return. As she walked to the station she smirked at the Superman emoji her sister Freya had texted her, then answered Dylan's call.

'Dylan, hi.'

'Morning, Jess. How's it going?'

'Not so bad. I meant to ask, how's your mum?'

'She's OK, thanks. Well, as good as she can be, I suppose. The girls at the home have got her on bed rest until some of the bruising goes down. It could have been worse.' Dylan shook his head. 'Dementia is a horrible disease. I've told Shelly if it happens to me, just chuck me down the stairs but make it look like an accident.' He offered a half-smile.

'Not sure you should be telling me that. What if you go home tonight and fall down the stairs?' Jessie grinned.

'Aye, very funny. Listen, I'm heading over to speak to Andrew Foster. I'll catch up with you later.'

Jessie really wanted to speak to Andrew Foster, but she also wanted to get a head start on Shannon's diary and laptop. They might contain vital information, and any leads at this stage were priceless. Shannon was last seen by Ben going inside Andrew Foster's house. Since then she appeared to have vanished into thin air. She didn't even have her phone with her.

'That's great news. Let me know how you get on. See you soon.'

Jessie thrust her shoulder against the door to the police station and made her way to the room that had been converted into her investigation room. She took the photo of a smiling Shannon from her bag and pinned it at the centre of the evidence board. She picked up the marker pen and scribbled Andrew Foster's name on it.

Shannon's diary and laptop had been brought up from Evidence and were on her desk, waiting for her. Jessie clicked on the kettle and retrieved a mug from the cupboard. While the water boiled, she stared at Shannon's smiling face. The photo Louise had given her was barely a month old. Jessie had worked missing persons for a long time before transferring to CID, but it never got easier when it was a child. It was now over forty-eight hours since Shannon had been seen last. She had no phone and no money with her. Whatever Dylan could get from Andrew Foster was vital.

CHAPTER TWENTY-THREE

Dylan couldn't believe Andrew Foster's appearance. Rather than the over-sedated, dishevelled zombie Jessie had tried talking to before, Andrew was sitting in the dining room clearly having showered and in clean clothes. His unruly burst of curls was tamed. His eyes were still heavy, but this was a huge improvement. The charge nurse took Dylan aside.

'He's better, but not as much as it might look.' She nodded at Andrew as she whispered, 'I'm still undecided whether he's ready to talk to you, but he's keen. Don't stay long.'

'I won't, don't worry. And you can stay too.'

Dylan reassured her, but if he was being honest, *he* would be more comfortable if she was nearby. He pulled out a chair opposite Andrew. Andrew nibbled his nails, then fixed Dylan with a silent, emotionless stare.

'How are you doing, Andrew?' Dylan said tentatively, and his words were answered with a shrug.

He opened his notebook and clicked his pen on. Then he inhaled a large, deep breath. He knew exactly what this interview meant to the investigation.

'Do you remember seeing Shannon Ross the night she disappeared? It was the night you were brought here.'

He waited and watched Andrew blink slowly and lift his thumb to wipe away a drop of saliva that had gathered in the corner of his mouth.

'I remember.' He spoke slowly, and it was clear it was a struggle to talk through his medication.

'That's good. How did she seem to you?'

'She's a good lass, Shannon. She gets me my bread and milk sometimes when I can't manage. She's not like the others. I know what they're up to.' Andrew Foster's eyes bore into Dylan as he tapped his head. 'They don't know their plan has been discovered.'

Then Andrew stopped talking. Instead he muttered something under his breath, closed his eyes and sighed. 'I'm sorry,' he finished in a murmur.

'What are you sorry for?' he asked.

'I didn't mean to push her so hard, but she was fussing, you know. I was confused, but it's clearer now. The fog has lifted a bit, but not completely. Some patches are still hazy.'

Dylan's heart raced. Was Andrew about to confess? Was it really going to be this easy? He pursed his lips but couldn't stop the involuntary bounce of his knee that he got when he was nervous.

'OK, tell me what bits you can remember.'

'I think I caught her lip with my nail and I cut her. I had to stop her fussing. She was in my face. I had to push her away, but I didn't mean to hurt her. I just had to escape. She was stifling me. She looked like she'd been punched but I swear I didn't hit her. I wouldn't hurt Shannon, I wouldn't. The look on her face when she ran out, I'll never forget it. She even dropped her phone. I should have gone after her to make it right, but I was so mixed up. My head was so cloudy, I couldn't think.' Andrew slapped his head twice.

Dylan glanced at Andrew's fingernails. They were long and ragged. Andrew's version of events sounded plausible, but Dylan wasn't sure if a cut lip was enough to spill blood on the floor.

'After she left, the voices screamed. They were so loud. They told me that if I stabbed myself they would stop, but they only laughed so I ran outside. I don't remember much after that.' He shrugged.

'So you don't have any idea where Shannon is now?'

Andrew sighed, then shook his head. 'I'm sorry.'

Another patient crashed open the dining room door and startled Andrew, who quickly scraped his chair backward to stand. Dylan barely got the chance to thank him for his help before he fled with the charge nurse a few paces behind him. He tucked his notebook away. He offered the new arrival a half-smile which was met with an eerie frown. By the time Dylan was in his car, he was relieved to be out of there.

Jessie sipped on her second cup of coffee. Starbucks it certainly wasn't, but it was passable.

10th October
I'm so happy I could burst. Being alone with him again today filled my tummy with the kind of butterflies only love can bring. Or is it lust, I don't know. I've never felt so strongly about anyone before and I know he feels the same way. Our love will have to stay hidden for now. People won't understand. When he lays his hands on me I feel so alive.

When she'd worked missing persons cases in the past, diaries were an important tool of the trade, but Shannon's was startling. Jessie quickly realised that there was far more to this quiet town than first appeared. First on her list was a visit to Eric Baldwin. Perhaps he could shed some more light on the revelations, being Shannon's best friend.

CHAPTER TWENTY-FOUR

Jessie was greeted at the door by a tall, slim woman with flecks of blue paint in her black hair and a strong German accent, who smiled warmly.

'Can I help you?'

'I'm DI Jessie Blake. I was wondering if I could have a word with your son, Eric. Is he in?'

'Of course, please come in.'

Agatha Baldwin opened the door wide and Jessie wiped her feet on the doormat, which she noticed read *Willkommen*; she thought that was cute.

'Eric!' Agatha called upstairs.

When she got no response, she pointed to the door at the end of the hall before heading upstairs.

'Go through. He might be wearing his headphones. I'll go and get him for you.' As she said it, she tapped her ears.

Jessie admired the paintings on the living room wall while she waited. The landscape watercolours were stunning. She recognised it as Queen's View, a little way up the road, a popular tourist spot overlooking the river Tummel. A visit from Queen Victoria had been the reason for the name. Agatha had captured the light beautifully and the breadth of the view, which was breathtaking.

Agatha took a seat opposite Jessie and could see that Eric's smile betrayed his anxiety when he pushed open the living room door to join them before flopping onto the sofa, his head down.

'Don't worry, you're not in trouble,' Jessie reassured him. 'Don't look so worried.'

'I know,' he answered solemnly. 'This is about Shannon, isn't it?'

'It is, yes. Well, more about her diary, actually.' Jessie nodded.

'Her diary?' Eric's confusion was instant.

'You didn't know she kept a diary?'

Eric shrugged. 'I know she was always writing, but not a diary. I thought she was writing a novel or something.'

Jessie had found no evidence of a novel. 'Is she?'

'Yes, it's about government conspiracy or a cover-up or something. She's really excited about it.' Eric's smile faded. 'You haven't found her yet, have you?'

Jessie sighed. 'Not yet, but we're doing everything we can. What can you tell me about Shannon's relationship with Calum Bailey and Rob Taylor?'

'What do you mean, relationship? Mr Bailey is our drama teacher and Rob is her dad's best mate.'

Eric was terrified his own friendship with Calum was in the diary. It would be catastrophic for Calum if their friendship was revealed. They had never been physical, so he had done nothing wrong. Calum understood what Eric was going through, that was all.

'Is it possible that Shannon was in a physical relationship with either of them, or both?' Jessie quizzed him.

The explicit nature of Shannon's writing had left very little to the imagination.

Eric screwed up his face.

'No, absolutely not, she wasn't like that.' Eric knew for a fact that she couldn't be having a relationship with Calum, but he didn't dare say. 'Shannon was a dreamer. She had a wild imagination. She must have made it up.'

'You keep talking about Shannon in the past tense, Eric. Why's that?'

Jessie's question startled Eric and tears filled his eyes. 'I don't know.'

'What's wrong?' Jessie was becoming increasingly suspicious of his behaviour. 'You seem nervous.'

'I just want my best friend back.' He dabbed his eyes with his fingers and sniffed away the tears.

It was then that Jessie noticed the eyeliner and mascara.

'Do you have any idea where she could have gone? Did she have a boyfriend that her parents didn't know about? Is he older than Shannon? Is she in trouble, Eric?' She handed the teenager a tissue from a packet she kept in her handbag. 'I'm sorry. I didn't mean to upset you. Shannon clearly means the world to you.' She smiled.

'She gets me, you know?' Eric wiped his face clean, then ran his fingers through his short, spiky hair. 'It's hard to be like me in a small town like this. She's always rooting for the underdog.' A little laugh escaped. 'And she hated bullies. When she saw Ben hassling Andrew, that drove her mad. I should have gone in there with her. Maybe if I had she wouldn't be missing.'

'You said to one of the other officers that she stepped in when her mum's younger brother, Ben, was having a go at a man named Andrew Foster, is that right?'

'That's right. Ben is a piece of work, he really is. Total arsehole.'

'In what way? Did he and Shannon get on?'

'Look up the words "arrogant bully" in the dictionary and you'll find the name Ben Randall written next to them. He's just one of those lads who find humour in other people's flaws and differences, you know.' Eric scoffed. 'Shannon said once I should feel sorry for him. I mean, seriously. She says he's got issues.'

Jessie took a moment to process Eric's reaction. It was clear he and Ben weren't the best of friends.

'What about Facebook, Eric?' she added.

'What about it?' Eric frowned.

'Was there anyone Shannon regularly spoke to on there that she might have arranged to meet?'

Eric shook his head vigorously. 'No way. Shannon was sensible. She wouldn't be that daft. In fact, she talked me out of doing it a while back. I got myself into a bit of trouble with a guy from Glasgow I'd been talking to on and off. He was hassling me to meet. I told Shannon and she talked me out of it.' He blushed because his mum was there, then repeated, 'She wouldn't be so daft.'

Jessie was beginning to build a better picture of Shannon Ross. It would seem she was a girl filled with good intentions and big, creative ambitions. She stuck up for the little guy, the oppressed and the misunderstood. She was loved by family and friends. A nagging doubt lingered in Jessie, though. Eric was adamant she wasn't in a relationship with either Calum Bailey or Rob Taylor, as the diary suggested. She wondered how Eric could be so sure if he didn't even know that his best friend kept a diary.

'Do you happen to know the password to Shannon's Facebook account?' she asked hopefully.

'Yes, sure. She knows mine, too. I thought we knew everything about each other,' he lied. He didn't think Shannon suspected anything about his friendship with Calum. 'Would you like me to log in for you?'

'That would be great.' Jessie was delighted with this development. 'Thank you.'

'I'll go and get it, hang on.' Eric stood up to leave as Agatha flashed him a soft smile of reassurance.

'Eric is being really helpful,' Jessie told her.

'He might not show it, but he is really worried. We all are. It's not like Shannon. She and Eric have been friends since nursery. This is just so awful.' Agatha sighed, then raised her eyes upwards. 'Where are my manners? I'm sorry, can I get you a cup of tea or coffee, detective?'

Jessie screwed up her nose. 'No thanks, I'm fine.'

'Here we go.' Eric sat close to her on the sofa as he logged into Shannon's Facebook account. The sight of her profile picture triggered more tears.

It was a picture of them taken just two weeks before at the edge of the river, the thrashing currents in the background. Eric handed the laptop to Jessie and wiped his face. She scrolled through Shannon's timeline to find several posts from concerned school friends asking her to get in touch. She checked Shannon's messages and found one that sparked her attention. It was from Calum Bailey, saying that he'd had time to think it over and they should meet to talk it through. Alarm bells rang loudly in Jessie's mind. She scribbled down the log-in details, then logged out of the account. The message had been left the morning of her disappearance. Shannon never sent a reply.

CHAPTER TWENTY-FIVE

Jason's legs burned from running. The heat spread rapidly from his calves to his thighs. He'd covered the three miles out onto the moor in a blur. He needed air. He needed to do something. He bent over, his hands gripping his knees to catch his breath. The first huge splat of rain didn't put him off. The increasing deluge couldn't make him turn round. Further he hiked through the bleak wilderness, the cold air trying to steal his breath with each step. Rain dripped from his cheeks and soaked into his clothes, but he had to keep moving. The call of the pink-footed geese overhead drew his attention and he followed their cries, his eyes drifting with the pattern of their flight. Every bird knew his place in the formation; even the stragglers. Where was Jason's place now?

Jason's chest tightened until it became hard to breathe. He coughed to clear the burning from his lungs. Within the isolated heart of the moor, Jason could be the last human on earth. The silence now encircled him, closing him inside the isolation. He stood to take in the whistling, gusting wind and the rain lashing his icy-cold cheeks, like he was trying to punish himself. He screamed into the wilderness around him – a long and guttural noise. He lifted his head to see the red deer stags scatter from their rut over the horizon, alerted to danger by his eruption and forcing an exodus of oystercatchers to rise, too. Again Jason screamed into the abyss until he was hoarse. He lifted his face into the driving, freezing rain, his teeth chattering in the chill. The sky darkened with his cries.

Ghillie Bobby Massie lifted his binoculars to his eyes and scanned the horizon for hares. He stopped dead when the sight of a man on his knees dressed in T-shirt and jeans caught his eye.

'Jesus, he must be frozen.' Bobby allowed the binoculars to dangle from his neck and used his walking pole to navigate his way towards the stranger. It wasn't until he got closer that Bobby realised it was Jason Ross. 'What are ye doin' out here? C'mon, I'll take you home, son.'

Jason didn't lift his head. Instead he remained motionless, the lashing rain battering against him and his sodden shirt stuck like glue to his torso. Bobby frowned and held out his hand.

'C'mon,' he repeated. 'Ye'll catch yer death out here.'

'Leave me!' Jason screamed. 'Would that really be a bad thing… would it?'

'C'mon, son, that wee lassie's going to need you when she gets back.'

Jason punched the boggy ground with the side of his fist. Then he hammered with such force with both hands, he created a pit in the earth. Bobby tugged his hat further over his ears against the biting wind out on the exposed moorland.

'Jason,' he murmured. 'C'mon with me. I've a flask a' rosy in the Jeep.'

Raindrops dripped from Jason's eyelashes as he lifted his eyes to see Bobby properly for the first time. As if he only now noticed the balding, Overweight fifty-year-old ghillie standing over him. Jason nodded and unfurled his mud-caked knees from the soil.

'That's it, c'mon with me.' Bobby placed an arm around Jason's soaked, trembling shoulder.

*

Rob Taylor sat and stared at his computer screen, then deleted the paragraph he had spent forty minutes writing. He allowed his head to drop into his hands and exhaled a long, slow breath. He hadn't slept at all last night, and his mind was blank. He was struggling to string a sentence together that made any sense.

He needed coffee, so he carried his mug to the kitchen to get a refill. The rain continued to lash outside his kitchen window. It seemed to Rob that the rain had started when Shannon disappeared and hadn't stopped. Each little drip raced towards puddles draining off the window ledge onto the pots of conifers below. All he could think about was Shannon and the agony Jason and Louise must be going through. He wished he could take the pain away, but he knew that would be impossible.

CHAPTER TWENTY-SIX

Jessie glanced down at her phone while she waited for Maggie to bring her breakfast. The text from her sister Freya made her smile, but it was the text from Carol that burned in her mind. She was still too afraid to call her, and she knew Carol wouldn't give bad news in a text. Perhaps if she didn't ever call it wouldn't be true. As she typed her reply to Freya, another of the pub's guests joined her in the dining room.

'Good morning,' Blair Crawford said as he sat down with his newspaper.

'Good morning,' Jessie replied, then looked away. The last thing she felt like doing was getting involved in small talk.

'It's a beautiful day out there,' Blair persisted, hoping his attempt at sarcastic weather humour would melt the ice.

She smiled and hoped he would take the hint. Blair could see that he would have to work harder to get her to bite. He would have to be more direct.

'You'll be here in connection with the missing girl, Shannon Ross. How is the search going?'

His question drew Jessie's attention from her phone.

'You should know I can't discuss the investigation with you.'

Jessie's eyes held Blair's as she delivered the answer he guessed he would get. Maggie Malcolm broke the tension with two plates of cooked breakfast for her guests.

'That looks good enough to eat,' Blair joked as Maggie laid his plate in front of him.

Jessie smirked. *How original.*

'Thank you,' Jessie said when hers was placed in front of her.

'Help yourselves to tea and coffee,' Maggie told them before returning to the kitchen.

'I know you can't discuss the case, but I just wanted to say I hope you find her soon. Shannon reminds me of another young girl. Another blonde teenager who didn't come home from school. One of my first assignments, actually,' Blair commented. 'Can't believe it was twenty years ago. It feels like yesterday.'

'Is that right, and, of course, I hope so too.' Jessie still wasn't biting. 'I'm getting a coffee, would you like one?'

She stood up from the table.

'Yes, that would be great, thanks.' Jessie poured the coffees as he continued. 'Do you remember Sophie Nicoll? She was a fifteen-year-old girl who went missing in the North East twenty years ago.'

Jessie frowned and attempted to recall the name, then shook her head.

'Sophie's body was found a few days later. She had been raped and murdered by two teenage boys she knew from school.'

'That's awful,' Jessie answered, and swallowed a bite of her toast.

'It's a story that's always stuck with me, you know. I spent a bit of time with Sophie's family for a while afterwards. Getting to know them. You know, the real Sophie, not just Sophie the victim. Stayed with me to this day. One of the lads committed suicide not long after. The other one, Daniel Simpson, served five years and is living God knows where, with a new identity and a second chance at life, which was more than they gave Sophie.'

'The boys were tried as juveniles, then?' Jessie commented.

Blair raised his eyebrows. 'Sadly, they were, yes. I'd have locked the bastards up and thrown away the key. Excuse the language.' He lifted his hand to apologise.

'Clearly the probation service felt he was no longer a threat then.'

Blair scoffed. 'Yes, sure, and they always get it right, don't they?'

Jessie washed her food down with the last of her coffee and checked the time on her watch. She wiped her mouth with her napkin and stood. Blair nodded with a smile.

'That was delicious,' Jessie called out to Maggie before she left.

'You have a good day, detective.'

'You too. See you later, perhaps.'

'Morning, Jessie. How's it going?' Dylan yawned, then greeted her with a warm smile as she walked into their compact incident room. 'Kettle's boiled, if you're after a brew.'

'Nah, I'm good, thanks. I've just had a cooked breakfast at The Black Witch. I'm stuffed.' She ignored the buzzing of her phone in her pocket.

Dylan frowned. 'You avoiding someone?'

'What?' Jessie snapped. 'No, why would I be avoiding anyone? Who would I be avoiding?'

She could see by the look on Dylan's face that she had over-reacted, but this was none of his business. The last thing she needed was Dylan's advice to distract her.

'OK, then.' Dylan refilled his cup with hot water and tipped in another spoonful of sugar. It was clear to him that she didn't want to talk about whatever was going on.

'Right, where was I?' Jessie ran her fingers through her shoulder-length black hair before pinning it into its usual messy bun. She tapped Shannon's diary with her finger. 'Right, the contents of Shannon's diary are an eye-opener, to say the least. If any of this little lot is true, there is a hell of a lot more to this sleepy little place that you might think.'

'I'm listening.' Dylan sipped his tea.

'Shannon, it seems, has quite the private life. There are entries in here to suggest her relationship with both Rob Taylor and her teacher Calum Bailey are not what they seem. Wait a minute, let me see if I can just find… ah, yes, here we are.'

She began to read. '"The moments we are alone are what I live for. He is so strong yet so very gentle. We both know what we feel seems wrong to so many people but how can something so wrong feel so right?"'

Dylan almost spat out his tea. 'What the hell? No way, let me see that.'

'Well, what with that and the cryptic message from Bailey on Facebook. What had he had time to think about, I wonder? Their relationship?'

Jessie passed him the diary then moved around to her evidence board, drew two lines from Shannon's smiling face and wrote the names Rob Taylor and Calum Bailey next to each one. Stranger things have happened. She lifted the lid on Shannon's laptop and logged into Facebook. She wanted to believe his reaction to Shannon's disappearance was genuine. The worry he expressed seemed real enough. Jessie scrolled down Shannon's timeline and read through some of the posts from concerned school friends, which were touching. Some suggested that they thought Shannon might have left Inverlochty because of something that troubled her, which intrigued Jessie. Had she simply run away? She scanned Bailey's message again. *What had he had time to think about?*

'You reckon Foster's in the frame, too, then? You reckon he knows more than he's letting on?' Dylan asked as he dropped the diary onto her desk and gulped the last of his tea, but not before spilling some on his tie.

'Jesus, Dylan, with a mouth that size how can you miss it?' Jessie laughed until her phone rang again, causing her expression to fall quickly into one of tension.

'Everything OK, Jess?' Dylan frowned. He was curious after watching her check the caller ID, switch it to silent and toss her phone down.

Jessie had to turn away, and she sniffed back the tears that began to sting the backs of her eyes. She coughed quickly to compose herself.

'Yes, fine, it's nothing, and yes, I'm not ruling anything or anyone out. Shannon is out there. Searches of the wood and Ben Lochty have turned up nothing.' She wiped the back of her hand across her nose and sniffed again. 'Right, I want you to talk to Bailey, and I'm heading to Rob Taylor's. See what he has to say about that.' She pointed to the diary as the buzz of a text rang out. 'Maybe one of those two can shed light on it. Or indeed, where the wee lass is. Has one of them arranged to meet her somewhere later?'

Dylan watched her take in a huge breath before opening the text message.

'Sure thing, boss.' Dylan nodded and pushed his chair under the table.

'I'll see you back here,' Jessie told him.

'If you're sure you're OK?' he answered with a wide-eyed nod of his head.

'I'm fine, Dylan, thank you. Please don't fuss.'

Dylan closed the door and she opened Carol's fifth message in two days. How could a short message with two innocent words fill Jessie with such terror?

Call me.

That's all she'd put. Jessie moved to the small rain-splashed window and stared out at the hills that surrounded Inverlochty, wishing she was on top of one of them right then, even if it was lashing down with freezing rain, while she waited for Carol to pick up. By the time she'd heard three rings, she feared her heart might explode.

'Hey, Carol, it's me.'

CHAPTER TWENTY-SEVEN

Louise opened her eyes and for one brief wonderful heartbeat Shannon wasn't gone, her daughter wasn't missing, and she would be there any minute. In her sleepy haze, everything in Louise's life was as it should be. Pain ripped into her when reality returned, and she pushed her face into the pillow and sobbed.

Her mobile buzzed on the bedside table. Through her tears she read a text from Cassie and laid the phone back down without answering it. Louise closed her eyes and tugged the duvet up round her neck. The more time that went by without any word from Shannon was crushing her. The not knowing was agony. She'd heard that expression in the past, but it was so true. They were currently enduring the gut-twisting limbo between hope and agony. It literally felt like torture to Louise.

Her mother wasn't helping, with her suggestions that perhaps Shannon had a secret boyfriend and she'd run away with him. If that was the case, she added, Shannon was probably having the time of her life. Even that detective thought Shannon had run away, but Louise knew her daughter better than either of them. She wouldn't keep a secret like that. Louise was sure of it. Eric would have told her by now anyway, especially after talking to the police. He wouldn't want to get into trouble.

Louise tucked her knees up into her stomach and hid her face from the light streaming in through the crack in the curtain. Maybe if she went to sleep again, Shannon would be there when she next woke.

*

'I'll get it!' Rob called as he went to answer the front door. 'Jason! Come in.' Rob pulled the door wide open, aghast at the state of Jason.

Rob had never seen Jason's eyes look so empty. They were dead, and it was clear he hadn't shaved for days. The stench of stale alcohol oozed through his pores.

'Where is she?' Jason's words were slow and deliberate, his expression fixed and staring as he walked past him down the long hallway towards Rob's living room.

'Come on, I'll make us some coffee.' Rob placed his arm around Jason's shoulders but, before they could get to the kitchen, there was a loud knock.

'I'll go this time,' Cassie whispered.

She was surprised to find a woman she didn't recognise standing on the doorstep with her badge close to her face.

'Hello, my name is DI Blake. I'm looking for Rob Taylor?'

'Of course, yes, he's in the kitchen, go straight through.'

'Thank you.' Jessie wiped her feet before going in, impressed by the antique oak sideboard and matching coat rack just inside the front door. She wouldn't have chosen the basic magnolia paint for such a large space, though. Jessie would have gone for more of a mocha instead. The wood floor looked real; expensive, too.

Jason's head appeared round the kitchen door on hearing Jessie's voice.

'Detective Blake? Have you found her? Why are you here? How did you know I would be here?'

Jessie nibbled her bottom lip. As much as she felt sorry for Jason, his presence here made the situation awkward.

'Jason, I'm not here for you.'

'What do you mean? Why are you here then?'

'Jason, mate,' Rob intervened. 'Let's get that coffee. Detective, can I get you a coffee?'

Jessie nodded. 'That would be great.'

Her chat with Rob Taylor would have to wait. For now.

CHAPTER TWENTY-EIGHT

1997

'Hey, Dan, wait up.'

The sound of Malky's Irish brogue travelled quickly towards Daniel as he cleared away his breakfast tray. The five-foot-six Irish lad had befriended Daniel the day Malky arrived. Being Irish and short made Jockey the ideal nickname, and Malky hated it. He wasn't shy about letting everyone know it, but he and Daniel got on well. Perhaps that was because Daniel had never called him Jockey. Not to his face, at least.

It hadn't been long before the reason for Daniel's incarceration came up in conversation. Malky said he hadn't heard but Daniel let that go. It was common knowledge in Carseview that Daniel was in for murder. Theft and GBH were Malky's speciality, and he had put a security guard in hospital with a broken jaw and several smashed ribs. Both boys had been raised in similarly dysfunctional homes, which bonded them immediately. Who knew having a junkie mother could be helpful because, before Malky, Daniel had kept himself to himself.

Even as a big lad, Daniel had been terrified of prison. It was a struggle to come to terms with the noise most of all. It was like nothing he had ever heard.

Daniel raised his head in greeting as Malky got closer. 'How's it going, Malk?'

'Not bad, not bad.'

'Where you been? You've missed your breakfast,' Daniel asked.

Malky smirked. 'Had a meeting with Cam, didn't I? She's coaching me for this parole meeting shit next week, isn't she?'

Daniel pushed his tray onto the pile and turned to face him. 'Lucky bastard.'

'Fuck off, they're not going to let me out. That security bastard is milking it, isn't he? He's still on crutches.' Malky grinned and squeezed Daniel's shoulder. 'You're stuck with me buddy.'

'You two get your arses in gear.' The prison officer's instruction tore into their laughter. 'Solomon wants you on time today, Malky.'

'Sir, just going, sir.' Daniel moved past him behind Malky, whose smirk was as big as his personality.

'Sir, just going, sir,' Malky mimicked.

'Fuck off,' Daniel retaliated.

'Nice to see you, Malky,' John Solomon greeted the last two students and closed the door quietly after them. 'Sit down, get your books out and turn to page sixty-five. Daniel, you start.'

Daniel would never admit this to anyone, but he didn't mind Mr Solomon's class. He enjoyed the education programme. It was different to school. He would certainly never admit it to any of the other lads. They would be merciless. But Cam knew. Instead, he had to join in Malky's ribbing. The sound of Malky's stifled laughter was something he had got used to. It was the soundtrack to their English class.

'Malky.' Mr Solomon guided Malky's book down onto the desk in front of him and pointed to the page. 'Enough.'

Daniel continued to read on, regardless, until the next reader was invited to carry on. He stared out of the window at the sunshine streaming across the golden fields of wheat, reliving that day over in his mind. In three weeks it would be exactly one year ago. If he had said no to Jack that morning. If he had helped his mum, like she had asked, instead; but he was angry with her that day. He didn't care that she was suffering. She had let him down again and he wanted to punish her; for her to feel the hurt he felt. But he couldn't go back. None of them could. The nightmares had stopped, at least. It was a long time before he'd forget the sight of Sophie's face; her hair streaked across her cheek, looking up at them as the soil hit her. That was an image Daniel would never forget.

'And that's it for today, everyone.'

Daniel looked up at the clock; an hour had passed. He got up to leave, as did the others.

'Daniel, I need to have a chat with you. Got a minute?'

Daniel spun round as he left the classroom to see Cam waiting for him. Daniel frowned at her serious expression.

'I'll catch you later, man.' Malky nodded to Cam before following the rest of their class into the gym.

'Hello.' Daniel eyed her suspiciously. 'Is everything OK?'

Cam unlocked one of the rooms that led off the main corridor. Now Daniel was worried.

'Have a seat,' Cam told him as she put her bag on the floor and hung her cardigan over the back of the chair.

Daniel's mouth suddenly felt like he hadn't had a drink for days. It was as if his tongue had become fixed to the roof of his mouth. He flopped down onto the chair opposite her, then shuffled uncomfortably until Cam spoke. She sorted through the papers in the folder in front of her.

'Tom Nicoll has managed to get a new lawyer to take on his case.'

Daniel's eyes narrowed. He couldn't understand why Tom Nicoll needed a lawyer.

'What do you mean? Tom Nicoll has a lawyer? What's that about?'

Cam nodded and offered Daniel a half-smile he recognised. The smile that was about to deliver bad news.

'Look, it's your right to know, but I don't want you to worry unnecessarily until there's something to worry about.'

'What?' Daniel sat bolt upright in his chair. 'What, worry about what?'

Cam ran her fingers over her forehead. There it was. That smile again.

'Sophie's family have hired Malcolm Richards to appeal your sentence. They will be petitioning the high court that your sentence was unduly lenient and should be increased. They're going to argue that time spent in juvenile detention isn't appropriate under the circumstances, and want you transferred to an adult prison for the remainder of your sentence.'

'What does that mean?' Daniel stuttered, his eyes darting around the room. 'I could go to prison?'

'First things first. We don't panic. Just because they want to appeal doesn't mean the appeal will even be granted but, as your social worker, I am obliged to keep you informed. You will be appointed a lawyer too if you need one, don't worry.'

Daniel rested his elbows on the table then dropped his head into his hands, shaking it as he spoke. 'This can't be happening. Not again. Please, not again.'

Cam reached out her hand and took hold of his arm.

'Look at me, Daniel, look at me.'

Daniel lifted his head. The fear in his eyes tugged at Cam's heart.

'Cam, I'm scared,' he whispered.

'I know you are, and I'm sorry this is happening to you, but you have to be brave.' She squeezed his wrist and Daniel grabbed onto her hand. 'You're not alone, OK? Whatever happens from here, you're not alone.'

Daniel appreciated she was trying her best to alleviate his fear, but nothing Cam could say would shift the gut-wrenching terror that had just thumped into his life. If only he could rewind the clock and go back to that day.

CHAPTER TWENTY-NINE

'Have you called Louise?' Jessie's patience was dwindling while she waited for Jason to finish his coffee. Her patience was wearing very thin. The longer she waited, the more chance Rob had of getting wind that she was really after him, if he hadn't realised already.

'She's not answering her phone,' Cassie answered, her face pale and tired. 'Shall I go and get her? Maybe she could take Jason home.'

Jessie had a better idea. The questions she had for Rob would have to be asked when she returned. 'No, I'll take Jason home.'

Rob and Jason sat in silence. Jason's fingers gripped the cup, but he hadn't drunk a drop. He sat motionless, staring out of the window. Rob looked up to see Cassie join them and was relieved to hear Jessie's suggestion.

'Come on, Jason, I'll give you a ride home.' She spoke quietly and rested a hand on his shoulder.

Her words were ignored until drips of cold coffee spilled onto Jason's leg, stirring him from his trance. He stared past her and placed his cup on the coffee table.

The pair drove in silence the short journey to Jason's home until he uttered words that Jessie dared not answer.

'She's dead, isn't she?'

Dylan rang the doorbell for a second time. When there was still no answer he moved to the living room window and screwed up his face as he peered in. The room was in darkness. He glanced down at his watch, then jogged back to the front door. He rang the bell again and listened before hammering it with the palm of his hand. Dylan wasn't giving up. The thought that Calum Bailey might be having a relationship with a fifteen-year-old girl alarmed him. He peered in at the window one last time, frustration coursing through him. He stepped around the puddles and tugged his hood up against the deluge, then headed back to his car. Perhaps Bailey was still at school.

Movement from the car park caught Calum Bailey's attention and his heart sank. Eric watched the colour drain from his face and turned to look out of the window.

'What is it?' Eric asked.

'You better go. He's probably here to speak to me.'

Eric's fingers lightly brushed Calum's shoulders. 'Text me later,' he said, then opened the classroom door to Dylan.

'Hello, Eric, you're keen. It's half past four.'

Eric smiled and walked away without answering. Calum stood up from behind his desk.

'Come in. Have a seat.'

'I'm DC Dylan Logan.' Dylan held his ID close to Calum's face before he sat down.

'Of course. What can I do for you?' Calum's throat was dry. He took one large gulp from his water bottle on the desk, hoping his nervousness wasn't too obvious.

Dylan glanced out the window to see Eric Baldwin staring back at him, but when Eric realised he had been spotted, he threw up the hood of his light jacket and hurried out of the gate. He noticed, however, that he was heading in the opposite direction to the Baldwins' home. Calum's cheeks flushed when he realised what he was looking at.

'Is this about Shannon?' Calum asked.

'I think it would be best if we come straight to the point.' Dylan's gaze bore into Calum's eyes. 'We know that you wanted to meet with Shannon the day she disappeared. You sent her a message saying you'd had time to think. What did you mean by that?'

'It was nothing, detective.'

'It couldn't have been nothing. I mean, how common is it for you to send private messages to your students on Facebook? What was the nature of your relationship with Shannon? It was clearly more than student and teacher for you to be contacting each other like that.'

Dylan continued to watch and wait as his words hung in the air. Calum sat back in his chair and considered his next move carefully.

CHAPTER THIRTY

Rob was rinsing the coffee mugs under the hot tap when Cassie wrapped her arms around his stomach from behind. She nestled her head in the lambswool sweater he always wore.

'I'm going for a lie-down,' she told him. 'I'm shattered.'

'Hey, come here,' Rob whispered. He gently cupped her face, then kissed her passionately on her lips. 'I love you.'

'I know,' she answered. 'I love you too.' She kissed his cheek and walked into their bedroom.

The doorbell rang. He ran to get it before the caller could ring again and disturb Cassie.

'Hello again, Rob, can we talk?'

'Of course, detective, but can I come to the station? Cassie's exhausted and I don't want her disturbed.'

'I'll give you a lift in my car.'

Rob considered her invitation for a moment, then nodded. The sooner he got there, the sooner he could get it over with.

Rob wiped his moist palms across his trousers. His mouth was so dry. The interview room she'd brought him to was cold, yet Rob was sweating. He peeled his sweater off and slung it over the back of the chair. The chair was hard and uncomfortable. Rob wished he'd declined Jessie's offer of a coffee. The wait for her to return with it was excruciating, although he knew these places weren't built for comfort.

'I'm sorry, I got held up. Here you go, milk and one sugar.'

Rob sipped slowly and tried to smile through his anxiety. 'Thanks.'

He licked his lips and waited.

'OK, you're probably wondering why I would want to speak to you.'

'Well, yes, but I imagine you need to speak to anyone with a connection to Shannon and her family.' Rob took a big gulp. Keeping his hands busy made him feel less nervous. Jessie placed the evidence bag with Shannon's diary in it on the table close to Rob. He picked the book up and frowned, then put it straight back down.

'What's this?' Rob pinched the bridge of his nose and frowned.

'This is Shannon's diary. This is where she keeps a journal, a very personal journal.'

'OK.' Rob spoke slowly, the sense of unease growing rapidly.

'An entry on page twenty-seven caught my eye, and that's why I need to speak to you.'

She removed the diary from the bag and turned to page twenty-seven. Rob gulped more of his coffee and felt a drip of sweat gather above his right eye. He was desperate to wipe it away but feared it would reveal his anxiety, so he left it and hoped his eyebrow would absorb it.

'I'll read a small extract to you.'

Jessie looked up and noticed a flush of red develop on his neck.

> Being with Rob tonight felt so good. I know he feels the way I do. He's always at the house and I know he wants to be alone with me.

She stopped reading and looked over at the shocked expression on Rob's face. His eyes were wide and staring.

'What the hell is she talking about? That sounds like we're—' Rob couldn't comprehend what he was hearing, and a sickening thud slammed into his stomach. Shannon was a clever girl with a fantastic imagination but never, in his worst nightmares, did he expect to hear this.

His hands are strong and powerful, but when he lays them on me I want to cry with pleasure, but I must remain in silent ecstasy.

'Can I please have a look at that?'

His heart thudded in his chest. Shannon's words made it look like she and him were in the midst of a passionate affair. He clasped a hand across his mouth and Jessie watched on without saying a word.

He flicked through some of the other pages and another entry caught his eye. Shannon suspected her mother was seeing another man, but didn't know it was him. Rob inhaled – a huge, deep breath – and handed back the diary.

'Shannon is an incredibly intelligent and imaginative young girl... Look, Cassie suggested a while back that she thought Shannon had some kind of teenage crush on me. I didn't believe her at the time, but now...' Rob pointed to the diary. 'That is pure fantasy. I can assure you, detective inspector, there's nothing going on between me and Shannon.' He gave in and rubbed away the drop of sweat with the back of his hand. 'Shannon is a child, for goodness' sake. I wouldn't do that. I'm not that kind of man. I can't believe this is happening.'

Jessie nibbled her bottom lip, the way she did when she was thinking.

'Where were you the night Shannon went missing?'

'I was in The Black Witch with Jason. There are at least forty people who can confirm that. Ask Maggie Malcolm, she'll tell you I was there.'

'And you haven't heard from Shannon since that night?'

'Of course not, why would I?' Rob frowned. 'If I had, you would be the first to know – I can assure you.'

'You won't mind me checking your phone, then, will you?' She held his gaze, just to be sure.

'Be my guest.' Rob grabbed his iPhone from his pocket and slid it across the table. He closed his eyes and shook his head. Jessie scrolled through Rob's call log and found a large number of calls to and from Louise Ross. She initially wondered if the affair had begun when Cassie became pregnant, until she saw that some of the texts were over six months old.

'It was you that Louise was having an affair with?' Jessie asked.

She handed him back his phone. Rob sighed as he pushed his phone deep into his pocket.

'I'm not proud of being unfaithful to Cassie, but what I had with Louise ended before the wedding. And what we did wasn't a crime. We're both adults.'

'Did Shannon suspect the affair?'

'I don't think so, but I don't know anything about her any more, after that.' Rob pointed at the diary. 'I just wish she would come home. Jason and Louise are struggling. Neither of them have slept for days.'

'We're supporting the family in every way we can.'

'You think Shannon is dead, don't you?'

Jessie stood, then held the door open for Rob and allowed his words to evaporate.

'We'll be in touch if we need to speak to you again.'

Rob stopped by the interview room door. 'Cassie doesn't know, and neither does Jason.' He searched Jessie's eyes for reassurance.

'Let's hope they never have to find out, then.'

CHAPTER THIRTY-ONE

1997

Daniel watched Gail Robertson pin her long, mousy-brown hair into a messy bun before she'd noticed him arrive for their session. He liked Gail. He liked her a lot. She'd told him she had been a support worker at Carseview for ten years and had seen lots of boys, just like him, make a success of their time there. She explained that punishment wasn't the only objective. She wanted her boys to thrive, she said. But that wasn't what Daniel liked the most about Gail. It was her double-D breasts the majority of the boys loved most of all. Not that she flaunted it, of course. That would be madness in a place like Carseview.

Her modesty was sexy, too. The fact that Gail Robertson was a forty-five-year-old mother of three sons didn't matter. Maybe it was a maternal attraction the boys had for her. The vast majority of Carseview inmates came from backgrounds without a nurturing mother figure, so it made sense. Although Gail was never alone with her boys, as she called them. Julia would not allow that.

'Good morning, Mrs Robertson.' Daniel offered her the widest smile he could manage.

'Hello, Daniel, come on in. Close the door.'

Daniel nodded to the prison officer in the corner, who reciprocated without smiling.

'I've brought the sheet you wanted me to fill in.'

'Oh good, let me see.' Gail reached out and took the booklet from him. She narrowed her eyes as she skimmed his answers. 'Have a seat, Daniel. I'll be right back. I need to pop next door to photocopy this for you. This will form the basis for the plan, going forward.' She turned back to smile at him as she bustled towards the door that separated her room from the administrator's office. Daniel blushed as he realised he'd been caught staring at her bottom.

'OK, this one is for you and I will keep this copy in your file.' Gail handed back his booklet, allowing her perfume to drift into Daniel's nostrils a little before she sat back down, causing a warmth to grow between his legs.

'Thanks,' he said sheepishly.

'So, have you got any questions?' she asked.

Daniel shook his head. 'No, I think the plan is pretty clear.'

'You're happy with your next steps?'

He nodded this time. 'Standard Grades and Highers won't be easy, I know, but I'll give it my best shot and I think choosing five subjects was enough, although I know you wanted me to do more.'

Gail's smile was infectious. 'It's better that you do the five you're comfortable with this year.'

'Even that will be a lot.' He shrugged.

'Don't be so hard on yourself. You're a clever lad, and I think you know that, deep down.' She glanced at the paper. 'Maths, English, Biology, Art and History. Good mix there.'

'I'm not looking forward to the maths.' He grinned.

'Nobody looks forward to maths.' Gail laughed.

Daniel stared into Gail's dark brown eyes and wished his mum had been like her.

'You're still enjoying the library shifts, are you?'

The ghost of a smile crept over Daniel's lips. 'It's not exactly a busy place but yes, it's fine. It's better than the laundry, I suppose, or the kitchen. Couldn't stand the thought of washing up every day.'

'Well, you won't be able to avoid that kind of thing for ever.'

Daniel shrugged with a grin. 'I can try.'

The sight of Gail glancing at her watch always created a sinking feeling in Daniel's stomach because it meant their session was over. It would be another week before he could spend time with her again, and Daniel missed her. Looking forward to their time together kept him going through those long nights alone.

CHAPTER THIRTY-TWO

Blair took his seat amidst the throng of television and newspaper journalists. He nodded to those he recognised and switched his phone to silent. There was the usual sense of anticipation, nervous excitement, in the room. The assembled press pack shuffled in their seats and then fell silent apart from the occasional cough, followed by the short blowing of someone's nose. Louise walked into the room slowly, head down, behind Jessie, wearing the same black jeans and dark blue T-shirt she'd had on since Shannon disappeared. Jessie guided her to the table and pulled out a chair for her before sitting down herself.

Jason wasn't there. It hadn't taken much digging to uncover details of Jason's unpredictable temper. A medical discharge from the army followed an assault on a senior officer during a drunken binge. He was diagnosed later with PTSD. Blair presumed DI Blake didn't trust Jason to cope with the stress of a public appeal. She was probably right. Blair's attention switched back to Louise. She appeared so fragile, like a little bird, that his mind was thrust back twenty years to the disappearance of Sophie Nicoll.

Jessie tapped a pile of papers against the table to the chorus of camera clicks. She cleared her throat, then took a sip of water.

'Good afternoon, and thank you for coming.' Camera flashes distracted Jessie briefly, but she persevered. 'Shannon Ross was last seen three days ago.' She held up Shannon's most recent school photo. 'It's imperative that anyone who knows where Shannon is, or who she could be with, contact the helpline urgently or any police officer. Over these last three days she has not contacted her friends or family. As far as we are aware, she does not have any money or clothes with her. Her disappearance is completely out of character. She hasn't been seen since half past three on Monday afternoon and, as you can imagine, we are all becoming increasingly concerned for her safety.'

Jessie reached under the table for Louise's hand and gave it a gentle squeeze. Louise sniffed and straightened up in preparation. The cameras snapped faster as she began to speak. Louise's legs trembled uncontrollably.

'Shannon, if you are watching this, please come home to us. We miss you. We need you home. Please, if anyone knows where Shannon is, tell someone. I just want you home. I need my baby home.'

Louise's words evaporated into a fresh bout of tears until she became inconsolable. Jessie intervened.

'I'm sorry, we can't take any questions, but please contact me or one of my colleagues if you know anything that can assist us.' She indicated to Louise to stand, but her legs collapsed underneath her. Her pain was so raw it hurt to see. Dylan ushered the press out quickly, so that Louise could receive medical attention.

Rob clasped his hands over his mouth and sniffed back his own tears. When he heard Cassie slam the front door shut, he quickly switched off the television and rubbed his eyes.

'I'm home. Could you get the rest of the bags? My back hurts like hell.'

Cassie was shocked by the state of Rob's tear-streaked face. She hurried to console him, fearing there had been a tragic development.

'What's happened? Is she—'

'I'm fine, no, there's no news. It's the appeal.'

He felt the tears sting his eyes once more. Seeing Louise's pain, he ached to hold her and tell her it was going to be OK. There was no way he could ever share that with Cassie.

'I'll call her.'

'Leave her for now. She's got that detective with her, and Jason. I'm sure he's there.'

Cassie scoffed. 'Aye, and what good is he? He's probably drunk, isn't he?'

Before Rob had a chance to contradict her in Jason's defence, Cassie cursed loudly from the hallway.

'Shit, I forgot to get your coffee.'

'It's fine, I don't need it that badly. I can wait.'

'No, I'll nip back out for it. It's your favourite.'

She grabbed her car keys and her bag until Rob took hold of her arm and kissed her.

'Put your feet up. I'll get the coffee,' Rob said to her with a smile. He needed to clear his head.

Rob walked to the little shop on the main street in just over ten minutes. As he passed the police station, a group of journalists joined him, taking him by surprise when a camera was thrust close to his face. The female reporter smiled and hastily asked if he knew Shannon and her family, and how the search was going. Rob froze. He wanted to run but his feet held him fast until the woman turned away from him.

'There has been no news on the whereabouts of local teenager Shannon Ross, and it seems the entire village is out looking for her. Sasha Monroe, ITV news.' Rob watched the news crew retreat as suddenly as they had appeared, his heart racing.

'Hello, Rob.' Maggie Malcolm startled him as she exited the shop. She shook her head. 'Terrible business. They must be so worried. Tell them if they need anything, to just ask. I'll be more than happy to help.'

Maggie nodded towards Louise being supported down the steps of the police station with DI Blake and DC Logan on either side of her. Maggie held the shop door open for Rob who frowned, then sprinted over to Louise.

'Louise!'

Louise looked up at him through the haze of tears. The pair stood silently staring at each other until she grabbed hold of him to prevent herself falling to the ground. Rob took the opportunity to comfort her. He closed his eyes and hugged her close to his chest and she sobbed, soaking his shirt with her tears. She held on so tightly that her nails dug into his flesh.

'I'll take her home, detective.'

'Thanks, Rob. I'll get back to the station to trawl through any new leads the appeal has generated.'

Rob kissed Louise on the head and held her close to his chest. Eventually she looked up at him with fear in her eyes, unable to speak.

'It's OK, I'll take care of you.'

Louise allowed him to lead her away from the station and the hustle and bustle of the main street. The pair walked in silence for half an hour, Louise holding onto him.

Then she noticed the silence. The scent of the Scots pine forest woke Louise from her fog. Memories of walks with Shannon as a toddler when they still had Max, Louise's old Labrador, slammed into her. Shannon would hold onto his lead, and although he could easily have pulled the tiny little girl off her feet, he never did. He was so patient with Shannon, even when she took his biscuits or his favourite toy. Shannon's heart was broken when Max had to be put to sleep when she was seven. She was adamant she didn't want another dog. So they didn't get one.

Louise reached out and ran her fingers over a damp tree trunk, snagging her thumb on a sharp piece of loose bark. She lifted her thumb to her lips and sucked the blood, then turned to face Rob, her eyes searching his for comfort.

'Where is she, Rob?' she whispered.

Rob would have done anything to take Louise's pain away.

'I don't know. But you need to be strong, Lou.' The temperature dropped as a black cloud threatened overhead. 'Come on, we'll shelter in here for a bit.' He led Louise into The Shieling, the abandoned cottage that had been empty for as long as Rob had lived there. Legend had it that it was old Morag McIver's cottage, where she fled the day the townsfolk chased her. Maggie Malcolm swore blind she had seen Morag herself around the crumbling property.

'Maybe auld Morag knows where she is,' Louise told him. 'Because nobody else does.'

Not that he believed in ghosts, but Rob quickly closed the door after them, just in case. The darkness of the woods cast shadows that played tricks on the eyes in this light.

'Hey, come here.' Rob held out his arms to her.

Louise snuggled her face close to his chest and inhaled his fresh sandalwood scent.

Rob was so different to Jason. He was gentle where Jason could be brash and clumsy. Rob soothed her when Jason added to her pain right now. They hadn't planned to have an affair. Louise had fallen for him in a moment of weakness. A drunken moment of weakness, to be more precise. Jason had passed out, he'd been so drunk, and Cassie had left the new year party early saying she had a headache. They got caught up in the moment, the celebration. A new year's kiss turned into something more passionate, which then morphed into secret, stolen moments that neither of them had planned. She knew Jason loved her, but Rob was different. She couldn't explain it.

She clung on, revelling in the warmth of his arms around her in the silence. Not that this was the first time they had snuck out to

The Shieling, but that wasn't what Louise was searching for today. They both knew it was over. He was about to become a father.

Blair began to regret his decision to take a walk in Inver Wood alone. Why did every tree look exactly the same, and why would his mind not allow him to forget the painting of Morag McIvor and her shadowy figure creeping between them? He couldn't help feeling small in the middle of such a vast, dense patch of woodland. The case was preying on his mind, too; Shannon's likeness to Sophie Nicoll was uncanny. He had never forgotten Sophie Nicoll's heartbroken family. Probably because it had been his first big case; but still, she was so like Shannon Ross. The sight of a small cottage tucked at the centre of the trees intrigued him as he got closer.

His phone buzzing in his pocket drifted into his thoughts.

'Hello, Blair Crawford.' He frowned. 'Hello, who is this? You'll have to speak up, I can't hear you.'

He gave up on the caller when it was clear he had a very poor signal and walked on, looking for anything that might tell him what had happened to Shannon. Maybe something the search team had missed. The cottage up ahead drew him until the heavens opened again, forcing another deluge on him. He turned back towards the pub, his search merely postponed for now.

Tom Nicoll dropped the glass he was drying, and it smashed into pieces all over his kitchen floor. Seeing that press conference was like a kick in the gut. His heart raced at a million miles an hour. He had to leave. He could be in Inverlochty by morning. Shannon's parents needed all the support they could get, and if anyone knew what they were going through, Tom did.

*

Jessie wasn't sure why, but she had to call. It seemed irrational, but she couldn't rest until she had. Talking to Carol had shaken her to the core. Her instinct was to run. To hide from whatever was coming; but she couldn't. Jessie had responsibilities, not least to Shannon. She was relying on her. She couldn't rush home to reassure herself that everything was OK.

'Hey, Jess, how is it all going up there?' Dave asked.

'Yeah, fine, well, not fine, but you know… Listen, I just wondered. Is Smokey OK?'

Jessie listened to the pause until her neighbour's answer soothed her racing heart.

'Of course he's OK. Listen.'

Jessie heaved a huge sigh of relief when she heard soft purring down the line. She squeezed her eyes tight shut and savoured every sound.

'He's been staying in my flat at night. I hope that's OK,' Dave told her. 'Has done since that first night. Must be missing you, Jess.'

'Thanks, Dave. You're a good friend.'

Dave's booming laugh rippled into Jessie's ear.

'You soppy article,' he teased. 'Smokey's no trouble. He's good company. When he's not nicking my ice cream, that is.'

Jessie stopped short of telling Dave to keep Smokey indoors. That wouldn't be fair on either of them. Not until she knew for sure what Dan's plans were. Until then Jessie would have to do whatever she could to stop the fear overwhelming her. But it wasn't the first time she'd had to do that, was it?

CHAPTER THIRTY-THREE

1998

'Simpson, come on, move yourself.'

The officer's words drifted through Daniel, but he wasn't listening. Instead he tugged his duvet further around his head and turned to face the wall, wincing from the pain in his wrists.

'Simpson, I'll remove you from the bed if I have to,' the officer repeated as he pulled back his duvet. 'Come on, Dr Hudson is waiting for you.'

'All right, I'm coming,' Daniel snapped. 'You don't have to keep on at me about it. I'm coming.'

'Do you need help?'

'No, fuck off, I can manage,' Daniel spat as the officer got closer.

'Watch your lip, boy. I'll be outside. Get dressed.'

Julia Hudson was shocked by the black circles around his eyes and the bandages on his wrists.

'Come in, Daniel. Sit down. Thank you.' She nodded to the officer, who closed the door.

Daniel slumped down on the chair and dropped his eyes to the floor. Julia took her own seat opposite him.

'Would you like a glass of water?'

Daniel answered with a short shake of his head as she rested her elbows on her desk, cupping her chin.

'Does it hurt badly?' she began. 'I can get you some painkillers if you need them.'

Daniel shook his head. Julia waited and watched, then wrote something in her notebook.

'Can you tell me why you did it?'

Daniel again answered with a short shake of his head.

Julia sighed.

'I can't help you unless you tell me what's wrong, can I?'

'Look, I've got nothing to say. I don't know why I'm here.' Daniel's eyes held hers briefly until he dropped his gaze again.

'I'm concerned that you're going to attempt to take your life again.' Julia explained. 'You must know that.'

Daniel shrugged.

'I thought things were going well for you. Before she left, Gail Robertson said she was so pleased with your progress.'

The mention of Gail Robertson's name caused Daniel to shift in his chair.

Julia observed the change in his body language.

'You were sad to see Gail leave, weren't you?'

Daniel shuffled himself further up the chair and sniffed. Julia was sure his eyes were moist.

'You miss her?' she continued as she rubbed her bottom lip with her thumb.

The whisper of a smile grew then fell away, and Daniel swallowed down his feelings. He didn't want Dr Hudson to know.

'Daniel?' Julia repeated. This wasn't the first time in her career Julia had witnessed an infatuation, but she hadn't seen this one coming. Daniel had kept it very quiet.

Daniel shrugged. 'I guess.'

'I think it's a little more than that, isn't it?'

It didn't seem to matter, Daniel thought, that he might not want to open up about something so private. Dr Hudson appeared to want to know everything about him. His whole life was under the microscope, it seemed.

'Do you want to talk about it?' she added.

Daniel scoffed. 'Would it matter if I said no?'

'I think it would help if you did. There's obviously something upsetting you very much. So deeply, that you tried to end your life.'

Daniel considered her words. End your life. *What life*, he thought. Without Gail, it didn't seem there was any point to it. How could she leave like that, without even saying goodbye to him? He'd been told something about her husband being ill, and her wanting to spend time with him. Where did that leave him? He needed her. Didn't she realise how much he depended on her? She was just another woman who had let him down.

'Daniel?'

Daniel sighed and stood slowly from the chair. 'Can I go now? There's really nothing to say.'

'Sit down.' Julia's tone changed, which shocked Daniel into doing as he was told. 'You have to understand something. While you're here, under my care, I am responsible for you. I need to know everything, however painful or uncomfortable that might be for you. It's my job to help you.'

Daniel dropped his chin to his chest. 'I'm sorry, Dr Hudson.'

Julia scribbled something into her notebook.

'So, let's start again, shall we?'

Daniel nodded. 'I do miss her.'

'You should have spoken to someone instead of—'

'I know. It all just got a bit much, then I wasn't thinking straight. I just did it without really thinking.'

Julia stared at Daniel. He looked so sad. Like Cam said, he was making such good progress. His fragile emotional attachments were difficult for him, as they were for so many of the boys in Carseview. Gail Robertson's sudden departure had had a huge impact on him. Paul Reekie, his new mentor, was clearly nothing like Gail. Gail's motherly aura worked with Daniel, and Julia understood completely why that was the case. She should have anticipated what had happened, and was so grateful Daniel was found in time.

'Thank you for sharing that with me.' She smiled. 'Eventually.'

'I'm sorry,' he whispered as his eyes filled with tears. 'I know it sounds stupid, but I loved her. Not in a creepy way, though.' He sniffed and rubbed his nose with the bandage on his wrist. 'I'm not a stalker.' He tried to laugh through his tears.

'I know,' Julia reassured him. 'It's normal for a boy your age to have feelings like that, and I'm sorry her departure wasn't better planned. I didn't realise the extent of your attachment, and that's down to me. I'm sorry, Daniel.'

Daniel shrugged. 'It's OK.'

'How do you feel now that you've opened up?'

He laid his elbows on Julia's desk and rested his head in his hands, then rubbed at his cropped blond hair. He shook his head.

'Empty,' he answered.

CHAPTER THIRTY-FOUR

Thoughts of Louise and Rob's affair drifted into Jessie's mind. She knew more than anyone the pain of infidelity in a marriage. Dan wasn't only violent and controlling. He was a serial cheat on top of that. Perhaps if she'd been stronger, sooner, Ryan would still be alive. She couldn't help but think about Jason. He didn't seem particularly strong emotionally as it was. He also had a history of violence. She wondered if he had ever been violent to Louise – or Shannon. Has he done something unthinkable to his own daughter? The niggling feeling in her gut was growing, but she had no evidence of guilt. She questioned how she would behave if her child was missing. But she would never know; not really.

A loud knock tore into her thoughts. She looked up and was surprised to see Dylan standing next to Calum Bailey. Jessie stood to greet her unexpected visitor. Dylan nodded once with a small smile and turned to leave.

'Thanks,' she called after him. 'Please take a seat, Calum. What can I do for you?'

The beads of sweat on Calum's brow piqued her interest.

'Can I get you a glass of water?'

'No. I'm fine, thanks.' Calum sat down. 'I have something to tell you. Something I should have said from the start.'

He wiped his forehead and Jessie reached for a bottle of water from behind her. She handed it to Calum with a reassuring smile. Calum gulped at it.

'OK, I'm listening,' she said.

'Shannon was writing a book. Did you know that?'

Jessie frowned in response. 'Why do you say "was"? We don't know what's happened to her yet, do we?'

Calum squirmed in his seat with his cheeks aflame. 'I meant *is*, I'm sorry. It's just got me so rattled, you know?'

'I understand. Take your time.'

Jessie recalled a brief reference to a novel from her chat with Eric, and wondered what this had to do with her disappearance.

'Eric Baldwin, Shannon's friend, mentioned it.'

Calum's breath exited in short, sharp bursts as he reached into his trouser pocket and slid a memory stick across the table to Jessie. This was not what she expected at all. She would have put money on Calum's confession of an affair with Shannon instead.

'What's on this?' She picked up the stick and examined it.

'I didn't know what she was writing until I agreed to read it for her. Once I'd read it, there was no way I could let her publish it.'

Rather than feeling relieved that he had shared his secret, Calum's anxiety soared, but it was too late now; he was committed.

'Shannon was talking to someone online, I don't know his name. She told me he was legit, and that the information he gave her was a hundred per cent accurate. He said he was taking a huge risk in telling her what he knew. She said it explained a lot about the way her father is.'

Jessie stared at the innocent-looking memory stick in the palm of her hand. 'I've been through Shannon's laptop and there's nothing to suggest what you've just told me.'

'Have you sent it to your tech support team? I bet they will be able to find Shannon's secret email account. There was no way she was talking about *that* in the open.' Calum nodded at the memory stick.

'What is this book about?'

'Look for yourself. I don't want to see that ever again.' Calum stood up to leave.

'Thanks for bringing this to me. Goodbye.'
Calum only had time to nod before he fled.
He barely made it outside before he vomited.

CHAPTER THIRTY-FIVE

The sign for Inverlochty couldn't come soon enough for Tom Nicoll. The stunning Scottish Borders landscape did little to soothe his nerves. How could something so dark and ugly be here? When the rolling Perthshire hills came into view, Tom was struck by the sheer isolation in contrast to the hustle and the bustle of North East England. He also spotted the reason people called it big tree country; the orange and red leaves were stunning. The change of season from summer to autumn was something Sophie had loved.

He pulled up outside The Black Witch pub and switched the engine off. He sat back, stretched his arms out in front of him and yawned. He was exhausted. A nervous anticipation ran through his whole body. What would he find in this small town?

Maggie Malcolm wiped the puddles of spilled lager off the bar. She couldn't fathom how a man can't lift a glass the small distance between the bar top and his mouth without spilling it.

'Can I help you?' She flicked her tea towel over her shoulder. 'We don't open until four, I'm afraid.'

'Would there be a room I could have for a couple of days, perhaps more?' Tom asked her.

'I'm sorry, we're completely full. I've only the two rooms, and they're both taken.'

When Maggie saw the crestfallen look on his face and the dark rings under his eyes, she took pity on him.

'Have you eaten breakfast?' she asked.

'No, I haven't. I'm starving.' Tom realised he hadn't eaten since eight o'clock the night before. He'd survived the long drive on coffee alone.

'Sit down and I'll get you a cooked breakfast. Then I'll see if a friend of mine has a room going. It's a wee bit out of the town, but he might have a vacancy. Help yourself to coffee. I'll not be long.'

She smiled at Tom, then disappeared behind the bar. Tom picked up his rucksack and moved over to one of the dining tables, away from the bar. He wasn't sure he could stomach more coffee, so he helped himself to orange juice instead. He spotted a copy of the local morning paper and grabbed that as he sat down. Shannon's smiling face stared back at him and Tom felt like he'd been kicked in the stomach. It felt like his little sister all over again. Sophie had been missing for almost a week before her body was discovered in a shallow grave. She'd been uncovered by two curious cocker spaniels and their horrified owner called the police. Shannon even looked like her. Same age. Same hair colour.

'There you go, you get that down you.' Maggie grinned as she laid a huge plate piled high with bacon, sausage, fried tomato, fried bread, fried mushrooms, black pudding, haggis pudding, fruit pudding and beans on the table in front of Tom. His eyes widened at the feast she'd prepared for him.

'This looks delicious, thanks so much for this.' Tom picked up the ketchup bottle and heaped a portion on the tiny patch of plate that wasn't covered.

'Oh, your toast,' Maggie patted his shoulder. 'I nearly forgot. I won't be a minute.'

Tom watched Maggie hurry away before he had a chance to say anything. The door to the bar opened and Tom was sure he recognised the man's face. He frowned and stared until the man did the same to him.

'Tom Nicoll?' Blair asked, and moved quickly to his table.

'Yes, I'm Tom Nicoll. I know your face but I'm sorry, I can't quite remember your name.'

Blair held out his hand to shake Tom's.

'I'm Blair Crawford. I worked for a newspaper which covered Sophie's story.' Blair hesitated, then offered Tom a small smile. 'I was friends with your mum.'

Tom closed his eyes and nodded in recognition. 'Of course, yes. Are you here to cover Shannon's disappearance?' Tom tapped the newspaper.

'That's right, yes. So, how are you, Tom? You've certainly changed since I last saw you. What brings you to Inverlochty? It's a long way from home.'

Tom wondered if Blair had seen *him* Maybe he could tell him where to find him but, before he could ask, Maggie bustled over to his table with a plate of toast, butter and marmalade. She dropped a hand onto Blair's shoulder and patted it.

'Yours will be about ten minutes,' she assured him.

Again, before Tom could quiz him, Blair's phone buzzed loudly.

'Sorry, I have to take this.' Tom was left wondering if Blair was on the hunt for Sophie's killer as well. This time he was not going to get away with it.

CHAPTER THIRTY-SIX

Ben Randall crushed the empty lager can and chucked it into the fast-flowing river. The rainfall in recent days had caused her to swell and thrash angrily through the town. He pulled another can from the carrier bag and opened it. He needn't have bothered because the other three he'd downed hadn't helped. He and Louise had argued again that morning. His big sister was on his back constantly. She seemed oblivious to the fact that he might be missing Shannon too. Ben heard footsteps behind him and turned to see who it was. A broad grin crept across his face when he realised he'd been caught. He stood and staggered forward with his hands up.

'It's a fair cop, detective. You've caught me red-handed.' The effects of the alcohol suddenly kicked in and caused a fit of the giggles.

'Come on, Ben, I'll take you home.'

'Were you looking for me?' Ben slurred. 'Or were you expecting to find Shannon here?'

He tripped and fell as he moved forward, spilling the contents of his carrier bag across the muddy bank. Before Dylan could say anything, Ben added, 'Have you looked in there yet?' He nodded in the direction of the choppy water.

Dylan grabbed hold of Ben's arm.

'Come on, lad.' Dylan pulled his car keys from his pocket as Ben snatched his arm back from his grip.

'I bet none of you would be this upset if it was me in there.'

Dylan stopped dead. 'What did you just say?'

Ben ignored him and kept walking ahead of him.

'Ben, stop right there,' Dylan called after him, his words startling two ducks on the bank who suddenly flew upwards out of the dense grass that grew there. Ben did as he was told and turned to stare at him.

'Well, where the hell else could she be? You've looked everywhere,' Ben said petulantly.

Once he'd caught up with him, Dylan ushered him to the car.

Rob dropped the teaspoon in the sink and carried the two mugs into the bedroom.

'Here you go.' He placed the hot peppermint tea on Cassie's bedside table.

'You didn't have to do that.' Cassie rubbed the base of her back and struggled to get comfortable.

'Is your back still sore?'

Cassie winced. 'I'll be fine, don't worry. I'll just stay in bed for a bit. You get on with whatever you need to be getting on with. I'll call you if I need you.'

Cassie smiled, but Rob saw the pain and tiredness etched on her face. He kissed her once, gently, on the top of her head.

'Don't get up. Text me if you need anything.'

'I will.' Cassie smiled weakly.

Rob's office wasn't far from their bedroom. He'd had the attic converted into his workspace not long after he bought the house. With the door closed it was so peaceful up there, and the view from the window was breathtaking. He could see right across the trees to the river as it wound its way to Dundee and beyond. His phone buzzed with a text message just as he got comfortable at his desk. He smiled when he saw it was from Louise.

You're welcome. I'm glad I could help.

CHAPTER THIRTY-SEVEN

Calum pulled his suitcase down from the top of the wardrobe; the dust spilled into his eyes and caught the back of his throat, making him cough. He wiped the surface of the case and remembered the last time it was used. He recalled fondly the excitement of emptying it, along with the boxes, the day he moved into this flat, but he couldn't stay in Inverlochty; not after giving that pen drive to DI Blake. It was only a matter of time before it was linked to him. He didn't want to be here when that happened.

He switched off the lights and locked the door for what might be the last time; he hadn't decided. He might come back, once the whole Shannon situation was resolved, one way or another. Calum ignored Eric's call again as he loaded the car. Saying goodbye to him had been awful, even if it was only by text.

He knew that Eric would be fine. He would be safer without him. Neither Calum nor Shannon had told Eric about the real story of the book. Once Shannon stumbled on that secret, she'd told Calum that she had not dared confide in Eric, even if he was her best friend. She said telling Calum was hard enough, but she needed someone she trusted to go over the manuscript. She never revealed her source. He'd pleaded with Shannon not to go ahead with the book and refused to help her with it. When begging didn't work, she had casually mentioned her suspicions that Eric and Calum were becoming more than teacher and student. She could have been bluffing, of course, but Calum didn't receive a reply when he sent Shannon a message saying he'd had time to think it over. Against his better judgement, he had told her he would help her. She left him little choice.

Now she was missing. Calum didn't want to hang about to find out if he was next. He'd warned her that messing with people like that would get her in trouble. She had even joked: 'What are they going to do, make me disappear?' Calum could hear those words as clearly as the day she'd said them.

The blue Mercedes behind Calum had been following his Seat Ibiza for more than ten miles now, he was sure of it. Stop being ridiculous, he told himself. He was just being paranoid, wasn't he? This was the only road north. Of course the Mercedes was still following him. There was no other route; nowhere for him to pass. This whole situation had him on edge. Every shadow, every noise made him nervous. There was a lay-by in five hundred yards. He would pull in there, and if the Mercedes driver did the same, then Calum would know. He held his breath then swallowed hard. He clicked the indicator on and waited. The Mercedes did not make any indication it was about to stop. Calum peered in his rear-view mirror and began to move into the lay-by.

'What the shitting hell?' Calum muttered when the Mercedes pulled in behind him.

His heart thudded while he stopped his car and waited. He struggled to control the trembling in his arms and gripped the steering wheel until his knuckles turned white; his heart was pounding. When he glanced in the mirror he saw a heavily built, well-dressed man in a grey suit getting out of the Mercedes and walking towards him.

Calum wasn't going to hang about to find out what he wanted. He thrust his car into gear and his wheels spun, kicking gravel at the man as he sped out of the lay-by. Calum had not noticed the lorry hurtling along the road. His little Seat Ibiza was thrown off the road and sent tumbling down the embankment, rolling as it fell, until it came to a halt on its roof at the bottom.

Calum Bailey died instantly on impact.

CHAPTER THIRTY-EIGHT

Dylan rubbed his eyes that stung from concentrating on a computer screen for so long. It had been a hard day; the kind of day that can fill your mind with fog. He could do with some baby Jack hugs right then. Since becoming a father, hugs from his son had the power to soothe his tired soul. Nobody had prepared Dylan for the overwhelming love he would feel for his child, or the sense of responsibility which made memories of his own father even darker. He would make sure Jack knew he was loved, and that Dylan loved Shelly the way a man should love his wife. Not the twisted control his own father had over them. Shelly's video message of Jack giggling helped. That and the voicemail Rivendell left to say his mum was comfortable. She was even eating again. That was a weight off his mind.

'Here you go.' Jessie slid a coaster out from under a pile of papers and placed a strong black coffee in front of him. 'How are you getting on?'

'Thanks. Yes, fine.' Dylan sniffed then leaned right into the back of his chair and stretched his arms above his head as he yawned. 'So far I've been able to find an email account in the name of J. Ross, which I assume is Jason's. Now, what I don't know is whether it's Jason's or whether Shannon has created an account in her father's name.'

Jessie was thrilled by this discovery. 'What's in it? Did she arrange to meet anyone the night she disappeared?'

'Sorry, the tech boys haven't had much luck with this. It's a Hotmail account, but don't worry, I will get it.'

'Here's an idea I'm going to put out there. I would love to hear what you think.'

'OK, I'm listening.'

Jessie pulled up another chair. 'What if Jason *has* done something to his daughter?'

'I have to say Jason seems genuinely cut up.'

'Yes, but what if the anguished father behaviour is down to guilt and grief at knowing what he's done? He has a history of violence, Dylan.'

'Yes, I know that, but—'

'Did he have an argument with Shannon about her book?' Jessie shrugged. 'There's more to that family than we know. I'd like you to keep an eye on Jason for now.'

Dylan nodded. 'Sure thing. And what about Calum, the teacher?'

'Mm,' Jessie paused. 'What does he have to gain from Shannon's disappearance?'

'Not sure myself, to be honest. Just a hunch, I suppose. And Foster? He was the last one to see her.'

'Try Shannon Ross, all one word.' Jessie tapped his shoulder and pointed to the laptop. 'I sometimes need to keep it that simple.'

Dylan typed it in and hit enter. The email account opened.

'Detective Inspector Blake, you are a genius.'

All of the emails were from someone named Dominic, and six of them remained unread.

'Wait a minute,' Dylan hesitated. 'Should we really be reading these? The account is in Jason's name.'

'Shannon is a vulnerable missing person. We can access this.'

Jessie considered the implications of any case she brought against anyone being tossed out on a technicality. But at the same time the urgency of the case preyed on her mind. 'OK, you go and talk to Calum Bailey again first. See if he knows about this Dominic. I'll call the super just for peace of mind. Get his go-ahead. One phone call won't hurt.'

Dylan closed the laptop and grabbed his mac from the back of the chair. Shelly had teased him about his likeness to Columbo when he first brought it home. Dylan hoped the physical likeness began and ended with the coat. He hoped the dark clouds would hold back the deluge they threatened until later tonight. He hated driving that winding back road home in the rain and the dark. He'd hardly seen Shelly and Jack recently but, as Shelly told him, this was a great opportunity. It would be worth it for his career.

Boom! The sudden crack of the farmer's bird scarer in the field across from the small, rural station startled Jessie.

'Shit's sake,' she muttered while her heart raced.

Her nerves were already frayed as it was. She saw his shadow around every corner, and tried to tell herself that it was impossible for him to know where she was. None of her colleagues would tell him if he asked, she knew that, but it still niggled at her. What if? What would he do if they met? What would she do? Why the hell did she still feel like this? Dan had no control over her any more. That ended the day he effectively murdered their child.

She looked up to see a flock of crows soar above the ancient oak that had probably stood in the corner of the field for longer than Jessie had been alive. The fast-flowing River Lochty meandered past the outer edge of the vast field of wheat, twisting and winding its way towards Dundee and then the North Sea. It was deep and dark and threatening as it poured through the small Highland Perthshire town. Despite being famous for its water sports, Jessie shuddered at the thought of getting in it, no matter the size of the boat. Her sister, Freya, often used to enjoy the thrill of white-water rafting upriver a short way from here. That was until her life unravelled spectacularly and she lost her marriage and job to alcoholism.

Dylan pulled on the handbrake and got out of his car to walk across the private car park of Calum Bailey's apartment building. He knocked and waited for an answer. When he didn't get any response, he rang his mobile number. He knew Bailey wouldn't be at school at the weekend, but when it went straight to voicemail he hung up. From the corner of his eye, Dylan saw a figure sitting alone on the steps of the adjacent building. He walked over to where Eric sat, his face red from crying.

'He's not there,' Eric told him.

'Do you know when Mr Bailey will be back? I need to talk to him.'

Dylan watched Eric keep his eyes fixed on the grass at his feet as he shook his head.

'Do you happen to know where he is?'

Eric lifted his head to speak. 'Your guess is as good as mine.'

'OK, well, if you see him, could you tell him to give me a call? I'm DC Dylan Logan.'

'He's gone.'

Dylan was confused. 'What do you mean, he's gone? Gone where?'

Eric shrugged. 'I have no idea where he is. Why should I? I'm just a kid, aren't I?'

Eric stood up and walked down the two steps to join Dylan.

'What did you need to talk to Calum about?'

A bit weird to call your teacher Calum, Dylan thought. He would never have been able to do that when he was at school.

'Thanks for your help, Eric.'

As Dylan turned to head back to his car, he wondered if Eric knew Dominic. He spun round.

'Eric, can I ask you something?'

'Sure, what is it?' he answered, hands thrust deep in his pockets.

'Did Shannon ever mention the name Dominic to you?'

The instant frown that developed on Eric's brow told Dylan that Eric couldn't help.

'Who's Dominic?' Eric answered. 'I don't know anyone called Dominic, and Shannon certainly didn't mention that name to me.'

Dylan got back to his car just as the heavens opened. He figured Jessie's mood would probably reflect the miserable weather when he got back.

CHAPTER THIRTY-NINE

Louise watched the rain from her bedroom window and worried that Shannon was out there, alone and cold. She lifted Shannon's school shirt from the laundry basket and held it close to her face. She slung it across the back of the chair ready for ironing. Shannon would need it when she got back, she told herself. She wished that Rob was with her, holding her close to him, stroking her hair. When she closed her eyes, she could feel him. She could smell him.

Her daydream was invaded by Jason's arm pulling her to him. He pushed her hair out of her eyes and pressed his lips against hers. Louise smelt the beer on his breath and felt nauseous. Instead of reciprocating his advance, Louise gently pushed her husband away and started to walk towards the door, shaking her head.

'Louise, please,' Jason pleaded.

Louise stopped and spoke without turning to face him.

'I can't, Jason, not now,' she whispered, then closed the bedroom door behind her with hot, stinging tears in her eyes.

The distance that grew daily between him and Louise was crushing Jason. He slumped down on the corner of the bed, and realised that he and Louise had not shared their bed since Shannon went missing. Louise had slept in Shannon's room from that night on. If it was space Louise needed then he would give it to her. He picked up his wallet from the bedside table and made his way to The Black Witch.

Louise watched as he disappeared. She knew exactly where he was going and what sort of state he would be in when he came home. Of all the times for Jason to show his utter selfishness. Still, it wasn't unexpected. The sound of footsteps going into the bathroom upstairs reminded her that she was still mad with Ben for his recent stunt; getting drunk in the middle of the day and skipping school to do it. She had yelled when Dylan kindly delivered him home. Ben had scurried into his room and they hadn't spoken since. Ben's face was white as a sheet when he cautiously poked his face round the living room door. Louise sighed, then held her arms open wide to her brother. Ben moved quickly forward and hugged his sister.

'I'm sorry,' he told her. 'I'm sorry for being such a dick.'

'Damn right you're acting like a dick, you little shit! Do you know how close I've been to sending you back home to live with Mum?'

Ben's eyes widened. 'I'm sorry.'

'Right, go and get a shower, because you stink. I'll make us a cup of tea and a sandwich.'

Ben returned the warm smile she gave him as she walked into the kitchen. Louise pulled the last couple of rashers of bacon from the packet and opened the grill, but something in the corner of her eye distracted her. A rustle of foliage from the tall beech hedge that surrounded the bottom end of their garden.

'Shannon,' she whispered, and dropped the packet on the floor. She raced out of the back door and into the garden. Standing at the centre of the garden, she stared all around her. 'Shannon!' she shouted. 'Shannon? Is that you?' Louise moved closer, tearing away great clumps of greenery with her bare hands. 'Shannon, I know you're there. I saw you!'

Maggie Malcolm was making her way to The Black Witch. She clasped her hand to her mouth and quickened her pace.

'Louise, sweetheart.' Maggie took off her jacket and wrapped it around Louise's shoulders, then knelt close to her on the wet grass. 'Hey, what are you doing, lass?'

'I saw her, hiding. I saw her. She was right here!' Louise began tearing at what was left of the leaves again. 'I saw her. I know I did. Why is she hiding from me?' Louise stopped and slumped onto the sodden ground, then turned her head to face Maggie. 'Why is she hiding from me?'

Maggie wiped away a tear and wrapped her arms around Louise. 'Come on, why don't we go inside, eh?'

'No, I have to find her.' Louise pushed Maggie's hand away and jumped to her feet. She jogged towards their shed, tossing aside Jason's bike and swiping things off shelves. 'I know she's here. I saw her!' Louise bolted from there to the far corner, where Jason had built the decking the previous summer. She leapt up the two steps and peered over the top of the hedge. 'Shannon!' Aside from startling a couple of seagulls who had come down for an easy meal, there was no reply.

Dylan was shocked by the expression on Jessie's face when he returned to the office. The clock above the ancient slate-grey filing cabinet that looked more at home in a 1980s police drama read just shy of eight o'clock. His first thought was that Shannon had been found dead.

'Thanks for letting me know.' Jessie gave Dylan a half-smile as she hung up the phone.

'Shut the door.'

'What's happened?'

'Calum Bailey is dead.'

'Jesus, what happened to him?'

'His body was found in his car ten miles north of here. His car was upside down at the bottom of an embankment. A lorry driver reported that Bailey drove right into his path. He didn't have a chance to brake and the lorry clipped Bailey's car, spinning it out of control and down to where it landed. Bailey was already dead when help got to him.'

'So, it was an accident?'

'Lorry driver says the only other witness was in a Mercedes that drove off before he could get the registration.'

Dylan moved over to pour himself a large mug of coffee despite the fact that he knew it would keep him awake if he drank it at this late hour.

'Do you want one?' he asked Jessie.

'I'd better not.'

Dylan sank half of the bitter liquid and told himself he would bring some from home tomorrow. As hard as he'd tried, he just couldn't take to the budget-brand rubbish on offer here.

'So, what now?' he asked.

CHAPTER FORTY

The silence of her bedroom enveloped Louise. It was deafening. She missed Shannon's laughter. The little snort she did when she found something hilarious. Then the hiccups that came after a really hearty laugh. She had always done that, ever since she was a baby. Louise could recall the first time Shannon laughed like it was yesterday. She was six weeks old, and Louise had scrunched up a paper bag. She couldn't remember what had been in the bag but when the paper crumpled in her hand, the sound triggered a fit of baby giggles that made both Jason and Louise laugh so hard. Jason had picked up the bag and crinkled and scrunched it until there was almost nothing left of it.

Louise dropped to her knees and opened her bottom drawer. When she couldn't find what she was looking for, she slid open the wardrobe door and reached up to the top shelf, stretching onto her tiptoes. She just wasn't tall enough to reach. She went into the hall and brought the chair from the top of the stairs and placed it in front of the wardrobe door. From her new vantage point she could see the box she was looking for. She pulled it to her. She blew the dust from the top, then coughed. She stepped down and flopped onto her bed. Yes, the video was there.

'Shit,' she said in a murmur, realising her new bedroom television couldn't play videos. Then she remembered Ben had her old set in his room.

'What are you doing?' Ben was startled by Louise bursting into his room.

He watched her frantically try to push the video into the machine.

'Wait, it's not plugged in. You'll break the thing if you're not careful.' Ben leapt off his bed, switched the plug on at the wall and then frowned at his sister. 'What's that?'

Louise hugged the remote close to her chest and watched the screen in silence, a smile growing across her lips as a single tear trickled down her face. Ben couldn't take his eyes off the screen. He swallowed hard and glanced from his sister to the screen and back. Shannon's smiling face staring back at him was too much. He grabbed his jumper from the floor and walked out.

Louise didn't even notice her little brother leave. She clicked rewind and watched Shannon again and again. Louise had been so proud, and maybe even a little smug, when Shannon was chosen to play Mary in the nativity that year. Shannon looked so pretty in the costume Louise had made for her. She remembered practising the lines over and over, all two of them. She was only six, after all. When the tape wouldn't play after she'd rewound it half a dozen times Louise hammered the button harder and harder until it spun out of control, spitting a roll of tape out of the ancient video recorder.

'No!' she screamed. 'No, no, no!' Louise fell to the floor and stuffed the tape back into the machine and pushed the buttons over and over. 'No!'

She clicked the eject button and after a loud whirring sound, the tape spluttered towards her. Louise lifted what was left of Shannon's nativity tape and squeezed it close to her chest.

'No,' she whimpered. 'No.'

CHAPTER FORTY-ONE

Rob hung his shirt over the back of the chair and took his towel into the large en suite bathroom. Despite everything, he'd had a productive day. Book six was being written by hand in a cute leather-bound notebook Cassie bought him last Christmas. He wasn't convinced at first, but the leather smell was growing on him.

When Rob was in full flow, words took him away from his reality. They always had, and that was probably what saved him. He was glad to see Cassie fast asleep, curled up in their duvet. He toyed with the idea of sleeping on the sofa again so that she wouldn't be disturbed by him coming to bed. The guilt Rob felt about his time with Louise still troubled him.

The hot water trickled over Rob's face and he stood under the flow to allow the steam to cleanse him until an ear-splitting scream disturbed his peace. He snatched his towel and raced to find Cassie, who was bent double with agony on the bed, clutching her belly under the duvet. She lifted her hand and trembled as she held it in front of her face. Her fingers were covered in blood, and when Rob ripped back their duvet he was terrified by the volume of blood soaking into the sheet.

'Jesus, OK, keep calm. I'll get help.'

Rob was horrified. He grabbed his phone.

'Help me!' Cassie screamed and clutched her belly tight. 'What's happening? Rob, help me. It feels like the baby's coming, but he can't. Not yet!'

'Ambulance, please hurry.' Rob gave the despatcher their details, then threw on his sweatshirt and jeans and wrapped his arms around her. He kissed her hand as she clung to him.

'Help is coming. Keep calm, it's going to be OK.'

Rob wanted to be strong for her, but they both knew what was happening.

'Mrs Taylor, hi, I'm Ruby, I'm one of the paramedics. I can see you're in a lot of pain, darling. Take this for me.'

Ruby handed Cassie a mouthpiece and rubbed her arm in an attempt to comfort her.

'Just take some deep breaths into this, sweetheart. It's a bit of gas and air for the pain. It should take the edge off for you until we get you to hospital, OK?'

Cassie's eyes were wide and panicked as she searched Rob's for reassurance. All he could do was step back and let the paramedic do her job. He wanted to cry. Rob feared this was his punishment.

'OK, Mrs Taylor, my colleague is going to get a chair and we're going to take you to hospital, darling. You just sit still and let us do all the work.' Ruby offered Cassie a warm smile as she took her pulse, which raced dangerously due to the heavy blood loss.

'Cassie, call me Cassie.' Cassie panted to control the pain that ripped into her. She had never felt anything like it in her life.

Ruby's colleague returned with the trolley and prepared it for her.

'OK, Cassie, we're going to move you onto this trolley and then we're going to carry you to the ambulance, sweetheart.'

Rob clasped his fingers behind his head as he looked on, helpless to do anything constructive. He didn't know what to do or say.

'I feel so sleepy,' Cassie whispered, and her head drooped forward as she was wheeled to the ambulance.

'Stay awake, darling, come on, Cassie.' Ruby tapped Cassie's shoulder and shot an uncomfortable glance at her partner.

Ruby moved Cassie rapidly inside, then Rob watched in horror as Cassie lost consciousness.

CHAPTER FORTY-TWO

Jason slid a ten-pound note onto the bar. 'Pint of lager and a whisky chaser, Maggie, when you've got a minute.'

'I'll get that, Maggie,' Blair told her.

'I'll put it on your tab.' She handed Jason his drinks and slid his money back towards him.

Jason Ross spent too much time in the pub, in Maggie's opinion, but under the circumstances she couldn't blame him for wanting a drink tonight.

Jason downed the nip of whisky in one gulp and waved his glass at Maggie.

'I'll take another.' He pushed his glass back across the bar.

Blair pulled a twenty-pound note from his wallet and held it up to show Maggie.

'Leave the bottle, I'll look after him.'

Maggie eyed Blair suspiciously at first but, as the pub was busy, she placed the bottle between them, along with two clean glasses. She walked away after relieving Blair of his money. Jason lifted the bottle and a glass and moved to a booth away from the bar.

'You're welcome,' Blair muttered and started to follow Jason.

'I'd rather drink alone, mate,' Jason said without lifting his head.

'I'm afraid half that bottle has my name on it, so you're stuck with me, I'm afraid.'

Blair took a seat opposite him and refilled Jason's glass and his own with whisky. Jason gulped it back and helped himself to another.

'Thanks,' Jason whispered, as the whisky burned his throat.

Blair raised his glass before he took a sip. 'Cheers.'

The two men sat in silence, the sound of raucous laughter ringing out from the other end of the pub. Blair topped up their glasses for a third time. This would be his last. He wasn't used to drinking whisky, and he was aware of its effects already. He took a deep breath before he spoke.

'How are you coping? It can't be easy for you and your missus. Is there any news?'

Jason filled his glass, then offered the bottle to Blair. Blair knew he shouldn't, but he took it to be sociable.

'I don't know how Louise is coping.' He tossed back another and held his glass up. 'This is how I'm coping.'

'Do the police have any leads at all?' Blair asked.

'Well, if they do, they sure as hell haven't told me. That Andrew Foster was the last person to see Shannon that night. He says she left his and doesn't know where she went after. I think he's lying. They found her phone and her blood in Foster's house. Now he's in the nuthouse and I can't get near him.' The effects of the alcohol had started to loosen Jason's tongue. 'I just want her back.' Jason's bloodshot eyes held Blair's.

'I know, mate, it must be shit for you right now, you and your wife.'

'Louise doesn't talk to me, hell, she doesn't even sleep in our bed any more.' He shrugged. 'She's slept in Shannon's bed since that first night.'

Jason's torment was palpable.

'I'm so sorry. I wish there was something I could say that might help.'

Jason poured another nip for each of them. This one really would have to be Blair's last, or he would suffer the consequences in the morning.

*

'Rob, I am so sorry.'

Louise rushed to the hospital as soon as she got his call. She understood his agony and wanted to help in any way she could. Miscarriage at any stage is awful, but Louise's last pregnancy also ended after only eighteen weeks. She still felt the physical pain of it as if it were yesterday.

Cassie would remain in hospital until she was fully recovered physically. She'd asked Rob to leave her; she wanted to be alone. The nurse explained that Cassie was in shock and suggested he come back in the morning, that he get some rest too. The next few days and weeks were going to be hard for both of them. But Rob didn't manage to move any further than the corridor before he called Louise. The operation had gone well but Cassie had lost so much blood that she needed three units to combat her dangerously low haemoglobin. The sight of all the blood appalled Rob, but seeing his dead baby son's tiny body would never leave him.

Rob lifted his wet face from Louise's shoulder and searched her eyes for comfort. All she could do was clasp his face in her hands and kiss his lips, then gently repeat her words.

'Rob, I'm so sorry.'

Rob lifted his sweatshirt and rubbed it roughly over his eyes.

'I'll take you home,' Louise murmured.

Louise stood and held out her hand to him. Without uttering a word, he stood and dropped his hand in hers.

Blair Crawford felt guilty for the state Jason was in. It was only right that he helped him home.

'There you go,' Blair said, and removed the arm that was propping Jason up and turned to head back to The Black Witch.

'You're a good man, you,' Jason slurred.

Blair waited for a moment to be sure he made it inside. After watching him drop his keys twice and tip sideways into the door frame before stepping into his hallway, Blair's conscience was clear. The walk back woke Blair from his alcohol-soaked fog. He was sure Louise passed him on the road, so he watched which direction the car was headed, because it certainly wasn't in the direction of her house. He was puzzled as to why she would be speeding up the hill the way she was; there were only two or three houses up there, it was so remote. He wondered who it was she knew, and why she would be rushing there at this time of night.

Louise pulled on the handbrake in Rob's driveway. Neither of them spoke until Rob reached for her arm.

'Please stay with me. I don't want to be alone.' One small tear trickled from his eyes and dripped from his cheek onto his sweatshirt.

Louise lifted her hand and wiped Rob's tear with her thumb with a soft smile and a gentle nod.

'Of course I'll stay with you,' she whispered as she pulled him close to her and he sobbed in her arms.

Ben was startled by the clatter of Jason's keys landing on the table. He got up to get a glass of water only to find his brother-in-law passed out on the sofa.

He shook his head and headed back to bed.

Ben popped his head round Shannon's bedroom door and, seeing his sister wasn't there, rang her. It went to voicemail.

CHAPTER FORTY-THREE

2001

Daniel Simpson glanced at the dining room clock. He moved his sausage and mash around his plate, his appetite all but non-existent. His stomach lurched with anxiety or anticipation, he wasn't sure which, or perhaps it was just absolute terror. He had been working towards this day for so long. The angry teenager was gone, and in his place Daniel hoped they'd found a good man; good enough to be trusted outside of Carseview. He stared at the boys who'd joined him at the table. He wouldn't miss them, that was for sure. His thoughts had turned to Jack again several times recently. He regretted that he wasn't getting the chance to start his life again, and he wished Jack had been given the opportunities he had been offered. But still, knowing Jack the way he did, he would have pushed them away.

For a boy with such loving, supportive parents, Jack MacKay always seemed so angry when, in reality, he had wanted for nothing. He had never struggled to school in filthy trainers that pinched his toes and rubbed so hard they peeled the skin. He had a winter coat when it was needed, and not some cheap knock-off either. He even bitched about the holidays he was dragged away on. Daniel knew Jack had got him into this mess, but on the other hand, Jack hadn't held a gun to Daniel's head. He could have said no at any moment. He could have walked away and taken Sophie with him.

Daniel should have stopped Jack grabbing her, pushing her to the ground. He knew tearing at her clothes was wrong. Sophie didn't want Jack to touch her like that. Perhaps what Daniel did was the worst betrayal, because he had just watched her go through the ordeal. He could have said no, but the atmosphere was charged with tension and Daniel had to admit that, for the first time in a long time, he felt alive. Finally, he had power. He had control, but he let Sophie down and she paid the ultimate price for his mistake. Daniel would never forget the revulsion that washed over him afterwards. His stomach churned when he thought about it, even today. He deserved every moment of the agony he'd suffered since. It was as a result of the decisions he made that day.

Daniel pushed his plate aside. He couldn't think about food. Even the smell turned his stomach. What if they said no? How long would he be locked away for if they did? What if Tom Nicoll got his wish and Daniel was sent to an adult prison? He'd sworn he wouldn't stop trying and had been true to his word. He had been right there, every step of Daniel's journey, like a ghost of the past. There's no way he would survive in an adult prison. He might as well do what Jack did if that happened. Maybe he'd done the right thing.

Daniel's mind raced with every possible bad outcome until the realisation crashed into him. What if they said yes? What if he had to face the world? What kind of world would he be welcomed into? He would be alone; he had no family to speak of. Daniel had never met his father. His mother selfishly deserted him when he needed her the most. There was no loving grandmother waiting to wrap him in her arms and tell him everything was going to be OK. Maybe it was on the outside that Daniel's real punishment would begin.

Cam Walsh knew Daniel's future hung in the hands of the board now. Five years had passed. She wished they could have witnessed his transformation for themselves. She'd submitted her report, and now she waited nervously to speak. Daniel Simpson wasn't just any inmate. Recent heavy press speculation over his imminent release had gathered an ugly momentum. Sophie Nicoll's brother, Tom, had been interviewed widely in the local and national press. He'd managed to get his local MP, Harvey Goldberg, involved in the case, who had managed to table a question in the House of Commons. The prime minister even said she would be happy to discuss his concerns. A crisis in the Middle East had then pushed Goldberg's concerns down her list of priorities, for which Cam was grateful.

There was no getting away from the fact that Daniel had committed a horrific crime, but he wasn't that angry teenager any more, thanks to the intensive programme of rehabilitation in Carseview. It was sad that it had taken such a dramatic event to change his life for the better. He'd gained qualifications he probably would have had no chance of achieving otherwise. Standard Grades and Highers. He should be proud of his accomplishments. Interview experience. Work experience within the unit. He had even been involved in mentoring a couple of the younger lads. Daniel was as prepared as he could be for life outside. He just needed the chance to prove it.

Tom Nicoll sat with his solicitor; she had advised him that she would talk to the board on behalf of his family. For such a young man Tom had campaigned tirelessly to prevent Daniel Simpson's release. He'd said he'd give his last breath to prevent another family enduring the agony his had gone through. Jack MacKay had at least done the decent thing and killed himself. Neither of them deserved to live after stealing Sophie's future. But it wasn't just Sophie's life that ended that day. Those that were left behind died a little, too. The life they once knew was extinguished in a heartbeat, along with all the hopes and wishes they had for the future. Tom would never be the fun uncle. His mum would never get the chance to hold Sophie's children. Never attend her graduation, or see her blossom into the beautiful young woman she would have been.

Daniel didn't deserve the second chance he'd denied Sophie. Tom didn't want the monster who'd murdered his beautiful little sister to ever be released; hence his petitioning for Daniel to be transferred to an adult prison. Laura and Ray Nicoll fully supported their son's efforts. Neither felt strong enough to attend the hearing, but Tom reassured them he was strong enough for all three of them and would never stop fighting for justice for Sophie, no matter how long it took.

CHAPTER FORTY-FOUR

Jessie was shocked by how quickly Dominic responded to the email. She was even more stunned by his agreeing to a face-to-face meeting. So, here she was, sitting, waiting and watching for his arrival. Dylan was not far away, listening to their conversation through the wire recorder she had securely tucked on her person for added security. Jessie wasn't taking any chances. If she felt threatened, he could be with her in minutes. From the witness report given by the lorry driver involved in the collision with Calum Bailey, Jessie anticipated a blue Mercedes would pull into the car park. She was surprised when a 2001 Land Rover with rusty bodywork arrived and parked close to her. The driver stared at Jessie over the top of his sunglasses and rolled down his window.

Dominic Wheelan was clearly confused by the sight of the pretty female detective as she smiled and held up her ID badge to him.

'You must be Dominic,' she said as she got in the passenger side.

'What's going on, where's Shannon? She emailed to say she wanted to talk.'

'I was hoping you would be able to tell me that.'

His perplexed expression disappointed Jessie.

'The revelations in Shannon's book are quite something, if they're true,' she continued.

Dominic's confusion deepened. 'What are you talking about? What book? I served in Iraq with Jason, and she said she wanted to know what happened to her dad. What might have made him the way he is. When she first reached out I thought it was Jason that emailed me. I loved the idea of catching up with an old mate. They treated him badly, they really did. It was wrong, what they did to him.'

Dylan listened in on the earpiece, rapidly realising that Shannon's book had nothing to do with her disappearance. Her foray into exposing a cover-up was a non-starter.

'So, is it true that a young girl was knocked down and killed while your battalion was on patrol?'

Dominic dropped his head and sighed. He gripped his steering wheel tight.

'Yes, it's true. A new lot had just joined us in Basra and this really young, shit-scared squaddie – first time deployed – hit and killed a six-year-old lassie. Fuck, it was horrible. It's surprising not more of us hit the bottle, but Jason got it bad. I'll never forget that scream, then just nothing.'

'And a senior officer covered up and protected the squaddie who did it? Is that part true?'

Dominic nodded without looking up. 'Aye, they buried her body at the side of the road.'

'And Jason's drinking? He was drunk when he assaulted a senior officer?'

Dominic nodded once more.

'The same officer who asked you all to lie, I'm guessing.'

A picture was emerging for Jessie. Calum Bailey's refusal to edit the book meant it was never going to be published. The army had never known anything about it. Dominic didn't even know anything about it. There was nobody trying to silence a young girl who had found out their dirty secret. All she had wanted to do was help her father.

Jessie would hang on to the pen drive for now. Calum Bailey's paranoia had been fed by a conspiracy theory after reading Shannon's manuscript. Jessie figured he'd left in a hurry to get away from what he saw as his own fate. But who was the Mercedes driver who drove off from the scene of the accident? Was Jessie being sucked into something that didn't exist? As she watched the Land Rover drive away, Jessie spoke directly to Dylan through the microphone.

'Did you hear all that?' she asked as she stared at her reflection in the rear-view mirror.

'I certainly did. So what now?'

'This whole book has been a wild goose chase. I'll see you back at the station.'

Dylan imagined she had meant to say it had been a red herring, but he agreed with her regardless. He didn't want to argue with the boss.

Sunlight flooded the room through the gap in the curtains. He watched Louise sleep, her blonde hair draped over her face. He gently brushed the stray strands away and leaned over to kiss her cheek. The way Rob felt about Louise was different to the feelings he had for Cassie. Yes, he loved Cassie, but he wasn't passionately in love with her; not the way he was with Louise. They hadn't meant to hurt anyone. When Cassie told him she was pregnant, Rob wanted to do the right thing for his child. Being raised by a single mother who dragged him from one stepfather to another almost destroyed him. No; Rob didn't want to risk that for his child. He would raise them in a proper family, no matter the cost. But all that was gone. His son was gone.

'Mm, Rob.' Louise licked her dry lips, then turned her body to face him. 'Good morning.'

Rob moved his mouth close to hers and kissed her, then he lay back so that Louise could cuddle close. Louise stroked his chest softly in time with the rhythm of his breath. She should feel guilty for spending the night with her best friend's husband, but she didn't. Selfishly, Louise wanted the comfort he gave her. The pain of not knowing where Shannon was had been crippling, but Rob's touch soothed the ache, just for a short time, and she wanted to hold on to that for as long as she could.

'Can we just lie here for ever?' Louise whispered.

Rob's fingers drifted over her back and he smiled at the idea. 'I wish it were that simple.'

Louise lifted her body up and rested on her elbow. 'I'd better go.' She started to get up until Rob grabbed her arm.

'Not yet, please.' His eyes pleaded with her to stay a little longer.

Louise clasped her fingers in his without saying a word.

Jason's head pounded with every beat of his heart. He didn't want to get up; not yet.

'Here.' Ben thrust a cup of hot, strong, sweet coffee in front of him. 'This might help.'

Jason managed to lift his aching body into a sitting position, slowly, and took the cup from him.

'Thanks.' Jason struggled to speak. His throat and lips were so dry.

Ben sat down beside him and smelt the stale whisky ooze from Jason's pores. Ben felt awful at the pathetic, broken shell of his brother-in-law. He wasn't Jason's biggest fan, but he did feel sorry for him.

'Go on, go and get a shower. I'll put some bacon on for you.'

Jason swallowed down the last drop of coffee, which partly quenched his thirst. He patted Ben's shoulder as he stood and staggered out of the living room.

'You're a good lad,' he muttered as he passed.

CHAPTER FORTY-FIVE

Dale McGilvery had fished on River Lochty since his father took him out on the water for the first time more than forty years ago. His wife of twenty years, his childhood sweetheart, Julie, packed him a sandwich and a flask of tea early that morning. Cheese and pickle; Dale's favourite. After the heavy rains the river was high, but calm enough to venture out for a bite. He loved that first push off from the edge of the bank. That was the first moment of freedom in his dad's little boat. Dale could feel the rest of the world float away from him, but in fact it was he who was floating away.

He cast his line and inhaled the scent of the river. The rainfall scent still lingered in the air to add to the mix that morning. Dale loved that smell. It didn't take long before his line tugged, and Dale began the dance with what he hoped would be a big salmon. He'd done this dance many times over the years. Giving, taking and twisting. Slowly winding in the reel to lift his catch from the darkness. When he struggled to haul in the line, he wondered how big this catch was, desperate not to let it escape. Julie was going to be pleased, he hoped. Not that she would relish the thought of gutting it. Dale would probably be assigned that job. A wry smile crossed his lips as he thought of her face when he walked in tonight. He tugged harder and began to wonder what kind of monster he'd snagged.

The shock of it made Dale drop his rod overboard and he stumbled towards the back of the boat, then fell back onto his seat. His heart raced as he shuddered and he whimpered with shock. His hand clutched at the stabbing pain in his chest. He'd never seen anything like it before. He reached for his phone, but it slipped from his grasp onto the boat floor before he could dial for help. It was like a gruesome doll. The face was like something out of a horror movie. The skin was bloated and her eyes stared blankly at him. One of her hands was raised just a little out of the water; enough to see her fingers, as if calling out to him for help. Or perhaps she was simply saying, *Here I am. You've found me.* His fishing hook had snagged on her hairband when Dale had wound in what he thought was an impressive catch – before realising he was about to reveal Shannon Ross's hiding place.

'Hello,' he stuttered. His mouth had suddenly become so dry. 'I've… I've just… there's a body. I think she's dead. She's white and staring. Please come quickly. I'm on the river at Inverlochty.' He tried to listen to what the operator was telling him but his words swam around Dale's head. He couldn't take his eyes off her, but the sight of her bloated flesh turned his stomach.

The girl in the river floated forward and backward as far away from the boat as the fishing line allowed. Her hair splayed out like a grotesque fan on the surface of the water. The current tried to steal her back, but her hair was fixed fast in Dale's line, holding her in place until help arrived.

CHAPTER FORTY-SIX

Jessie Blake fastened the zip on her white forensic suit and tucked her hair inside the hood. She walked the short distance from the road to where the body of a young woman had been brought up. A break in the rain had produced a rainbow that lit up the peak of Ben Lochty as it loomed over the scene of such heartbreak.

A forensic team from Dundee was already on the riverbank. Dale McGilvery was receiving medical treatment for shock, and Jessie sent a uniformed officer to take his statement. Whether this body was Shannon or not, it was still a horrific discovery for a sleepy little place like Inverlochty. As she approached, it was obvious which forensic pathologist had been assigned. David Lyndhurst's six-foot-six frame and booming, deep voice was unmistakable. David had helped Jessie through her first murder. Like all rookies, she had succumbed to the smell. She thought she was prepared, but it quickly became apparent that her breakfast was headed in only one direction. Onto the grass in front of the crime scene. David gave her some Vicks to help her through it. She'd never forgotten his kindness.

'Great to see you, David. Shame about the circumstances. Have you any idea how long she's been in there?'

David Lyndhurst spun round. 'Jessie Blake. This is your case, is it? Can't tell you very much yet, I'm afraid, except that your girl here is young; probably mid-teens, if that. Does she look like your missing girl?'

Jessie looked at the bloated corpse on the riverbank as the tent was erected around them. There was no doubt about it. It was Shannon.

'Aye, I'm afraid it looks very much like it. Thanks, David, let me have your report as soon as you can, will you? This one's pretty urgent, as you can imagine. I need to rule out foul play sooner rather than later.' She offered him a smile. 'It's great to see you.'

'You too, Jess. Don't be a stranger.'

Jessie turned to walk back to her car, but stopped short. 'Are you taking her to Dundee? Her mum is going to want to see her.'

David frowned and shook his head. 'No, I'd tell her no, Jessie.'

Jessie sighed. 'I know. You're right, I'll tell her.' She nodded. 'I'll hear from you soon.'

CHAPTER FORTY-SEVEN

Louise dropped Rob off at the hospital entrance. She knew she should go in and visit her friend, but she couldn't face her; not after spending last night with her husband. What kind of friend does that? She wondered if she would ever be able to face her again, especially as Louise understood exactly the agony Cassie was going through.

'I hope she's OK, Rob,' Louise said when Rob leaned in and kissed her cheek.

'I'll call you later,' Rob answered as he got out of her car.

Louise drove away with tears pouring down her face.

Louise spotted DI Blake lock her car then walk up the path to their front door. Jessie knocked. When Ben opened the door, she asked if Jason and Louise were home. Louise looked on in horror as Jason met Jessie in the doorway. She clasped her hands to her face as he fell to his knees. Jessie didn't have to tell her. Louise heard the scream before she recognised it as her own.

'I'm so sorry.'

Ben paced up and down with tears stinging his eyes. He grabbed his jacket and fled. He had to get out. If he stayed, he would suffocate.

Jessie put a cup of hot, sweet tea into Jason's trembling hand. Jason and Louise stood apart from each other, lonely in their shared grief, unable to stand it alone or together.

'I need to see her,' Louise murmured.

'We do need someone who can give us a positive ID, but I don't think it should be either of you. Is there anyone else?'

'I can do it, I'm fine,' Louise insisted.

Jessie shook her head, but before she could disagree, Jason piped up.

'I want to do it.'

'Are you sure there isn't anyone else you would prefer to do it?' Jessie gave him the opportunity to change his mind.

'No, she's my daughter.' His words became choked in his throat as he fought the urge to break down. 'I'm her dad. She needs me.'

Louise looked at him and, for the first time since their daughter went missing, allowed him to comfort her. She fell into his arms.

Ben watched from a distance as Shannon's body was loaded into the back of the ambulance. She looked so small from where he sat. He rubbed at the tears that soaked his face and drank from one of the beer bottles. He sat and drank long after she was gone. His mind raced at a million miles an hour and his stomach churned. He held the packet of painkillers in his hands and gulped more and more alcohol. His sister didn't need any more hassle from him, and that's all he created these days. Louise and Jason would be better off without him.

Visiting the hospital had been a mistake. Cassie had told Rob she didn't want him to stay with her, so he left her again. She said she would rather be alone. Couldn't she see how he was hurting? What now, Rob wondered? He didn't love Cassie the way he loved Louise. She was everything to Rob. He wasn't going to let Louise slip away. His relationship with Cassie would have fizzled out had it not been for the baby.

Rob couldn't think straight. He switched off the engine and reached for his wallet. He removed the ultrasound scan picture of his son and ran his fingers over it. A single tear trickled out. All they had left now were memories of the dreams they had for their son. Rob had promised he would read to his son from the minute he was born; he would have taught him to use his words and not his fists. He would have shown him how to love and respect the women in his life. They could have watched England and Scotland play rugby and, if he was any good, he could have chosen either country to play for. He had a choice, after all. But none of that was ever going to happen now.

Rob tucked the photo away and tried Louise's number. When she didn't answer, he started the engine and made his way to her house.

CHAPTER FORTY-EIGHT

2001

Daniel Simpson lay in bed staring at the ceiling as he contemplated the way forward. He would have to live under strict conditions but, this time tomorrow, he would be as free as he could possibly be. He couldn't believe it when Cam told him the board's decision. The initial feeling of exhilaration was quickly replaced with crippling anxiety, followed by terror. Cam had explained that all those feelings were perfectly normal. He listened to the morning routine clatter around him, unable to imagine what it was going to be like not to have it as the soundtrack to the start of his day.

'Good morning, Daniel,' Dr Julia Hudson greeted him.

'Morning.'

Daniel sat down.

'How are you feeling? Are you nervous?'

'I'm not going to lie. It's scary, you know. This place feels like all I've known for so long.'

'You won't be alone. You will continue to see me for some time, and Cam Walsh, of course, will continue to support you, as you know. You will stay in the supported accommodation for as long as we all agree you need it. It's not like you're walking out of here alone, and you understand the conditions and restrictions.'

Daniel liked the new name they had chosen for him. The notoriety made it impossible for Daniel Simpson to have a normal life, Tom Nicoll had made sure of that. He also made it clear to the board that he would never stop watching the man who stole his sister from him.

Tom Nicoll was devastated that his efforts to keep Daniel Simpson in jail had failed. He watched his mother go through the horror of losing Sophie all over again. The grief was intolerable. The day they were told of Daniel's release was almost as bad as the day they were told a body had been found. The expression on his father's face after identifying Sophie's body was unforgettable. So much for Harvey Goldberg's promises. He had found another, more voteworthy cause to attach himself to. Tom felt like he was the only one left who could see through the mask Daniel Simpson wore. He knew the real Daniel Simpson. The master manipulator who had pulled the wool over everyone's eyes. Nobody had forced him to abuse Sophie. He could have saved her, but he didn't. Daniel Simpson chose to take his turn in their evil game.

Tom didn't believe Daniel's defence that he was the victim of neglect, which meant he didn't know what he was doing. That he didn't know right from wrong. The influence of hardcore violence in movies was just a convenient excuse for his defence. It took two to commit the awful crime they committed that day. Daniel was not an innocent victim in all this. Had anyone ever asked him why he did it? Did Daniel even have an answer? One day, Tom would have the opportunity to ask him. He would make damn sure of that. Tom saw the monster that lay within and feared that by the time the world saw it as well, it would be too late, because by then another young girl would be dead.

CHAPTER FORTY-NINE

Jason had told Jessie that he wanted to go to Dundee straight away and, after a call to David Lyndhurst, it was agreed that she could drive him later that afternoon. Jessie wasn't happy about leaving Louise alone, but she had assured her that Ben would be back soon. She and Jason had left for Dundee to confirm whether it was Shannon one way or another. The forty minute journey from Inverlochty to Dundee had gone faster than Jessie feared it might despite the agonising silence. Jessie didn't blame him for not talking. Of course he would be lost in his thoughts. Jessie tucked her Ford fiesta into the last available space in the small car park. She could see the fear and pain ooze from Jason as he walked, head down in front of her towards the mortuary door. She placed a hand on his shoulder.

'Are you ready?' Jessie asked.

'No, but I would never be ready for this.'

Jessie couldn't disagree. Her question had been stupid, but it's what people say, isn't it? Like, are you OK? That's another one. Of course Jason and Louise were not OK. It's never OK to lose a child. Your life is never the same again. There will always be a part of you missing. Jessie knew that.

'Mr Ross, would you like to come with me?'

Jessie looked up to see Jason being led away by a tall, attractive, Mediterranean-looking man in his early thirties, she guessed, who she didn't recognise. He offered her a smile of acknowledgement as he passed. Jessie reciprocated his warm greeting with a blush, chastising herself for it. She followed behind them and stood next to Jason as the sheet was removed from her face.

Jason's legs threatened to give way beneath him and he whimpered. That was all Jessie needed for a positive identification. No parent ever had to tell her. Their pain revealed the truth every time.

'I'm so sorry for your loss,' the handsome stranger said as the sheet again hid Shannon's face.

'No, leave it, don't cover her, not yet. Can I have a moment alone with her?'

The man nodded and indicated to Jessie to follow him outside.

'Never gets easier, does it?' Jessie sighed. 'Watching families go through that ordeal.'

David Lyndhurst's assistant shook his head and reached out his hand. 'It does not. I'm Benito Capello, by the way, but people usually call me Ben. Italian parents.' He shrugged as if to explain. 'I'm working with Dr Lyndhurst for a few months.'

'Lovely to meet you, Ben.' Jessie smiled and turned her attention back to Jason, who was now hugging Shannon's lifeless body and sobbing hard.

'I'll go and see him,' Ben told her.

Jessie was touched by the gentle way he comforted Jason, and enjoyed the way he held her gaze as they left, but that was as far as relationships went. Jessie was adamant of that. No man would ever get close enough to hurt her again.

CHAPTER FIFTY

Shannon's room was cold. Louise wrapped Shannon's blanket around her shoulders against the chill, the call of migrating birds outside. Their arrival heralded a new season. Louise wasn't ready for that. Shannon was lost. How could the world carry on? Louise and Jason would be for ever trapped in the past. How could they have a future now? The world continued to turn, but Louise wanted it to stop so she could get off. So she could escape the pain; the gut-kicking agony of her loss. She sat on the edge of the bed and lifted her pillow to her face to smell her. She gripped the pillow so tight that she dug her nails into the palms of her hands, unaware that she'd broken the skin until a drop of blood landed on the bed sheet. Louise sucked her palm to stop the drips without releasing her grip on the pillow. She had to smell Shannon. She needed to feel her. Perhaps they were wrong. Perhaps Jason would call to say it wasn't her.

When Rob didn't get an answer, he tried the door handle and found it unlocked, so he let himself in.

'Jason?' he shouted. 'Louise, are you in?'

'I'm up here,' Louise called as his voice stirred her from her fog.

Rob climbed the stairs two at a time, then found Louise on Shannon's bed, still gripping the pillow. When Louise didn't look at him, he whispered her name.

'Louise, what's happened?'

Rob watched the silent tear drop down her cheek. He knelt close to her and tilted her face to him, then pressed his lips softly to hers before wiping her tear away.

'Tell me, Lou.'

'They found her.'

Panic gripped Rob. His gut clenched and he wanted to run; he didn't want to listen to those words.

Louise's eyes lingered on his.

'They found a body.'

Her words ripped at Rob's heart. She needed him more than ever now, but he didn't think he could face the truth.

'Where's Jason?' he asked.

Louise stared blankly. 'Identifying her body.'

Rob could only clasp his fingers over his mouth and exhale loudly through them.

'I'm so sorry,' was all he could say, over and over. 'I'm so sorry.'

Rob held her in his arms. He was surprised to find that she was no longer crying. He just held her and stroked her hair while they sat in silence.

CHAPTER FIFTY-ONE

Eric Baldwin screwed up his eyes at the figure in the distance with their head slumped forward. When he got closer, he saw it was Ben. Usually they avoided each other because of Ben's relentless bullying, but with Shannon missing he had to put that to one side for now. He needed to know if there was any news.

'Hey, Ben.' When his words were ignored, he stuck his fingers between his teeth and whistled.

Eric spotted the cans and the empty pill packet as he got closer. He felt for a pulse. He was alive but unconscious.

'Ben, you fucking idiot.' He shook Ben's shoulders, then reached for his phone.

'Ambulance, hurry, please.' Codeine and paracetamol. 'Shit, what have you done?'

'What's his name?'

'Ben Randall, and he's taken these.' Eric handed over the empty packet. 'Can I go now that you're here?'

He walked home, bewildered by Ben's behaviour. He was desperate to knock on Shannon's door, but Agatha had told him not to disturb her parents. She assured him they would let him know when there was news. Eric was Shannon's best friend, after all.

*

Louise snatched her phone up from the table at the first buzz. The unknown number ID puzzled her. Rob saw her frown as he sat on the sofa finishing his coffee.

'Yes, this is Louise Ross.'

She closed her eyes and heaved a huge sigh, but Rob couldn't interpret from that what was wrong.

'Thanks, I'll be there as soon as I can.'

She threw down her phone and put her head in her hands.

'What the hell's happened?'

'It's Ben, he's taken a load of pills. Eric Baldwin found him and called an ambulance. They've taken him to Perth.'

Rob hugged her.

'Shh, come on, I'll take you. You'd better pack him some pyjamas and a toothbrush. They'll probably want to keep him in overnight.'

'Thank you. I don't know what I would do without you, Rob. But what about Jason?'

'Worry about that when you get back.'

The harsh lighting above his bed made Ben cover his eyes. The blood pressure cuff tightening periodically irritated him. Ben's mouth was so dry, and he felt sick, but he was alive. So alive, in fact, that the stench of disinfectant turned his already nauseous stomach. It felt like his brain was pulsing inside his skull, bouncing off the inside so hard it was agony. The clattering of trolleys and shouts from what Ben thought was clearly a mentally disturbed woman across the corridor didn't help. The nurse assured him this was normal and would ease with time.

She had also told him how lucky he was that his friend had found him when he did. He wasn't sure if he was relieved or not that Eric had helped him. How ironic that it had been Eric. Ben had been such an arsehole to him. Seeing Louise standing at the

end of his bed didn't make him feel much better. Louise wanted
to be angry. She wanted to scream and shout out that he was a
selfish son of a bitch. Didn't she have enough to deal with? Wasn't
she hurting enough? Instead, she dropped his overnight bag on
the floor and moved to him. She scooped her little brother up in
her arms and he clung on tight, sobbing that he was sorry.

CHAPTER FIFTY-TWO

Rob turned into his drive, confused by the stranger sat on his doorstep. He switched off his engine. He got out of his car and started walking towards his front door. The stranger's gaze fixed on Rob without flinching.

'Can I help you?'

The stranger stood.

'Hello, Daniel.'

'My… my name isn't Daniel,' Rob stuttered. 'I'm sorry, you must have me mixed up with someone else.'

Tom Nicoll smirked. Rob struggled to find his front door key in panic. When he eventually found the right one, his hands trembled so much it was difficult to put it in the lock. Tom Nicoll laughed at the terror in his eyes.

'What's wrong, Daniel? Are you not pleased to see a face from the past? I told them back then that I wouldn't stop looking for you, and now there's another teenage girl missing – right in the very village they hid you. Do they know? Shannon's parents, do they know who you really are?'

Tom moved forward just as Rob slammed the front door shut. He hammered his fist on the door before turning to leave.

'I'm sure I'll be seeing you again soon, Daniel.'

Rob gasped for breath. Pain ripped into his chest and his head thumped. He tugged at the collar of his shirt and gasped for air. His breathing quickened into short, sharp puffs, gulping as much air as he could take in. Rob fell to his knees, panting and struggling for his life as the world went black.

CHAPTER FIFTY-THREE

Cassie couldn't understand why Rob hadn't come to see her. Yes, she'd asked for space, for time to recover, but the text message had been clear. She needed him to collect her this morning because the doctor said she was well enough to go home. She and Rob hadn't argued, which made his silence even more puzzling. They had so much to talk about. She wanted to apologise for shutting him out. That was wrong of her. Rob had lost a baby, too. His son. Rob had been so excited when the scan showed that she was carrying a boy. She assumed he would feel the same if their baby had been a girl, but the look on his face was amazing and he'd cried. She hoped he was OK. She had been wrong to send him away like that. She had left messages on both their home number and his mobile.

'Rob, it's me again. Look, I need picking up. I'm being discharged.' Cassie sighed. 'Never mind, I'll see you at home. We should talk.'

She nibbled her bottom lip and hoped that Louise would be awake. It would take her mum an hour to get there from Dundee where she and her father had bought a retirement villa in a development in the north of the city, and Cassie was anxious to get home to her own bed. To her own surroundings, although when she would be able to go back into the room they had only recently decided would be their son's nursery she didn't know. She had looked forward to filling the house with children. Even Rob agreed that five bedrooms was too much for two or even three people.

Louise answered her call within two rings.

'Hi. Listen, I hate to ask under the circumstances, but I can't get hold of Rob. Could you give me a lift home?'

Louise wiped sleep from her eyes. She glanced at the time on her bedside clock. 'Yes, of course, what time do you need me?'

Louise and Jason had talked late into the night after DI Blake had dropped him off. They had really talked. More than they had for years, it felt like. They talked about everything and nothing. It was like they saw each other for the first time since Shannon disappeared. The look on Jason's face when he walked in the door told Louise all she needed to know. He was a shell of his former self. When Shannon's body was released to them they would have so much to organise. As Jessie had told them, there would be a post-mortem to establish what had happened to Shannon and she would keep them informed at every stage.

Louise put her phone back on the bedside table and turned to face Jason. Last night they'd slept together in the same bed; neither of them wanted to be alone. They didn't have sex but wanted to be close, joined together by their overwhelming grief. The thought of being alone terrified them equally, the agony of grief ripping at them.

'I have to get Cassie from the hospital.' She bent down to kiss his cheek and he reached for her arm and begged her to stay.

'What? Where the hell's Rob? He should be picking his wife up. We've just lost our daughter, for fuck's sake.' Jason's words trailed off into tears which he hastily wiped away as he lay back down on his pillow. 'Whatever, you go.'

'She says he's not answering his phone, and there's nobody else.'

Louise stroked Jason's hair softly. 'I won't be long.'

She kissed his forehead before she got up to get dressed.

*

Jessie met with Dylan in the incident room in anticipation of David Lyndhurst's findings. This was not the outcome any of them wanted.

'As you know, a body was pulled from River Lochty yesterday morning, which has been formally identified as Shannon Ross.'

'Have you spoken to Louise and Jason this morning?' Dylan asked. 'How are they doing?'

Jessie shook her head. 'Not yet.'

'I'll go over and check on them.'

'Could you hang fire until we get David's report? He's doing Shannon's PM as a priority.'

Just as she finished that sentence, her phone rang.

'Talk of the devil,' she said. 'Hi, David. How are you?'

Dylan waited and watched as she nodded at what David was telling her. When she closed her eyes and exhaled, he knew the news wasn't good.

'Thanks, yes, speak soon.' Jessie licked her lips and dropped her phone onto the desk. 'OK, we now officially have a murder investigation on our hands.'

'Jesus Christ.' Dylan brushed his hands roughly over his neatly cropped hair. This was the first murder he knew of in Inverlochty.

'Dylan?'

'What? No, sorry, I'm fine, it's just a shock. I mean, this is Inverlochty, for Christ's sake. At worst I thought we were looking at an accident, which is obviously horrendous enough, I know, but murder?'

Jessie continued with David's findings.

'Shannon Ross was dead before she hit the water because there was no water in her lungs. Probable cause of death was a massive head injury as David found Shannon's skull had a large crack across the back, most likely from blunt force trauma.'

'What now, boss?' Dylan asked. 'Who would want to do that to someone like wee Shannon? Are we looking at Foster for this? The blood in his bathroom? Her phone in his kitchen?'

Jessie perched on the edge of her desk and stared up at Shannon's smiling face. She pointed at the photo.

'I don't know yet, but what I do know is that when we find out who has done this, we prepare the best airtight motherfucker of a case against the bastard and nail his sorry arse to the wall. He's going to wish he'd never been born.'

CHAPTER FIFTY-FOUR

Cassie's heart broke for her best friend. She couldn't believe Louise had the strength to stand, let alone come and collect her, after Louise told her the awful truth about Shannon. Louise was on autopilot. She was moving with the tide of whatever came along, and for now that was collecting Cassie. She had lost the ability to oppose the forces that jostled for her attention.

'Thank you for this,' Cassie whispered. 'If I'd known.' She stopped. She didn't know what else to say.

It hurt to look into Louise's empty eyes, so filled with pain.

As Louise turned into Cassie's drive, she was troubled by the fact that Rob's car wasn't there. Louise knew he'd taken the miscarriage hard, but he wouldn't go without telling anyone; without telling her. That wasn't Rob's style. She opened the passenger door for Cassie and helped her walk slowly inside.

'Rob, are you here?' Cassie shouted into the empty house.

Cassie saw that the messages she'd left for him on the answering machine hadn't been listened to as the number four flashed up at her. Louise sat next to her friend, but before she had the chance to speak, she spotted a white envelope with Cassie's name on it and panicked. What if Rob had confessed to their affair?

'What's that?' Cassie's eyes narrowed as she reached for the white envelope propped up against the plant on the coffee table.

Dear Cassie,

I know you won't understand what I must do but I want you to know that I loved you and our baby with all my heart. This isn't about you or our son. I really thought I had a chance to have the family I never had as a boy, but perhaps it's only fair that I'm denied that chance. I'm so sorry that you're alone and hurting. I never meant for that to happen. I hope that one day you will find it in your heart to forgive me. I've done a terrible thing, and you're about to find out the truth about me. I guess I'm a coward for not wanting to stick around to face the consequences.

Love always,

Rob x

Louise dropped the paper. 'I have to go, I'm sorry.'

'Louise, wait.' Cassie tried to follow her but her weakness meant that Louise was gone by the time she reached the door, which had been left wide open in her haste. Before she had a chance to close the door, a man she didn't recognise appeared at the bottom of the drive and called out to her by name.

'Cassie Taylor, I wonder if I could have five minutes of your time?'

The man continued towards the door and smiled as if he knew her.

'Do I know you?' she asked, feeling vulnerable and alone suddenly.

'Forgive me, my name is Tom Nicoll. Your husband and I go back a long way.'

CHAPTER FIFTY-FIVE

Tom Nicoll was disappointed but not surprised not to find Rob at home this time, but he didn't have to be present for Tom to destroy his life. The look of terror on his face last night would have to do for now.

'You're a friend of Rob's?' Cassie asked as Tom moved past her into the hall.

Tom eyed the hall, then allowed his eyes to drift up the staircase, briefly coming to rest on the huge bookcase at the top. Oak, if he wasn't much mistaken. *Expensive taste for a murderer*, he thought.

'Yes, your husband and I go back more than twenty years. He hasn't mentioned me?' He paused before turning to face her. 'Or my little sister Sophie?'

Cassie leaned on the front door as it clicked shut. Her mind still spun after Rob's note, and now this stranger was claiming to be an old friend.

'So how do you know Rob?

In that moment Tom felt truly sorry for her. Her eyes searched for the truth when she had no idea what the truth really was.

Cassie had cried, and she had shouted; screamed even. She had insisted Tom was lying. Then she was adamant he was mixing Rob up with someone else. Anger and denial at the loss of the man she once knew. A normal reaction. It was painful to watch, but it had to be done, Tom reflected as he walked from there to the police station.

'I need to talk to the detective in charge of the investigation into Shannon Ross's disappearance.'

'I'll tell DI Blake you're here. What did you say your name was?' The desk sergeant picked up the phone.

'I'm Tom Nicoll. Tell her I have information that someone should have told her from the beginning.'

'Send him straight through,' Jessie told the desk sergeant.

Before he left them alone, Dylan told Jessie that he was about to head over to Louise and Jason's, which piqued Tom's interest.

'How are they coping, Shannon's parents?' His expression softened at the mention of their names.

'As well as can be expected, I suppose. I don't know when I'll be back, so—'

'Take as long as you need,' said Jessie. 'I'll call you if I need you back.'

Dylan left with a nod and closed the door behind him, leaving Jessie with her mysterious visitor.

'Please take a seat, Mr Nicoll. You have information that could help my investigation, is that right?'

Tom pulled a chair out from the table and sat down opposite her. 'Yes, I certainly do.'

The echo of the key turning in the lock sent chills down Dylan's spine. There was something about this place that really bothered him.

'Andrew is in the day room. Go straight through.' The nurse disappeared into a side room before Dylan had a chance to thank her.

Dylan walked in the direction he'd been ushered to find Andrew sat at a table alone, scribbling notes in a notebook.

'Andrew Foster. I'm DC Dylan Logan.' He held up his ID, which Andrew glanced at suspiciously, then went back to writing in his book.

'What's that you're writing?' Dylan asked enthusiastically, to open a dialogue.

'What business is that of yours?' Andrew Foster frowned, then closed his book and tucked his pen into the wire margin.

'It's none of my business, you're right, I'm sorry.' Dylan tried again. 'So, how are you, Andrew?'

'I'm fine, I suppose.'

'That's good, I'm glad. And your arms, how are they doing?'

Andrew's gaze wandered to the bandages on his forearms and he nodded.

'Aye, I'm OK. It could have been a lot worse, I suppose.'

A short silence settled over them while Dylan considered how to approach the subject of Shannon's disappearance and now murder.

The nurse who had let Dylan in appeared behind them and nodded towards the small ward kitchen.

'Help yourself to a cup of tea, or perhaps Andrew could get you one?'

'No thanks. I'm fine, really.' Dylan lifted a hand at the offer.

'So, what can I do for you, officer?' Andrew asked. 'I'm sure you're not here just to see how I'm doing.'

Dylan exhaled a huge sigh, which caused Andrew to frown.

'What's wrong? Has something happened?'

'I'm sorry to have to tell you that Shannon Ross was found dead yesterday morning. A fisherman discovered her body. She was murdered, Andrew.'

Andrew threw himself back in his chair and sat bolt upright. 'No! That can't be true. You're lying!' He clasped both hands across the top of his head. 'I pushed her!' he shouted. 'But I didn't kill her, did I?' The doubt in his voice was palpable. He hammered his fists on the table and screamed, then turned his fists on himself, punching his head hard. 'No, she can't be dead. Not Shannon, she's a good girl. The voices, they were so loud. They made me do it. I wouldn't have done it if they hadn't been screaming at me like that. No, no. She can't be gone. I didn't mean to hurt her. I just wanted it to stop.'

A group of nurses ran to their table to check on him and one of them shook his head at Dylan.

'I'm sorry, but I'm going to have to ask you to leave now. Andrew is too distressed to continue this conversation.'

Dylan watched with horror as Andrew received an injection which had an immediate effect. Foster's thrashing, tormented body softened quickly before he was helped to his feet and guided towards his room.

If Andrew Foster *had* done something to Shannon, it was going to be incredibly difficult to find out what or why.

Jessie stared at Tom Nicoll, unable to utter a single word. Everything she had just heard was whirring around in her brain. When Tom produced the newspaper clippings and photographs, there was no denying that the man she knew as Rob Taylor was in fact Daniel Simpson. It was the eyes. His eyes were distinctive and unmistakable. Why hadn't she been informed the moment she arrived? Sophie and Shannon looked alike; blonde and blue-eyed. They were even the same age. Jessie's head swam with different scenarios. Was Taylor using Louise to get to Shannon? Did he kill her the day she went missing? Had he been lying to her, to everyone since that night? Surely someone must have been supervising this man?

'How did you find him?' Jessie wondered.

'Quite by accident, detective inspector. I saw his face on the news and I recognised it in an instant. Twenty years might have gone by, but there are days that it feels like yesterday to me.'

Tom's steely composure began to slip.

'I'm sorry that happened to your sister.'

The sadness in Tom's eyes was obvious. 'You have to find him.'

'What do you mean, find him?'

'He's gone, detective.'

CHAPTER FIFTY-SIX

Dylan knocked at the door and prepared himself as best he could. He couldn't decide if he was relieved or not to see Ben answer the door.

'Hello, Ben, is your sister in?'

'They're in the kitchen.'

Ben's head thumped. The hospital had kept him in overnight for observation, and had given him an emergency appointment with the community psychiatric nurse at his GP surgery at the end of the week to assess his mental health needs.

Dylan wiped his feet and followed Ben inside. He loosened his jacket as he walked towards the kitchen. Louise stood and moved closer to him.

'Tell me.'

'I'm sorry, Louise. Shannon didn't drown.'

Jason's chair scraped across the vinyl floor as he stood. 'What do you mean?'

Louise pulled Jason's arm away. 'Let him speak.'

Jason allowed his arms to fall by his sides.

'Shannon died from a blow to the back of the head. I'm so sorry. She was dead before she hit the water.'

Jason raced to the sink and only just made it before he vomited. Louise tried to ask Dylan a question, but the words wouldn't come.

'DI Blake will come and talk over what will happen next. I know this is a lot to take in.'

Louise's legs felt uncertain underneath her and Dylan helped her into a chair. Jason wiped the vomit from his mouth.

'Who would do something like that?' And then a horrifying thought hit him. 'Did he hurt her, you know? Was she—?'

Dylan interrupted him with a shake of his head. 'No, there was no evidence of any sexual assault.' He kept his voice low.

The front door slammed shut behind him and Ben ran. He didn't know where he was going, but he had to run.

CHAPTER FIFTY-SEVEN

The shock of Jessie's words stopped Dylan in his tracks.

'I'll meet you there. I'm on my way now.'

He tossed his phone onto the passenger seat, stunned by the revelation of Rob's identity. He vaguely remembered the case from the mid-1990s, but why hadn't they been informed he was living in Inverlochty?

When he arrived at the top of the hill he found Jessie's car tucked behind the hedge at the entrance to the driveway. Jessie waved for Dylan to stay out of sight, so he did as he was told and parked behind her car.

'Is he in?' Dylan whispered.

'I'm not sure. I guess we'll find out soon enough.'

After a long, heated discussion with a senior social worker called Camilla Walsh, Jessie was given all the information she requested. After his release in 2001, Daniel Simpson ceased to exist, replaced by Rob Taylor. He was moved into a halfway house, a supported accommodation project in Glasgow. His former life in the north of England was wiped from history, apart from the few people who needed to know. Jessie learned that he was one of a handful of convicted killers living under this licence. Camilla assured her that she would report the matter to the probation service authority as a matter of urgency, and couldn't understand how such a potentially disastrous oversight could have happened.

'Hello, can I help you?' Cassie answered the door to Jessie's ID badge in her face.

'Is Rob here? It's a matter of some urgency that we speak to him.'

'You had better come in.' Cassie waved them both through the door. 'Rob isn't here. He's left me, but I know why you're here for him.'

Dylan closed the front door and followed the two women inside. 'Where is he?' Jessie asked.

'He's not here, I told you,' Cassie said. 'So you can stop searching.'

'I just need to check your house, Cassie. Is that OK?' Jessie asked.

A shrug of Cassie's shoulders was enough for Jessie to begin her room-to-room search.

'When did you last see your husband?' Dylan asked.

'My husband? And who is he, exactly?' Cassie laughed bitterly as she sat down slowly on the sofa, still finding movement uncomfortable. It was clear that Rob had run when he realised he was about to be exposed.

'When did you last see Rob?'

'Rob? Don't you mean Daniel?' Cassie called back. 'I can't believe this is happening! Two weeks ago I was expecting my baby. Shannon wasn't gone. Everybody was happy.' Cassie broke down. 'Why did he do it? To Shannon. To Louise. To me?'

'I know this is hard.' Dylan placed a hand on her shoulder. 'Have you any idea where Rob would go? Somewhere he might go to get away from everything? Does he have a holiday home, any relatives nearby? Anybody, anywhere?'

'He told me both his parents were dead.' Cassie dropped her head in her hands, then shook her head. 'God, I've been so stupid. It's all my fault. If I hadn't got together with him he wouldn't have been able to get close to Shannon.'

Jessie made her way back to the living room and shook her head at Dylan.

'I told you he wasn't here! I don't know where he is. He didn't even collect me from hospital after I lost our baby.'

'I'm sorry for your loss, Cassie. I had no idea.' Jessie knew the pain all too well. *Poor Cassie. She must be going through hell*, she thought, *and now this*. 'Is there someone I can call for you? Someone who can be with you?'

Cassie appreciated her gesture. 'I'll be fine, thanks. I'm going to my mum's. Just find him, please. Before anyone else gets hurt. Promise me?'

Jessie glanced at Dylan, then back to Cassie.

'I promise,' she whispered.

Finding that letter under the door to his room was the holy grail for a journalist and, as he sat at his laptop, Blair Crawford opened another bottle of beer and toasted Tom Nicoll.

CHAPTER FIFTY-EIGHT

2010

Rob knew he could be happy in Inverlochty; especially in a house on the top of a hill just on the outskirts of town. There was a good vibe about the house, and the town. He'd worked hard to afford this house. He deserved it. The past few years had been hard. Rob would never deny that; instead he would use it to become the man he should be. Book three was coming along well, and he still enjoyed the buzz of five-star reviews as much as he had the very first one. Writing book one had been more a form of therapy than a deliberate literary effort. He had no idea what lay ahead when he first put pen to paper. Cam bought him the notebook and pen because she knew he liked to write, but even she had no idea what was about to come.

'That's us all done,' the hefty, balding removal man called upstairs in his harsh Glasgow accent. 'We're heading off now.'

'Hang on, I'm coming down.' Rob grabbed two twenty-pound notes from his jeans and walked downstairs. 'Thanks, guys, for all your hard work.'

'Thanks, pal. Good luck in your new place.' The removal man held up a twenty-pound note. 'And thanks for this. Much appreciated.'

Rob nodded and smiled as he closed the front door after them. He listened to their truck disappear into the distance, leaving behind it only silence. Rob closed his eyes and breathed slowly, revelling in the peace. All he could hear was the sound of his own breath and he loved it. He wanted to savour every moment. He clicked on the kettle and slid his finger across the worktop. It was smooth, and so clean; cleaner than his last place. He wasn't sad to leave that old flat behind.

Cam was apprehensive at first. She wasn't sure he was ready to take on something so big, but Rob talked her round in the end. Something caught Rob's attention from the corner of his eye, right outside his kitchen window. He narrowed his eyes and peered round the side of the curtain so as not to scare his visitor. He watched in awe as the kingfisher bobbed and bowed its graceful head in search of lunch in the burn that ran along the back of his new house. Rob smiled as the kettle came to a boil. He unwrapped a mug and rummaged in another box for coffee.

'Shit.' He was worried he'd forgotten to pack the coffee in the 'need it quick' box. He moved aside his notebook, then gasped. He ran his fingers over the dog-eared pages, then pulled out his copy of *The Hitchhiker's Guide to the Galaxy*. Her leaving gift. She had given a small token to everyone, but still, it meant a lot to him. The book had that effect every time; it was like it had some strange hold on him. But he knew it wasn't the book; it was the person who had given it him that he remembered the most. Thinking about Gail Robertson still filled Rob with a strange feeling he couldn't quite put his finger on even now as a grown man. She had had such an impact on his life.

The dark clouds seemed to follow Rob into town as he walked down the hill past the huge oak trees on either side. The legend of The Black Witch made him question every shadow and crunch he heard until he quickened his pace. The ten-minute walk was enough to refresh him. The tiredness he'd felt was gone. A high-pitched squeal startled him out of his daydream. He couldn't help but grin at the sight in front of him until guilt made him jog forward.

'Hey, I'll get them for you,' he said. 'Hang on.'

'Thank you so much. Bloody bags. You know what the problem is, don't you?'

Rob continued to retrieve the oranges from the pavement and shrugged with a smile.

'They use cheap bags. Paper-thin, they are. As much use as a chocolate kettle.'

'You might be right.' Rob handed her back her escaped shopping. 'Here you go.'

'Thanks. I'm sorry, I don't think I know you, do I? Have we met before?' She frowned.

Rob smiled. 'No, I'm Rob Taylor, how do you do? I've just bought the house at the top of Scroggie Hill.'

The young woman frowned again, then her eyes lit up before she blushed and gasped a little.

'You're Rob Taylor! The author. I heard a rumour that an author had bought that house. Sheila didn't say it was you she sold the property to. Wow, I can't believe this. I love your books.'

Rob's heart raced. 'Yes,' he replied awkwardly, and turned to walk away.

'Don't go,' she urged. 'Can I buy you a coffee as a thank you? Please.'

Rob closed his eyes and swallowed hard before he turned back with a smile. 'Sure, that would be great.'

Her soft blue eyes caught his and held his gaze. 'It's so good to meet you, Rob. I'm Cassie.'

CHAPTER FIFTY-NINE

Rob sat bolt upright in the hotel room bed, sweat pouring from him. The bed sheets were soaking wet. The nightmares always stayed with him, but this one was particularly brutal.

The alarm clock read three o'clock in the morning. He ran his fingers through his damp hair then wiped his hands on his T-shirt. He had left the house with one suitcase, his phone and laptop. Tom Nicoll left him with no choice. Cassie probably knew the truth by now, but what mattered more to Rob was that Louise knew. The thought that she might believe he had something to do with Shannon's death hurt him so badly he felt sick. It burned so deep inside that Louise might think that. He'd picked up the phone to call her so many times, but what could he say? He laid his head back down on the pillow. In the morning he would have to figure out what he was going to do and where he should go, because he sure as hell couldn't go home, thanks to Tom Nicoll.

Jessie was walking up to the Ross's house when she noticed Blair Crawford sitting in his car across the street. She narrowed her eyes as she knocked on their door.

'Come in, DI Blake.' Jason opened the door wide for Jessie. 'Louise is still in bed, I'll go and get her. Go through, I won't be a minute.'

Jessie smiled and made her way into the living room. She picked up Shannon's school photo and imagined Rob Taylor seeing that photo every time he was there. She thought about him spending time with her. Had he planned it? Did it just happen, like he said it did with Sophie? Did she believe that?

'Hello, sorry, I didn't know you would be here so early.' Louise yawned then rubbed sleep from her eyes.

'I'll go and make us some coffee,' Jason offered.

He ran his hand across the back of Louise's shoulders and Jessie was touched by the way Louise reached for his hand with a soft smile. The way Jason looked at her tugged at Jessie's heart. Louise sniffed and brushed her bare arms against the early-morning chill, and pulled the blanket from the back of the sofa around her shoulders.

'DC Logan visited you yesterday to let you know how Shannon most likely—' Jessie paused while Jason returned with coffee for the three of them.

'There isn't any easy way to tell you this.'

Jason and Louise glanced briefly at each other then back at Jessie. Part of Jessie wished they weren't listening so intently, patiently hanging on her every word.

'We have a suspect that we are very keen to talk to in connection to Shannon's death.'

Jason slammed his mug on the table, some of its contents cascading over the sides.

'Who is it?' he growled.

'Jason, let her speak.'

Jessie feared what Jason would do when she told him.

'How much do you know about your friend Rob Taylor?'

Jason stood and paced the floor, his fingers clasped so tight that his knuckles turned white.

'Rob! I'm going to fucking kill him.'

Jason snatched up his car keys and went to leave. Louise blocked his path. She clutched at his shirt.

'Let her finish.' Louise directed her words straight into Jason's eyes, her own mind spinning out of control. Jason lifted his hands up and retreated after throwing down his keys, hard, on the chair by the living room door.

'OK, let's hear it.' His voice was tense, full of anger.

'Sit down, Jason. Come on, I want you to calm down. I need your help.'

Jason perched on the edge of the sofa and dropped his head in his hands, rage simmering. He snapped his head up to hear what Jessie had to say. Louise reached for his hand. She nodded at him with a gentle smile, which made him settle back into the cushions and kiss her hand once.

'I'm sorry,' he whispered.

'This isn't easy to hear, I know,' Jessie told them.

Jason shook his head and Louise tugged the blanket further around her.

'Rob Taylor is not the man you think he is.'

'Clearly!' Jason leaned forward and released his grip on Louise's hand.

'Rob Taylor was not his birth name.'

Louise frowned and joined her husband on the edge of the seat. 'What do you mean?'

She knew Rob better than she knew herself. She would know if something wasn't right; if he was lying. She wouldn't have let him get close to her or Shannon if she suspected he was any kind of con man.

'In 1996 a teenage girl was raped and murdered by two boys from her class.'

Louise clamped both hands over her mouth and stood up. 'Oh God, no, no! I don't want to hear this.' She put her hands over her ears, then squeezed the blanket tighter around herself. 'Jason, this can't be happening. I know Rob, it's not him. It can't be him.'

She pressed her face into Jason's shirt and sobbed.

'Finish what you've got to say,' Jason spoke calmly, controlling his rage with a clenched fist.

Jessie nodded. 'Her name was Sophie Nicoll and the two boys were Daniel Simpson and Jack MacKay. They were tried as juveniles and sentenced to five years in Carseview young offenders' institution.'

Louise sobbed as she listened in horror.

'Jack MacKay committed suicide not long after his incarceration, but Daniel Simpson completed his sentence and, following intensive rehabilitation, was released in 2001 with a new identity. 'Rob Taylor.'

Jessie watched the couple attempt to absorb her words.

'Right now, we have no evidence to suggest that he has done anything. We only have the fact that he is missing and, of course, his history.'

'What do you mean, he's missing?' Louise exclaimed.

'When the information eventually arrived on my desk, we had to consider Rob a suspect, and by the time we went to talk to him he was already gone.'

Then Louise remembered the letter. He wasn't abandoning Cassie. He was running away from what he'd done.

'Louise, I wonder if you, with your connection to Rob, could perhaps—'

Jason glanced from Louise to Jessie and back again, puzzled by her suggestion.

'What connection? What's that supposed to mean?'

The flush on Louise's face helped connect the dots.

'Louise, tell me you didn't, you haven't…?' He pulled away from her when she reached out for him. 'How could you do that to me, to us?'

'I'm so sorry,' she tried to whisper through her tears.

Jason slapped her hands away.

'You fucked him, the man who killed our daughter.' He spun on his heels and walked out of the front door, slamming it hard behind him.

'I should go after him,' Louise cried.

'I'm sorry, I didn't mean for that to happen, but please, I need your help. Do you know where Rob could be?'

'God, I've been so stupid.' Louise tossed the blanket onto the floor. 'I have to talk to Jason. I've hurt him so badly.'

Louise opened the front door but it was too late, Jason was gone. So was Blair Crawford, Jessie noticed, once she'd caught up with Louise.

'Come back inside, we need to talk.'

'Ben, you scared me,' Jessie said as they bumped into him in the kitchen.

'Sorry, I just need something to eat,' he answered, his face sombre, the black rings under his eyes evidence of another sleepless night.

'You go up, I'll bring you a sandwich in a bit.' Louise smiled at her brother as he turned to head back to his room. 'He misses Shannon, too.' She choked back her tears. 'He took a load of pills the other day. This is all affecting him so deeply. Ben is so much more sensitive than he makes out.'

'I'm sorry. Can you think of anywhere Rob would go? We need to talk to him,' Jessie urged.

'Look, if I knew I would tell you. Do you think I want to help him hide from you?'

'I want you to call him.' Jessie instructed her.

Louise felt nauseous at the thought of hearing his voice. How could she talk to him when he might have harmed her daughter? Still, she relented. She had no choice.

'What do you want me to say?'

Blair Crawford paid Maggie for the bottle of Glen Moray whisky and took it and the two glasses up to his room. Jason Ross had been in such a mess when he'd stumbled in front of his car that he couldn't leave him like that. He gave Jason his room key to clean himself up. It wouldn't be a problem if he hid out for a while. The two men had a lot to talk about.

'Thanks.' Jason sank the entire glass in two large gulps then waved it in front of Blair for a refill. 'Same again.'

'This is the good stuff, take your time with it.' Blair placed the bottle on the dressing table and watched Jason sink that glass, too.

'Just keep pouring, my friend. I've got stuff in here I need to forget.' Jason tapped his fingers on the side of his head. 'Stuff you wouldn't believe. Fuck, stuff *I* cannot actually believe.'

'Do you want to talk about it?' Blair refilled his glass.

'I told you, you wouldn't believe it if I told you. Man.'

Jason pinched his eyes with his thumb and forefinger.

'Try me. I'm a great listener.'

CHAPTER SIXTY

The sound of his phone vibrating on the hard floor woke Rob from a deep sleep. A sleep that hadn't come easily after that nightmare.

'Louise, I'm so glad you called. It's so good to hear your voice.'

When his words were greeted with silence, he spoke again. 'Louise, is that you? Please talk to me,' he begged.

His voice tore through her, ripping at her emotions. He still sounded the same. None of this could really be true, could it?

'Tell me the truth,' she murmured. 'Did you hurt Shannon?'

'Please, Louise, you have to believe me. I haven't hurt Shannon. I would never hurt her. I love her like she's my own flesh and blood. You must know that.'

Rob's heart thundered, and his chest tightened like a vice. He struggled to breathe.

'Is that the truth?'

All Louise could make out were rapid, panting breaths until a deep, gravelly voice she didn't recognise spoke.

'I didn't do it,' he insisted. 'I would never hurt you or Shannon.'

The silence that followed felt like for ever to Rob. 'Louise, are you still there?'

'But you have hurt someone before, haven't you?' Louise rubbed a tear from the tip of her nose.

The vice tightened around Rob and he sucked in as much air as he could, but it wasn't enough.

'Rob, where are you?'

*

Jessie rang the bell on the reception desk and was greeted by a chirpy, middle-aged woman wearing a badge with the name Madge written in capital letters, who bustled towards them with enthusiasm in her walk.

'Hello there, what can I do for you?'

Jessie held up her ID and pulled Rob's photo out of her pocket while Dylan reached for his. 'I am Detective Inspector Blake, and this is my colleague Detective Constable Logan. I would appreciate it if you could let us have access to a room booked in the name of Rob Taylor. I believe he arrived a couple of nights ago. Six foot three with blond hair. This is him here.'

Jessie handed her Rob's photo, but Madge shook her head. 'I don't recognise him, I'm afraid.'

'This is rather important, so if you could check your books, that would be great.'

'Wait here, I'll go and get the diary. I won't be a minute.'

'Thank you, that's really helpful.' Dylan smiled politely.

Jessie's phone buzzed in her pocket. When the caller ID read unknown number, she tapped the reject button without hesitation. Seconds later the buzzing returned, this time forcing her to put her phone on silent and stuff it back at the bottom of her pocket.

Dylan shot a concerned glance in Jessie's direction. That wasn't like her.

'What?' she asked when Dylan stared at her.

'I didn't say anything, Jess,' he answered.

'What have you heard?' she barked, then instantly regretted it. 'I'm sorry, I didn't mean to snap. I know you were only trying to help.'

'It's none of my business, I know, but it's obvious there's something going on, that's all.' He shrugged.

Neither of them could continue the conversation as Madge bustled back towards them. Jessie was grateful for that. Any longer and she might have told him.

'I'm sorry to keep you waiting.' She laid the huge diary on the desk and lifted her glasses from the chain that dangled above her ample bosom. 'Right, Rob Taylor, you said.' She flicked through several pages, backward and forward, then removed her glasses. 'I'm sorry, there's nobody here in that name. There's not even anyone who arrived two days ago. All of our rooms are booked for a convention in Dundee. Most of the guests have been here for a week.'

Jessie glanced at Dylan, who was staring at her in confusion. Louise had lied to them.

Rob answered the door after only one knock.

'I'm so glad you came. You have to believe me. I had nothing to do with it. I would never hurt Shannon or you.'

Louise felt guilty that she'd sent the two detectives to the wrong hotel, but she had to see Rob first. She would know when she saw him if he was guilty. She would see it in his eyes. He still looked the same. His eyes still melted her heart when she looked at him.

'But you have hurt someone, haven't you?' Her voice struggled to be heard.

Rob's head dropped as he turned away from her. He sat on the edge of his bed and sighed.

'I'm not that mixed-up teenage boy any more. They helped me. They made me a better man. You know me, Lou, better than anyone ever has.'

Louise scoffed. 'How can you sit there and say that? I don't know. Nobody knows you, Rob. Or do I call you Daniel? Which is it? Does Cassie know?'

'Louise, please, it doesn't matter who knows. I haven't done anything to Shannon.' He gazed into her eyes. 'I just want to get on with my life. I've been punished. Forgive me, Lou, please. I didn't deliberately deceive you or Cassie. I had strict conditions I had to adhere to, that's all.'

'I'm sorry,' Louise murmured as she turned for the door. 'Goodbye, Rob.'

Louise had been wrong to think she could do this. Her baby was dead. It might not be at Rob's hands, but he was capable of it all the same. She couldn't forgive him. Not for the lies. Not for his past.

'Lou,' he called after her until her car was a fleck in the distance, unaware of the figure tucked behind the neatly clipped beech hedge that circled the entire hotel car park.

CHAPTER SIXTY-ONE

2001

Daniel Simpson dropped his bag onto the floor of his new room, which was bigger than his room in Carseview. But not by much, and it was colder. The cold was the first thing he noticed. Sharing a bathroom with three other people wasn't a problem. It was preferable to sharing with twenty teenage boys with varying degrees of personal hygiene ranging from zero to poor at best. He looked forward to having a bath. Being able to choose how long he soaked, and even when. The view from his window was the railway station and, for a minute, he watched the commuters rushing quickly towards the waiting trains and wondered if that would be him one day. Dark clouds gathered overhead before huge drops of rain hammered down on the rush hour travellers, who quickened their pace. He gazed at the variety of umbrellas and hoods being yanked up to protect them from the deluge.

His daydreams were interrupted by the train rumbling away from the station. A noise he wondered if he would get used to. Along with the unpredictable, tempestuous Scottish weather. Then again, staring out at the exquisite Charles Rennie Mackintosh Glasgow school of Art in the distance wasn't a bad way to start the day. Maybe one day he might even study there. For the first time in a long time, Daniel believed in possibilities. The possibility of having a life outside Carseview. The possibility of finding happiness, despite everything. Within walking distance was the factory that would be his first-ever job. The bottling operation ran a scheme for ex-offenders, and Cam Walsh had successfully managed to find Daniel a place. Although it wasn't Daniel Simpson they were hiring, because he didn't exist any more. Cam explained that he had been replaced by Rob Taylor, which was fine. It wasn't like it was a hard name to remember.

'What do you think?' Cam joined him in his room after organising the paperwork with Mary Dalgleish, senior support worker of the supported accommodation project. Cam was lucky to find him a place; Mary's project had a fantastic reputation, and the fact that her client was outside the catchment area had made it that bit harder, but Cam persevered. The fact that one of the boys had got drunk and trashed the house kitchen meant his place had become available, but even Mary and her team weren't told about Daniel's past. As far as they were concerned, a young man called Rob Taylor would be joining them. Daniel's new life began the moment he stepped out of Carseview by order of Judge Rylance, who rubber-stamped his release. They couldn't risk the press finding him. He would have no chance if they did.

Rob Taylor turned to Cam and smiled. 'It's perfect.'

'Good, I'm glad you like it. It's basic, but it's all you need, right, isn't it? To get you started, that is.'

'Cam, I don't know what to say. I still can't believe I'm actually here.' Daniel sat down on his bed. The mattress was soft, maybe even a little lumpy, but it was his. He ran his fingers over the duvet and straightened up the pillow. He would treat himself to a new duvet set as soon as he could, and maybe a couple of towels. Towels of his choice of colour.

'OK, well, I'm going to head off.' Cam hoisted her bag further up her shoulder. 'If you need anything between now and when I come back on Thursday, tell Mary or call, OK?'

Daniel nodded with a smile and stood to see Cam out. He opened the door for her. 'Thanks. I'll be fine.'

He watched Cam cross the car park from his window as she struggled to keep her hood up in the rising wind and inhaled a huge breath before blowing it out slowly between his fingers. He turned and stared into the room, which was empty except for his bed, a bedside table, a small pine chest of drawers and a little old-fashioned television with a remote control whose buttons had long since lost their numbers. An electric wall heater gave off a slight burning smell when he turned it up; he figured it must be dust trapped inside.

Daniel opened the fitted wardrobe and pulled out a handful of metal coat hangers, some barely resembling their original shape but still usable. He hung up his white shirt and draped his navy tie around the collar. His smart suit. The one he needed to convince the parole board he was a responsible, safe human being, which he must have done otherwise he wouldn't be sitting here trembling in the cold. He grabbed a jumper from his bag and tugged it over his head, then rubbed his arms to create some heat.

A sound erupted from the hall outside his room. Men with thick Scottish accents roared with laughter, deep in conversation, about what Daniel had no idea, but they sounded happy. They didn't sound angry, which was the overriding emotion at Carseview. Daniel had once been filled with so much anger himself. Anger that he had been so stupid. Anger that his mum had let him down again. Anger that left him to take the blame.

He took one last look down at Cam, down in the street, and smirked, then shook his head. He kicked off his boots and flopped down onto his bed, struggling to exhale through his own laughter.

CHAPTER SIXTY-TWO

The knock on his hotel room door confused and excited Rob in equal measure. He hoped Louise had changed her mind and come back to him.

'Hang on,' he shouted as he unlocked the door. 'I'm so glad you came ba—'

He tried to slam it shut, but the foot jammed in the door stopped him.

'You need to leave,' Rob hissed.

'Or what? You'll call the police?' Rob's uninvited guest laughed and shoved his way inside. 'You're quite the comedian, Daniel.'

'My name isn't Daniel,' Rob growled. 'Get out of here. This won't help anyone.'

'Oh no, and why's that, Dan?' Tom spat. 'I think it's about time you and I had a chat, don't you? It's long overdue, I would say.'

Rob's six foot three muscular frame might dwarf Tom Nicoll, but that didn't stop the fear. His years of hate had made Tom a giant. The look in his eyes bore right through Rob. Who could Rob call for help? He had burned every single bridge he had, and the police were the last people he wanted to talk to. They thought he'd repeated the crime for which he'd lost his freedom all those years ago.

'What do you want, Tom?' Rob would have to talk his way out of this. He smelt the beer on Tom's breath from across the room 'I don't know what you're expecting me to say.' Rob had to fill the disturbing silence before panic struck him dumb.

The hatred that Tom Nicoll felt for Daniel Simpson, as he would always remember him, was as powerful right there in that hotel room as it was the day Sophie's body was discovered. He wished his dad was alive to see the terror in Sophie's killer's eyes.

'There's nothing I can say to make this any better,' Rob's voice trembled. 'I can't change what's happened.'

'Do you ever think about her?' Tom finally spoke.

'Of course I think about it.'

His body language betrayed him with its tense, clenched, rigid posture.

'My little sister was an "it", was she? Is that how you saw her?'

'No, of course not, I meant "her", I do think about her.' Rob stopped to lick his dry lips. 'Sophie,' he ended in a whisper.

Tom lurched forward and stabbed a finger into Rob's collarbone. 'You don't get to say her name,' he spat.

Rob's entire body shook as he pushed Tom's arm away, relieved to see him stumble backward and come to rest on the bathroom door frame, steadying himself as he slipped.

'I'm sorry. Is that what you want to hear? Of course I'm sorry, but no matter how sorry I am, and no matter what you do to me, Tom, Sophie will still be dead. Do you think I want this? If I could go back to that day, that morning. If I had known what he had planned, Tom.'

Tom was shocked by the tears that stung his eyes when Rob said her name.

'You have no idea the things I've wanted to do to you over the past twenty years. The things I still want to do to you. Maybe if I'd got to you sooner, little Shannon Ross would still be alive.'

Rob pointed his finger aggressively at Tom. 'I did not hurt Shannon. I would never hurt Shannon, or Louise, and don't you dare suggest otherwise. I'm not that boy any more.'

Tom grinned. 'Touched a nerve, have I?'

Rob glared without answering.

'I have, haven't I? Louise is your fucking kryptonite, isn't she? It was her that led me here, by the way.'

The horror on Rob's face betrayed the terror he felt when he saw Tom reach into his pocket and pull out a knife.

Sweat trickled across Rob's brow, dripping down, nipping at the corners of his eyes. His throat was tight, but his heart didn't race, and he wasn't gasping for breath. Instead a calmness washed over him. Tom's words became inaudible; morphed into a distorted message Rob couldn't understand. Maybe this was the justice Sophie had deserved all along. Tom tightened his grip on the knife's handle.

'Come on then, do it. I deserve this for all the pain I've caused.' He pulled Tom's hand closer and pressed the knife to his chest. 'Just do it.'

'You would love that, wouldn't you? Nice and clean and simple.' Tom spat. 'Do you really think I want to spare you any pain?' He laughed. 'You're very wrong indeed, Daniel Simpson. I'm going to enjoy making you suffer, slowly. The way you and Jack did my little sister.'

'Well, what are you waiting for?' Rob yelled into Tom's face, his eyes wide and staring before ending in a whisper, 'Just do it. Finish it.'

Rob closed his eyes and waited. Time slowed and one small drop of sweat ran over Rob's nose and another trickled onto his lips until he licked the salty liquid away. It was then that the hammering fist battered on the door, startling Rob out of his daze. He pushed Tom away, sending him toppling into the bathroom door frame before hitting the floor.

'Rob Taylor, this is Detective Jessie Blake. Open the door.'

CHAPTER SIXTY-THREE

Jessie waited while Rob was assessed by the paramedic. She watched a dazed Tom Nicoll being led away in handcuffs, his knife safely sealed in an evidence bag.

'OK, you're good to go.'

Jessie smiled to the paramedic as she passed on her way back to her waiting ambulance.

'I swear I didn't hurt her, but I'll come with you, detective inspector.' Rob offered a ghost of a smile then turned away. Jessie slipped her hand around Rob's arm and led him to her car.

'I'll get it,' Eric shouted to his mum, and was stunned to see Ben Randall standing on their doorstep.

'Can I come in?' Ben asked, his eyes struggling to focus as he swayed.

'God, look at the state of you.' Eric opened the door wide and helped Ben through.

'Who is it?' Agatha's voice carried towards the boys at the front door.

'Come on, you can sleep it off in my room.' Eric tucked one of Ben's arms around his shoulder, so the teenager could lean on him for support.

'It's fine, Mum, don't worry,' Eric shouted.

'Thanks, mate,' Ben slurred. 'I don't want to go home.'

Eric couldn't help but wonder exactly why Ben sought sanctuary with him after spending the past two years bullying him constantly with taunts of 'faggot' and 'queer boy'.

'Stay here as long as you like,' Eric lied.

He hated the idea of Ben spending time there but, under the circumstances, he would let him sleep it off for a bit. Ben slumped on the bed and Eric draped a blanket over him.

'You're a good guy, Eric Baldwin,' Ben muttered as Eric helped him out of his shoes. 'I wish I was more like you.'

'Shut up and go to sleep, Ben.'

'It's my fault she's dead,' Ben slurred. 'My fault.' Then his words disappeared into loud snores.

Eric scowled. 'You're such a fucking drama queen, Ben Randall. You think everything is about you, don't you?'

He shook his head and pulled his bedroom door closed behind him.

CHAPTER SIXTY-FOUR

Dylan Logan looked on as Rob signed his name on his release form. No matter how hard Jessie tried, there was no evidence to suggest he had anything to do with Shannon's death. Nothing on Shannon's body linked her death to Rob and, at the time of her disappearance, Rob was in a room full of his readers. He was free to go, and Jessie was back to square one.

Dylan couldn't believe Rob was capable of the crimes he'd committed as a child. He had always seemed to calm, so in control. Since Rob's identity was exposed, Dylan had searched the internet for details of Sophie Nicoll's murder. He couldn't blame Tom Nicoll for going after him like that. If someone had done those things to his sister, Dylan would be inconsolable, and perhaps his anger would never disappear either.

Louise waited outside the station for Rob because he had nobody else. It was as simple as that. Rob was utterly drained. Jessie's questioning had sucked every ounce of energy he had left after his ordeal.

'Come on.' Louise reached out her hand to him and tried to ignore the photographers who had assembled outside as word spread of Rob's arrest. The couple were followed by the group until they reached Louise's car.

'Where do you want to go?'

Rob rubbed at his tired eyes. 'Just drive, I'll figure out the rest once we're away from here.'

*

Dylan Logan showed his ID to the nurse in charge, who pointed him in the direction of Tom Nicoll's bed. The sound of their voices stirred Tom from his sleep and he watched the young detective approach. He didn't regret a single part of what he'd done, aside from the fact that Daniel Simpson was still alive.

'Hello, detective, I've been expecting you.'

'How are you doing, Tom?'

Tom smiled. 'Shall we just cut the niceness and get down to it?'

His abruptness didn't surprise Dylan. Tom was an intelligent man. He knew perfectly well that attempting to murder Rob wouldn't go unpunished.

'I'm sorry, but I'm going to have to ask you to accompany me to the station. Doctor says you're fit to be discharged, is that correct?'

Tom nodded. 'Can I have a minute to get dressed?'

'Sure, I'll be right outside.'

Dylan tugged the curtain around the bed, but he didn't leave Tom for a moment, even though he was on the other side of the curtain. Tom was soon dressed and ready to go. He held his hand out in front of Dylan.

'No handcuffs, Tom. We won't need them, will we?' Dylan raised an eyebrow. He wanted to avoid Tom's humiliation, which didn't go unnoticed.

'Thank you,' Tom whispered, his eyes glistening with tears.

CHAPTER SIXTY-FIVE

'Do you want me to come in?' Louise asked.

'No, this is something I have to do alone. She deserves that much. I don't want to hurt her any more than I already have.'

Rob leaned his body closer to Louise and kissed her cheek. 'Thank you, Louise.'

Louise instinctively pulled back from him. 'Go, please.' She flinched at his touch. 'Be gentle with her. Cassie is vulnerable and hurting. Make this easy for her.'

'Can I call you later?' he asked, and tried to run his fingers over her hair, brushing the stray strands out of her eyes. Her rejection was killing him.

Louise closed her eyes while she shook her head. 'I don't think that's a good idea for either of us.' She swallowed hard and exhaled a trembling breath. 'Goodbye, Rob.'

Rob watched Louise's car disappear before moving across the drive, wiping hot, stinging tears from his face, gravel crunching underfoot. He didn't recognise the car parked outside his front door. He inhaled two deep breaths and slowly exhaled them as he reached for the door handle.

'Cass, it's me,' he said as he approached the living room. His heart threatened to burst out of his chest with the anticipation of their confrontation. She had every right to be angry, and Rob feared the nightmare conversation ahead. He tried to imagine what it would be like to be in Cassie's shoes, and it was impossible. He couldn't imagine what he would have done. Cassie was an open book. He didn't think she was even capable of having a secret.

'Hello, Rob.' A familiar face greeted him instead. 'I thought I'd better pay you a visit.'

CHAPTER SIXTY-SIX

The house was in darkness by the time Louise arrived home. She wished Jason was there so that they could get it over with. She hated herself for the extra pain he was going through but couldn't help it. Rob had given her the passion and pleasure that Jason didn't, not any more. She couldn't remember a time when he had ignited the flame inside her the way Rob had.

She squeezed her eyes shut, not allowing a tear to trickle onto her cheek. Not being able to touch or hold her daughter again was crushing her. The agony of her loss gripped her body in the pitch black. The grief was physical as well as emotional, and Louise clawed her stomach and wept. This time she didn't hold back, and cried into the silent blackness of her kitchen. Her tortured body let out a moan of complete anguish. She felt her stomach tighten and her gut twist.

Louise's legs weakened, and she slid down the kitchen wall until she reached the floor. She curled into a ball, hugged her stomach and just cried. She screamed into the emptiness, fearing her heart was broken for ever. She was so absorbed in her grief that she didn't hear the front door open.

'Louise?' Jason called out as he walked into the house. He made his way to the kitchen and switched on the light unaware that Louise was there.

'I didn't hear you come in.' Louise lifted her aching body slowly from the floor, rubbing at her stinging red eyes and wiping away the tears. Jason's face didn't wear the rage Louise expected to see on it. Instead he held out his hand to help her up from the floor. He took out two mugs and tea bags, then made them both tea without uttering a word.

'Thank you,' Louise whispered when he handed her a mug before walking away.

'Jason,' she called after him, but he didn't stop. Louise joined him in the living room and sat down opposite him. 'We need to talk.'

Jason stared up from his drink. 'Come on then, talk.'

His stare unnerved her. It wasn't anger in his eyes. It was something she didn't recognise, and it scared her.

'I'm sorry, I didn't mean to hurt you. Rob and me, we just... happened.'

'It's Rob and me now, is it?' Jason shouted.

Louise didn't answer him. Instead, she stared into her mug.

'So what happens now?' Jason's eyes pleaded for hope that their marriage wasn't over. 'Will we bury our daughter together, or is this it?'

Louise couldn't think about that. 'Don't, Jason.'

Jason's anger started to fizz. He slammed his mug on the coffee table.

'Don't what? Don't mention our dead daughter? Don't mention you've been screwing the animal that probably killed her?' he screamed. 'Why, Louise, what the hell did I do wrong?'

Louise knew he wasn't being rational. Jason had always viewed life from his perspective; she should have known better.

'Where the hell do you think you are going?' Jason lashed out and grabbed her arm.

'Stop it, you're hurting me!' she cried as his grip grew tighter.

He pushed her back against the wall and pinned her there with an elbow on either side of her head. He squeezed her chin in his hand and forced her to look at him.

'Jason, please, let me go.'

The look on Jason's face terrified her. Sure, she'd seen the wrong side of Jason's temper before. That went with the territory with him, especially after he left the army. PTSD, they said he had, but Louise was unconvinced. She knew it was images of the little girl left lying in the road that ate him up, even all these years later. Being forced to cover up the crime had stayed with him. She didn't blame him for his drinking. Now Shannon, and her infidelity. In truth, their marriage was over.

'How could you, Lou?' Jason spat. 'With him?'

'I didn't know who he was, did I?' Louise whimpered.

'And that makes it OK?' Jason scoffed and squeezed harder.

Louise froze, fearing what Jason would do next.

Rob wasn't sure whether it was relief or horror he felt when he saw Cam Walsh sitting on his black leather sofa, under the print of the Glasgow School of Art building. Rob couldn't explain why he liked that picture he'd bought in a charity shop in Perth several years ago. He just did, he told people. He noticed Cam was alone, and wondered where Cassie was. Rob passed the arm of the sofa and dropped a hand on Cam's shoulder, then squeezed.

'Where's Cassie?'

Cam froze, then smiled a little. 'Cassie let me in about half an hour ago. She said I could wait for you. She put some boxes in her car, then left. She said she would be back for the others in a while.' Cam nodded towards the hallway. 'I'm sorry for your loss. Cassie told me about the baby.'

It was then that Rob spotted the assortment of boxes and bags lined up in the hall at the bottom of the stairs.

'It's all such a mess, Cam,' Rob sat on the sofa next to her. 'Life was so good, you know?' He shook his head and she let out a mournful sigh. He could be himself with Cam. She knew everything about him, more than any other living person.

'DI Blake called me. I've had to order an inquiry into why she wasn't told about your status. I'm also in the middle of an investigation into my own professional conduct.'

'Shit, Cam, I'm sorry. God, this whole situation is so fucked up. I didn't do it. I wouldn't. I couldn't. I'm not that boy any more.' Rob heard himself lose control. 'I loved her. Shannon, and Louise. I loved them both, and Jason was my best mate.'

Cam moved closer and placed an arm around his shoulder. 'Look, we'll sort this, somehow. Your identity is compromised, so we'll have to consider our options.'

Rob stood. 'I'm not leaving Inverlochty. My life is here.'

'Let's talk about it, at least.'

'There's nothing to talk about,' he answered as a car pulled into the drive. Rob moved to peer out of the living room window. 'It's Cassie.'

'I'll be in touch soon. You know that it's not your decision to make, don't you? You know that we will decide what's best for you and for everyone here?' Cam patted his arm and smiled softly at Cassie when they passed each other. When Cassie spotted him, she went to turn and leave until he called her name.

'Cassie, wait. We need to talk about what's happened. What you've been told about me.'

Cassie interrupted him angrily. 'What, so you can lie to me some more, this time to my face instead of by omission? How could you keep it from me? I loved you. I was having your baby!' Cassie's pitch rose the more she yelled, until pain gripped her stomach.

Rob moved forward to comfort her, but as soon as he was close enough, she slapped his face. Hard.

'Get away from me!' she screamed. 'Does Louise know what you are? You're a monster!'

Cassie reached for her suitcase and Rob tried to help her.

'Back off, you make me sick!' She ripped her wedding ring off and threw it along the hallway. She hurled her house key at Rob's chest, then rushed outside. Rob tried to follow her. 'Stay away from me. I'll send for the rest of my stuff.'

That was the last thing Rob heard as Cassie's car spun the gravel and flew out of the drive.

Louise froze in terror. She wanted to fight back, but Jason was too strong. His weight overpowered her.

The sound of Louise's helpless sobs broke into Jason's rage before he did something he would regret. They were like a switch that flicked his anger off just in time. He pushed Louise away and watched her fall to her knees, horrified by what he had almost done to her. He choked back the anger and tried to help her up.

'Get away from me!' she cried.

'I'm so sorry,' he sobbed. 'I'm sorry.'

He wanted to pull her to him and show her he loved her, but she hated him now. She couldn't bear to be near him. Jason fled out through the back door, leaving Louise in floods of terrified tears.

Her phone rang in the kitchen and snapped her from her shocked stupor. She straightened her clothes and limped to answer it. When she saw it was Rob, she erupted into anguished tears again.

'Louise? Louise, what's wrong?'

Louise couldn't speak.

'I'm coming to get you.' He didn't care if Jason was there or not.

'No, leave me alone!' Louise yelled, then tossed her phone across the room and screamed out in agony. The pain was ripping through her until she thought she would be sick. Even her skin ached. Fear and grief overwhelmed her.

CHAPTER SIXTY-SEVEN

'Jason, how are you doing?' Dylan asked as he walked into the waiting room at the police station where Jason Ross sat with a look of pure anger on his face. 'Come on, we can talk in here.'

Dylan took Jason into one of the interview rooms and offered him coffee.

'I don't want coffee. I want answers.'

'I completely understand your frustration, but we're doing everything we can to find out what happened to Shannon, I can assure you.'

'So, do you have any leads?'

Dylan wished he had something constructive to tell him. 'We're following several lines of enquiry.' That even sounded lame to Dylan.

'So, no, you're no closer to finding my daughter's killer. Why was Rob Taylor released?'

Just saying his name sent a chill running through Jason. He'd trusted Rob with everything that was precious to him and Rob had stabbed him in the back.

'We have no evidence that Rob did anything to Shannon, and he has an alibi for the hours covering her disappearance.'

'He might as well have killed her. He's taken everything else.'

Rob had to get out. The walls were closing in on him and he feared they would crush him. He grabbed his car keys. As he drove away, he scoffed at the irony of the rainbow of vibrant colours above him now that the rain had finally stopped.

Driving through his tears became impossible. Rob had to stop and wipe his face, but when he looked up he came face to face with Jason and, as both men stared at each other, they failed to see Louise in the car behind.

Jason raced to Rob's parked car. He ripped the door open and yanked Rob out.

'I trusted you!' Jason screamed, with Rob at his mercy. 'She's my wife, you son of a bitch.' Then he punched Rob, hard. Blood sprayed from his busted lip and Jason punched him again and again. His jealous rage was out of control. Louise rushed to pull him off, but she was easily swept aside with one shove. Seeing her fall to the ground strengthened Rob's resolve. He got to his feet and pushed Jason to the ground.

'That's enough, Jason. I'm sorry.'

Rob's words were like petrol on a flame. Jason surged forward and slammed his shoulder into Rob's body, both men toppling to the ground. Louise shrieked, and it was this that attracted Ben's attention as he made his way back from sleeping off his self-pity at Eric's. He ran as fast as he could, his head pounding, to help his sister. Jason sat astride Rob, who had no means of escape, and the blows rained down. He punched Rob's face over and over until Rob offered no resistance. Dylan had been alerted by Louise's screams and was first to try and help Rob, but his attempt was quickly swept aside as Jason pushed him on his arse with ease before resuming his onslaught. Ben looked on in horror, not knowing what to do. So he did what he always did, and fled.

'Jason, you're killing him!' Louise screamed and ran forward again in an attempt to save Rob's life. 'Stop, please!'

'Stay out of this!' Jason growled back at her. 'This is between me and him.'

Dylan pulled himself onto his knees, then lurched forward to tackle Jason again.

'Get off me!' Jason barked, struggling hard as Dylan held him in place with a knee until back-up arrived. 'Get off! This isn't finished, Rob. Mark my words, I'm not finished with you.'

'Shut it!' Dylan boomed as he fixed the handcuffs on him. 'Don't go making threats.'

He pulled Jason to his feet and gripped his arm. Louise dropped to her knees and felt for Rob's pulse, which was faint, but he was alive.

Jason winced from the pain in his knuckles as he sipped from the cup of water, his eyes fixed on the floor. Jessie hated herself for being right, especially now. Perhaps it had been an accident. Had he hurt his daughter during a fit of rage, the type of outburst he'd just displayed? She checked the time on her phone and wished Jason's lawyer would hurry up, when a heavily made-up woman walked through the door.

'My name is Loretta Sweeney. I will be representing Jason Ross,' the middle-aged, silver-haired woman told them as she bustled in and took a seat next to Jason.

CHAPTER SIXTY-EIGHT

'Ben, what's happened?'

Ben didn't respond, but stood on the doorstep crying and rambling to himself.

'You had better come in.' Eric grabbed hold of Ben's arm and guided him inside.

'Who is it?' Agatha called out before joining them. 'My goodness, Ben, what is wrong?'

Eric shook his head. 'I don't know what's wrong with him. He just keeps sobbing. Is he in shock or something? Ben, what's happened? Look at me!' Eric pulled Ben's face towards him. 'Ben?'

Agatha draped her arm around Ben's shoulder and helped lower him to the sofa. She too was unable to understand what he was saying. She knelt down in front of him and placed her hand on his chin in an attempt to get him to focus on her, but Ben leapt away from her touch and fled out through the back door, repeating the same words over and over. Eric's heart raced as he finally heard what Ben was trying to tell him.

'Detective Inspector Blake,' Loretta Sweeney interrupted her. 'This is a highly irregular line of questioning. I must insist that you—'

'Must insist that I what?' Jessie stood up. 'Stop asking Jason what happened the night he got angry with Shannon? Why he tossed her body in the river? Why he lied to his wife, to all of us?'

Jason's eyes widened and he shook his head. 'What are you talking about?'

'Jason, don't say another word,' Loretta urged.

'But…' He tried to answer, then stopped and slumped back in his chair.

'We know you have a temper, Jason. We've all seen what that temper is capable of. I'm not saying that you planned to kill Shannon; on the contrary, I think you loved your daughter very much.'

Jason dropped his head into his hands and sobbed.

'My client needs a break,' Loretta announced as Jessie glared at her.

The tension in the room bubbled hot just as the knock came.

'Come in,' Jessie shouted, and frowned at the uniformed officer's expression.

'I think you'd better come now.'

CHAPTER SIXTY-NINE

Ben had one of Agatha's craft knives and was threatening to slit his wrists. Only this time he was stone-cold sober. Eric didn't know if he was relieved or not that Ben had only gone as far as his mother's studio after racing after him in search of answers.

'Why did you do it?' Eric asked, but Ben continued to stare straight ahead.

Eric sighed and tapped his fingers across Agatha's marble worktop. A man's voice from outside the studio deepened Ben's agitation. He was struggling to focus.

'It's OK, I'll talk to him.' Eric raised his hands to reassure Ben as he moved closer to the blocked door, which was piled high with chairs and a large wooden table.

Ben needed time to think. He had to stop them getting to him; distracting him. He had to straighten out the jumble of thoughts that swirled around his head.

'Eric, is that you?' Dylan called out.

'Eric, are you OK?' Agatha's anxious voice followed Dylan's.

'Yes, we're OK in here. Mum, don't worry, I'm fine.' Eric was shocked by the calmness that flowed over him. But he had to stay calm, for Ben's sake. Trapped in the workshop without anything to protect him, all he had was this calm. It was the only thing likely to get him out of there alive.

'Good, I'm glad,' Dylan called back.

Ben lifted a finger to his lips. He stuffed another small knife into his pocket before climbing out through the window in the back wall of the studio. It took Eric a moment to realise that the siege was over. He began pulling chairs away from the door, then opened it, stunned by what had just happened. He just couldn't get his head around it. He didn't understand any of this.

'*Mein Liebling!*' Agatha rushed forward, cradled Eric in her arms and buried her face in his cheek.

Jessie and Dylan surged into the room and scanned the space for Ben.

'Where is he?' Jessie shouted at Eric.

'He went out the back window,' Eric replied from within his mother's embrace.

Dylan ran round the boundary of the building, cursing the fact that Ben had got away. He squinted into the distance, but Ben could have gone in one of three different directions.

'Shit,' he muttered under his breath.

'Have you got any idea where he's heading?' Jessie exclaimed.

Eric shook his head. 'He's got a knife with him.'

CHAPTER SEVENTY

Louise was confused by the sight of Dylan and Jessie approaching her door. She sniffed and wiped her nose, then checked her reflection in the hall mirror. Louise didn't recognise the woman who glanced back at her; her eyes were blank and staring. The doorbell startled her despite the fact that she knew it was coming.

'Come in, detectives.' Louise opened the door wide for them.

'Thank you,' Jessie murmured as she wiped her feet.

Dylan offered her a smile Louise hadn't seen before. She frowned as she closed the door. 'Please go through.'

Louise squeezed her eyes tight shut, inhaled a huge breath and exhaled it slowly before following them inside.

'Come and sit down,' Jessie told her. 'Is Ben here?'

'No, he's not, why?'

Louise began to tremble. Something very bad was about to happen. She could feel it. But what the hell could be worse than losing your daughter?

Jessie nodded to Dylan, then towards the kitchen. He had known Jessie long enough to know what she meant.

'I'm fine standing.' Louise swallowed hard. 'Please, just tell me whatever it is you've come here to say.'

'Come on.' Jessie moved closer to her and dropped a gentle hand on her arm. 'Come and sit down.'

Louise pulled her arm back. 'I can't stand this! Just tell me.'

'OK. Listen,' Jessie began just as Dylan returned with three mugs of tea. 'Evidence has been brought to me that suggests your brother Ben was involved in Shannon's death.' Jessie watched confusion take the place of Louise's anxiety before morphing into disbelief.

'What? Don't be ridiculous,' Louise stuttered. 'How could he? I mean, that's just not possible. Ben loves Shannon. No, no, no, that's not true. It can't be true.' Louise collapsed onto the sofa, her legs uncertain beneath her. 'You're lying.'

Jessie sat down next to Louise and placed a hand over hers. 'I wish I was.'

Before Louise could respond, her phone rang under the album of photos that was full of Shannon as a toddler. Louise's favourite time. She glanced at Jessie.

'It's Ben,' she exclaimed. 'What should I do?'

Jessie shot a glance at Dylan.

'Answer it, Louise, but don't say we're here. Just ask him where he is. Don't repeat what I've just told you.' Jessie's words were stern as she perched on the edge of the sofa.

'Hello, Ben,' Louise stammered, her heart pounding hard in her chest. A headache burst across her temples. She sighed to keep her composure.

'I'm sorry.' Ben was crying.

Louise wiped away her own tears. 'Tell me where you are, and I'll come and get you.'

Jessie nibbled her bottom lip, anxious to grab the phone from her. She could even see Dylan's anticipation grow. It was only in situations like this Jessie ever saw his composure slip. Nibbling his thumbnail was Dylan's vice at times like these.

'Ben?' Louise called out. 'Ben, are you still there?'

Jessie leapt up from the sofa. 'Well?'

'He hung up.' Louise sobbed. 'Oh God, I can't believe this is happening!'

'Did he say anything to indicate where he might be?' Dylan asked. 'Anything at all?'

Louise dropped her head in her hands, then shook it vigorously. 'No… but wait.' She snapped her head back up. 'I heard the river thrashing in the background. It only makes a noise like that at the back of Andrew Foster's place.'

Jessie grabbed her bag and headed for the door, just as Louise tugged on her jacket.

'I'm coming with you.'

CHAPTER SEVENTY-ONE

Rob leaned heavily on the sticks the hospital had reluctantly given him. He hadn't wanted to stay there a minute longer. The doctors had explained that he'd taken a considerable beating, and as he'd been knocked unconscious, he needed to stay in at least overnight for observation after sustaining a head injury. Rob took the sticks and the information leaflet, then signed the 'discharged against medical advice' form. They'd given him a couple of days' supply of painkillers, but urged him to see his GP for more later, saying that he would need them for a few days. The cracked ribs would be painful for a few weeks yet, as well as his broken nose, which was what hurt the most, if Rob was honest. The taxi from Perth had cost him over a hundred pounds, but he had no choice. Who could Rob call? Cam might have come, but she would also tell him he had to stay in hospital.

'Hang on, mate. Just let me out here,' Rob told the driver when he saw the silhouette of Ben Randall pacing up and down close to the water's edge.

'Are you sure?' the taxi driver asked.

'Yes, yes, I'm sure.' Rob winced from the pinching pain in his ribs. 'Jesus,' he exclaimed.

He steadied himself on the sticks and limped towards Ben.

'Don't come any closer!' Ben held the knife up, then turned back to face the angry, rushing current.

'OK, OK, I won't, but what are you doing, mate?'

Ben turned his head back round and stared. 'You wouldn't understand.'

Rob exhaled loudly in a bid to ignore the searing pain in his head. 'I don't know. You won't know until you give me a chance, will you? Come on, step back a bit. I won't come any closer, just tell me what's happened.'

The sound of a car pulling into the car park startled Ben, who stepped even closer to the water's edge.

'Whoa, whoa, it's OK, Ben!' Rob shouted out and waved Jessie to stay back.

Louise glanced from Rob to the direction of the swollen river and clasped her hand over her mouth.

'I need to go over there!' Louise shouted, but Jessie held her back.

'Just sit tight for now. I'll call for back-up.'

Until it arrived, all she had was Rob Taylor.

'I won't come any closer if you don't want me to, but we need to talk, don't you think?' Rob shouted over the deafening sound of the rushing water. 'I could really do with a seat, and you've found a nice big rock to rest on. Perhaps I could come and share it. Your brother-in-law did quite a number on me.'

'Why do you care if I die?' Ben waved the knife in Rob's direction.

'Of course I care. We all do.'

'Louise will never forgive me for what I've done.'

It dawned on Rob what was happening. But not Ben, surely? Rob didn't have an answer for that. 'I can't promise you whether your sister will forgive you, you're right, but she deserves to know the truth, doesn't she? She deserves to know what happened to Shannon, and only you can tell her that. But listen, can I be honest with you? If I tell you something, will you let me help you?'

The bewildered expression on Ben's face told Rob that he didn't know about his past. He had obviously been too consumed by his own guilt.

'I killed someone, Ben, a long time ago.'

Rob allowed his confession to sink in. He didn't talk again until his words had been absorbed. He limped forward and kept going when his first few steps weren't met with resistance.

'Can I sit?' He pointed to the space next to Ben, made more than a little uncomfortable by its proximity to the water's edge. The racing water was hypnotic as it rushed past.

'Help yourself,' Ben invited.

Rob moaned as he lowered his body down awkwardly to Ben's side.

'He really did work you over good, didn't he?' Ben released a small laugh.

'You're not kidding.' Rob hugged his ribs while he tried to get comfortable.

'Who did you kill?' Ben asked, and Rob noticed his grip had loosened around the knife.

'If I'm honest with you, will you be honest with me in return?'

'I guess so,' Ben agreed.

Even after all these years, saying the words out loud was difficult. Rob hoped he would never have to revisit this, but if he'd been honest with himself, something like that can never be forgotten. A young girl had died, and not by accident. He hadn't put his hands on her throat, but he was there. He could have stopped it. He was complicit.

'So, what's it like in prison?'

'It's not nice. There's nothing good about it, but you'll be OK. You're just a kid. You won't go to prison. You'll go to a place like I did, a young offenders' place.'

'Do you ever think about her, that girl you killed?'

Rob swallowed hard. 'Of course. Sophie has always been with me. Her death affected so many people. She was an innocent victim. What I did changed so many lives, not just mine and Sophie's. You won't stop thinking about Shannon, and you won't stop loving her either. She was family.'

'Did Sophie's family ever forgive you?'

The truth and Rob's commitment to it would have to part company for Ben's sake, he had to lie. 'I don't know. I can't control that, and neither can you.'

Ben permitted the knife to slip from his grasp and they both watched until it was swallowed under the angry current.

'Thank you, Rob, for telling me, for trusting me.'

'Can you do the same for me? Will you tell them what happened to her?'

Ben hoisted himself up and offered his hand to Rob, who waved it away.

'You go, I'll manage.'

Rob watched Ben's back as he moved further and further away. He winced from the pain in his ribs when he tried to stand. Perhaps he deserved the beating Jason had given him. It might have been better if Jessie hadn't saved him from Tom Nicoll. He might not have hurt Shannon, but he was guilty. Guilt that he had carried with him for over twenty years.

The weight was becoming unbearable, these days. Shannon's death was forcing Rob to relive his previous life over and over. A life he never thought he would have to think about again. He inhaled a huge breath and turned to face Louise before tossing the sticks aside. The calmness Rob felt was refreshing and unexpected. There was no fear. His heart didn't race. He wondered if this was how Jack had felt. It was the right decision, and something he should have done a long time ago. Perhaps it would have saved Louise and Cassie some of their pain. Cassie. She hadn't deserved any of it. Rob rubbed away a tear when he thought of his son. He had hurt so many people with his lies.

Louise frowned before screaming out his name. Jessie and Dylan spun to see Rob fall backward into the fast-flowing, angry current which tossed and thrashed his already beaten body until it was sucked under the blackness.

Jessie frantically called for help before surging towards the riverbank, almost slipping on the soggy grass at the edge. She stared into the deep, murky water, unable to catch even a glimpse of him. The river had claimed him as her own now. Dylan raced forward to join her, then stared back at Louise's distraught face.

'No!' Louise dropped to her knees. 'Rob!'

CHAPTER SEVENTY-TWO

Dylan placed a paper cup in front of Ben and took his seat beside Jessie. Cam Walsh had offered to act as Ben's adult representation for the purposes of this first interview, and Jessie was grateful that she was available. She didn't want to wait.

Ben sipped the water slowly. He thought about what Rob had told him, and images of what he said swam inside his head. The sound of a chair leg scraping across the floor made Ben jump and spill a little of his water on his shirt. He quickly wiped it, heat rising in his cheeks.

'OK, Ben. In your own time, if you can, tell us what happened to Shannon.'

Ben slid his cup back over the table. Dylan shot a glance at Jessie, who was staring at Ben with narrowed eyes.

'Ben, are you OK?' Cam asked.

'Yes, I am, sorry.' He snapped sharply back into focus and met Jessie's glance. 'Me and my mates were ribbing Andrew Foster because he was shouting to himself as usual, and Shannon got angry. She pushed me in front of everyone.'

Ben paused but Jessie didn't speak. She didn't want to interrupt his train of thought. She waited.

'I saw Shannon running out of Foster's back door later. She had a cut on her lip. I teased her about being Foster's girlfriend or something. I can't remember exactly what I said, but I've never seen her so mad. She ran at me and tried to slap my face, but I caught her arm.' Ben paused again. It was obvious that the memory of what happened next was playing out in his mind. He swallowed the last of his water.

'You're doing really well, Ben,' Cam encouraged him, and was met with a half-smile.

'I just pushed her away, that's all I did, I swear.' His voice rose. 'Then she fell back and hit her head. She didn't move after that.' His tears began to fall. 'I didn't mean it to happen.'

'So, you pushed her away. She fell and banged her head. She wasn't moving. What happened then?' Dylan was keen to keep Ben talking. 'Did you check to see if she was breathing, or if she had a pulse?'

'I panicked. Foster's house backs on to the river.' Ben sobbed into his sleeve.

'Do you need a break?' Cam placed a hand on Ben's arm.

Jessie's eyes widened. That's all she needed, Ben taking a break. She was relieved to see him shake his head and hoped he wanted this over as quickly as she did.

'I knew it was wrong, but I wasn't thinking straight. I had done it before I knew what I was doing. Then I couldn't go back. She was gone.'

'I'm going to have to ask you to tell us what you did,' Jessie insisted. She needed to hear him say it.

'I pushed Shannon's body into the river.' Ben closed his eyes as the words tumbled awkwardly out of his mouth.

Jessie sipped the hot, sweet coffee, savouring every mouthful. She closed her eyes and enjoyed the silence of the incident room. The sound of Dylan's voice woke her from her trance.

'Hey, Jess.'

Dylan looked as tired as Jessie felt. She admired the way he was handling what his life had thrown at him without complaint. It can't be easy watching your mother deteriorate the way he was. *Perhaps having Jack to distract him helps*, she wondered.

'Hi, kettle's not long boiled. You fancy a brew? I'll make it. You look knackered.'

'Cheers for that. Yes, I'm shattered.'

He flopped down onto a chair as Jessie put a mug on the desk in front of him.

'There you go. Get that down you.'

'Thanks.' He took a sip. 'Not bad, Jess. You're getting better.'

'Hey you, cheeky sod.' Jessie smiled.

'Leaves a bad taste all this, doesn't it?' Dylan added. 'Not just Ben, but Rob Taylor, or whoever he was.'

Jessie couldn't disagree, not really.

'Aye I know, Dylan. Still, the reality is that Rob had to live somewhere, and it does seem he genuinely changed his life.'

'Yes, but it's fucked up, though, isn't it? Him acting like nothing's wrong. Probably not a bad thing he jumped.' Dylan shrugged. 'When you heading back home? You had it easy. Getting put up in The Black Witch like that. Mind you, isn't it supposed to be haunted?'

'It's the living we need to worry about, Dylan. Ghosts don't scare me. I'm going to stick around for a bit, you know. Super says I'm due holiday leave. It'll be nice to enjoy a bit of downtime.'

'Sounds nice. Shelly booked a wee cottage on the Moray coast a while back. We're heading up there in a couple of weeks. Can't wait.'

'Listen, Dylan, it's been nice working with you again. I'd forgotten what—'

'What a great guy I was?'

His comment made Jessie laugh. 'Yes, right. You're one of a kind, Dylan Logan.'

'You're not so bad yourself, detective inspector.'

'That does sound bloody good, doesn't it?' Jessie grinned, still revelling in her relatively new role as her phone rang in her pocket. 'Hello, DI Blake.'

Dylan sank the last of his coffee, concerned by the frown growing on Jessie's face before she hung up.

'Who was that?' he asked.

'Erm, wrong number, maybe.' Jessie pushed her phone deep into her jacket pocket until it rang again. Her eyes met Dylan's. Dan couldn't possibly have her new number. Could he?

CHAPTER SEVENTY-THREE

Two weeks ago

With his footsteps slow and determined, Andrew Foster shuffled across the park, weaving in and out and counting in sequence as he moved. His light T-shirt billowed in the wind that whipped across the grass. He had to get it right. If he missed one number, there would be trouble. Created in the mid-1800s, Inverlochty Park was a Victorian indulgence. Cherry trees that had long since shed their blossom encased the park on all sides. Where once there stood an exquisite boating pond where families would queue for their turn on the water was a dirty, sludge-filled pond that was home to the swans and mallards who could bear the smell. A group of teenagers gathered around the last remaining bench, guzzling from cans of beer and smoking cigarettes they'd smuggled from home.

Andrew didn't have time to worry about them. He glanced at his watch. If he didn't hurry they would be so mad with him, and he didn't want to face their wrath again. Not after last time. He scurried on out of the park and towards home. He counted on his fingers again to be sure and cursed under his breath. Those noisy teenagers had made him lose count again. He'd had enough of them. Always there, invading his mind, stealing his thoughts. He turned around and yelled across the park. Andrew wanted them to know that he was on to them. He knew what they were up to, and they wouldn't get away with it any longer. What if they started stealing the minds of other people? People who were not so alert as to what to look for. This had been a long time coming.

Andrew decided he would confront the problem head on. He didn't want to hide away.

'Shit, Ben, look.' Ben Randall's best friend Craig punched his shoulder and pointed to the edge of the park. 'It's that freak that's always talking to himself. He's shouting at us this time. Look.'

Ben took a last draw on his cigarette and coughed as he stubbed it out with his trainer.

'What the hell is his problem?' Ben swallowed the remainder of his lager and tossed the can under the bench that read *For Lisa Roberts. She loved this place.* Not that you would know it now, with the overgrown berberis skimming the edges of it and weaving over the back.

'I know what you're doing!' Andrew called out, counting out a sequence of ten on his fingers as he moved towards them. 'I won't stand for it, you hear? Leave my mind be.' He tapped his thumb across his forehead. 'You hear me? These are *my* thoughts. Not yours to steal.'

Ben stared at Craig, who burst out laughing. 'What the hell is he banging on about? Bloody nutter.'

Ben watched Andrew turn back towards the park gate.

'Come on, you want to have a bit of fun?'

Craig tossed his can aside and jogged after him, closely followed by the others.

'Oh go on, I'm paying,' Eric Baldwin playfully tapped his pocket and Shannon Ross couldn't help but smile.

'OK, you've twisted my arm.' She beamed and tied her long blonde hair back to tame it in the breeze.

'Shit, look. Ben and his group of merry dickheads are at it again.' Eric nodded at Andrew Foster's approach, with Ben and Craig close behind him, laughing and taunting him.

Shannon could see Andrew clutching his ears and shuffling to get away from his pursuers, who blocked his every weaving motion. Andrew reached into his pocket, but the keys slipped from his grasp before he could get them in the door. Ben snatched them up before Andrew had a chance to react.

'Get me in a strawberry thick shake, will you? I won't be long.' Shannon slammed her bag into Eric's chest and raced over to Andrew's aid.

'Don't get involved,' Eric called out, but he knew he was wasting his time.

'Ben, give me the keys or I'll tell Mum what an arsehole you've been. Not to mention the fags and booze.' Shannon held out her hand, her eyebrows raised. 'What the hell? Hassling a defenceless man. Real mature.'

Ben sneered, then glanced at Craig before glaring back at her. 'Come and get them then, snitch.'

'Stop being a dick, Ben.'

Andrew Foster slumped onto the ground outside his cottage. The same cottage that had stood on that spot since 1646. Bonnie Prince Charlie himself was said to have visited it on his brief, disastrous trip to Scotland in 1746, exactly a hundred years later. Nobody could find evidence that this was the case, but Andrew's mum was adamant it was a true story and she was proud to share it. Andrew cradled his head in his hands.

'Stop, stop, stop shouting.' He rocked back and forth. 'It's so loud. Make them stop.'

'Ben, are you proud of yourself?' Shannon's tone sharpened. 'Give me Andrew's keys.'

'I said, come and get them.'

Ben's mood darkened as he raised the keys in front of her.

'Shit, man, just give her the keys.' Craig blasted. 'It's not worth the aggro.'

Shannon stared Ben down, then lunged for them but missed.

'Too slow!' Ben teased, then dangled them out in front of her again.

Shannon saw red and lurched forward, this time knocking Ben to the ground as she grabbed them.

'Come on, Andrew, let's get you inside. I'll make a cup of tea.'

'It's loud, it's too loud,' Andrew muttered. 'I'm late. They're going to be so mad with me.'

Shannon switched on the kettle and searched for two clean cups, but decided she probably wouldn't have a cup after all. Not after seeing the thick, cheese-encrusted plates stacked by the sink, some with mould forming a fine layer across the rim. She found a mug for Andrew and rinsed it under the tap, troubled by the hot tap producing no more than a lukewarm trickle. She wondered if her dad might have a look at it for him. She opened a window to allow in some fresh air. The kitchen smelt stale, like it hadn't been aired for a long time. The sound of the kettle clicking off startled Andrew, who leapt up from the chair with a scream. Shannon moved forward to reassure him. She'd never seen him so agitated, his limbs flailing in all directions.

'Get off me!' he screamed, his sharp thumbnail scraping her lip.

'Ouch!' Shannon yelped and pressed the cut with her finger. When she removed her finger and saw the blood, she jogged upstairs to assess the damage in the bathroom mirror.

'Shannon, I'm sorry, I didn't mean to.' Andrew's agitation increased. 'Stop screaming at me, I know I'm late, I know I'm late.'

A couple of drops of blood trickled from Shannon's lip and dripped onto the floor before she made her way back to Andrew.

'Look, it's OK, I'm fine, Andrew.' She struggled to get him to focus on her, but eventually he smiled at her as if he was returning to reality. 'I'm going to pop out and get you a couple of things from across the road, OK?'

She wasn't sure if Andrew had understood completely, but the shop wasn't far so she wouldn't be long. It was probably a good idea for her mum to look in on Andrew too.

'What are you laughing at?' Ben growled. 'I let her knock me down. Got to let them win sometimes.'

Ben did his best to cover up his embarrassment but inside, he was seething. He watched Craig disappear towards home and wandered for a while to gather his thoughts. It would be better if he had a chance to calm down a bit before he faced Shannon. Ben perched himself on the edge of the riverbank and tossed branches into the fast-flowing current, mesmerised by the speed at which they were sucked in and chewed up by the angry flow.

'Andrew, it's just me.'

Shannon returned from gathering a few bits for him and coughed with the dust choking her throat. She moved past newspapers piled high on either side of the hallway. Asking him to tidy up was a waste of time, and doing it for him was not an option. The stress of that was likely to cause more harm than good.

'Andrew, what have you done?' She dropped the shopping bags. 'What have you done?'

'It's nothing, leave me alone!' Andrew snarled and continued to scratch at his arms with the fork, causing blood to pool and trickle onto his trousers. 'I have to. It's my punishment. They warned me not to be late again, and the numbers. They are all wrong. They are all so wrong. This will teach me to get it right. I have to try harder.'

'Andrew, stop that, you'll hurt yourself.' Shannon tried to move forward with her phone in her hand, ready to call Louise.

Her advance only agitated Andrew further, who cut deeper into his arms.

'Get out! Get out of my house!' he screamed. 'Get out!'

Andrew lunged at her with the fork, sending her phone tumbling to the floor. Shannon fled out of the back door and straight into Ben, who was startled by her sudden arrival. He leapt up from his place close to the water's edge and moved swiftly towards her. Ben hadn't forgotten the humiliation she'd caused. Who the hell did she think she was? Mummy's perfect angel.

'Well, look who it is,' Ben taunted her. 'Andrew Foster's girlfriend.'

Shannon didn't have time for Ben's nonsense. 'Go away, Ben.'

Ben scowled and grabbed her arm. 'What did you just say?'

'I said, go away.' Shannon shrieked and lunged forward to push him over again.

This time he caught hold of her and forced her away from him. The sickening crack when her head hit the boulder almost stopped his heart. She wasn't moving. Ben dropped to his knees and grabbed hold of her shoulders. He shook her violently, but there was no response.

'Shit, shit.' He got to his feet and paced back and forth, his fingers clenched across the top of his head. 'Fuck.' He glanced left and right, then covered his mouth with both of his hands. 'Shannon?' he called out to her, then kicked her arm with his trainer. The sound of the fast-flowing river invaded his thoughts. *Oh my God, I've killed her. No, no, no, Shannon. Wake up.*

Ben panicked. He struggled to pick up her lifeless body, dragging it part of the way to the water's edge. He glanced down at her. She looked so peaceful. Even the anger that gnarled her features was gone. She just looked like she was sleeping. His heart thundered in his chest as he tossed her down into the abyss. The swirling, angry current pulled her away from him instantly. It was only a matter of seconds before he couldn't see her at all.

He had to get out of there. He didn't think he'd been seen, but he couldn't be a hundred per cent. He tugged the hood of his jacket over his head and scurried towards the park, almost bowling into Rob and Cassie Taylor. He muttered an inaudible apology but kept his head down until he was well past them.

CHAPTER SEVENTY-FOUR

Jason had never needed a drink more in his life. The small church that had stood at the heart of the Highland Perthshire town since the time of the Reformation was filled with mourners, and there was barely a pew left empty. John Knox himself was rumoured to have given a speech to the enthralled congregation of the day. The sixteenth-century building had withstood the years well. Today it was filled with the scent of lilies, donated by Wilma's flower shop. She wanted to fill the space with love. The love she wanted Louise and Jason to know was there for them. The whole community grieved along with Jason and Louise. Shannon was one of theirs, and her loss was felt deeply. The weight of Agatha Baldwin's hand on his shoulder stirred Jason from his thoughts of whisky.

'I'm so sorry,' she whispered, then took her seat further back in the church.

Jason smiled and nodded at her kind words. He wished Louise would hurry back. She'd told him she needed a few minutes to gather her thoughts. That was half an hour ago.

'Louise. How are you doing?'

Louise lifted her head to see Jessie and Dylan standing over her. She stubbed out her cigarette and stood to greet them.

'Hi, I don't usually. Today I just needed something, you know?'

'I'll see you inside, Jess,' Dylan murmured and nodded to Louise as he passed.

'I didn't expect to see either of you here. I really appreciate you coming.'

'I'm heading back to Perth later. Dylan wanted to show his respects, too.' Jessie ran a hand over Louise's arm. 'How's Jason?'

Louise shrugged. 'Not good. Having the assault case hanging over him isn't helping, but that was all him. Nobody forced Jason to kick the shit out of Rob. He was damn lucky to get bail.'

Jessie couldn't disagree. 'I guess the CPS looked at the bigger picture, Louise. I suppose they thought you needed him more. Listen, if I don't see you later, take care of yourself.'

'You too, DI Blake, and thank you for everything.'

Jessie moved towards the huge church doors. She took her seat next to Dylan at the back of a packed St Mark's, and nodded to Louise as she passed to join Jason. She was pleased to see the church so full, for Louise and Jason's sake. She spotted Maggie Malcolm, who gave a small wave in greeting. Even the fisherman who had stumbled upon Shannon's body was there. Blair Crawford too acknowledged her. Jessie smiled grudgingly back at him.

Jason looked up from the pew and gripped Louise's hand before she could sit down. She offered him a soft smile, her eyes filled with heavy tears and she grabbed his hand in hers. Reverend Malcolm's words disappeared into a fog of grief when Shannon's simple white coffin passed them. It wasn't until the sound of 'Over the Rainbow' was being played that Louise lifted her head to face him and he acknowledged her with such a warm smile. It was then that she recognised the beautiful girl he was talking so fondly about. She was a kind girl. A generous soul. A funny girl, full of fun and mischief. Her heart was huge and filled with love for her family and her best friend Eric.

Jessie watched Eric's mother squeeze him tightly when they heard his name mentioned, as he swallowed down the surge of emotion it released. It would seem Shannon Ross was truly loved, and that made her premature death even more tragic.

Maggie Malcolm put a glass of lemonade in front of Jason and leaned in close to his ear.

'I'm proud of you, Jason,' she murmured. 'It can't be easy, today of all days.'

'Aye, thanks,' he answered. What else could he say? If only Maggie knew how much he wanted to shove her aside and drink himself into oblivion.

'Hey.' Louise touched the base of Jason's back. 'I'll have the same, Maggie.'

'You don't have to do that.' Jason planted a soft kiss on her lips. 'Have a glass of wine if you want one. It's OK.'

The past couple of weeks had been hell on their marriage, and it would take time, but they'd both agreed to try. They owed that to Shannon's memory.

Louise held his gaze, then turned to Maggie.

'Lemonade, Maggie, thanks.'

He kissed the top of her head, then wrapped his arm around her shoulders as Louise snuggled her head into his chest.

A lump filled Blair Crawford's throat as he stood there watching them standing so close in their grief. His mind couldn't help drifting to Tom Nicoll and the grief his family had been through, grief that led to years of hate and a quest for justice that consumed him. He hoped, for Tom's sake, that one day he would be able to find the peace he so needed. He lifted the handle of his suitcase and held the door open for a face he recognised before walking across the car park to his car.

*

'Louise?' A voice piped up from behind them. 'Jason?'

'Cassie.' Jason reached out to hug her warmly. 'It's good to see you. How are you?'

'That was a beautiful service,' Cassie said quietly. 'I won't stay, I just wanted to pay my respects.'

'Would you like a drink?'

Cassie turned to face Louise, who struggled to hold her gaze until Cassie reached for her hands. She squeezed them both firmly in hers, then wrapped her arms around Louise.

'I'm so sorry,' Louise sobbed. 'I'm so sorry.'

Louise clung to her tightly and allowed the tears to flow. First slowly, them tumbling furiously, then faster and faster until she felt like she was going to pass out.

'I'm sorry,' Louise cried, 'I'm sorry, Cassie.'

CHAPTER SEVENTY-FIVE

Two months later

'Are you sure?' Jessie asked her sister, who shrugged gently, the sound of raucous laughter emanating from a staff Christmas lunch at the other end of the restaurant.

The news of Moira Blake's diagnosis still came as a shock, despite Jessie knowing how sick her mum was.

'Mum's being her usual chirpy self, but I think, deep down, she's scared. I know I would be.'

'How long?'

'A few months at best, maybe a year?'

Jessie clasped her fingers over her mouth. All those years spent apart, and now her mum was dying.

'Can I get you ladies something to drink?' the waiter piped up from behind them.

Jessie wouldn't have blamed Freya for ordering a beer, and was so proud of her when she asked for a lemonade instead.

'We're going to have to be strong for her, aren't we?' Freya asked. 'I don't know if I can—'

Jessie's eyes misted over and she sniffed back her tears while she reached her hand out across the table. 'Yes, you can. We both can, and we will. We'll be there for Mum, come what may.'

*

Jessie parked her car and checked the lock three times for peace of mind. She gripped her keys in a fist, the sharp edge pushing through, and walked into the garden she shared at the back of her apartment block, jumping with fright when Smokey appeared from behind Dave's bike shed. Smokey rubbed himself around her ankles, almost tripping Jessie up. She scanned her surroundings before picking him up and nuzzling him to her cheek. Jessie continued to check for any disturbance: footprints, anything out of the ordinary. When she was satisfied, she made her way upstairs. She undid the two locks and scanned the hall before closing the door and fastening the locks then fixing the two chains across.

The sight of two messages blinking on her machine filled her with dread. Dan didn't have her number, but it was a fear that never left her. She tapped and listened to message number one, then smiled at Dylan's silly message about turning forty and that Shelly couldn't wait to see her. 'It's been too long,' he added.

The second message was from Moira Blake, struggling to speak without becoming breathless, to check that Jessie was still coming for dinner on Sunday. Of course Jessie was coming for dinner. There weren't many dinners left for them. Jessie swept from room to room, checking every window was closed and bolted, just in case. She opened her wardrobe and pushed aside the hangers. She tossed open the shower curtain.

She drained the remnants from the bottle of Chardonnay into her glass and peered down at the lights of Perth, glowing as far as the eye could see. With a population of fifty thousand, she had no evidence to believe he was one of them. It was just her gut. In many ways Jessie had chosen the location of her flat in the same way Rob Taylor had. It was close enough, yet far enough away from the chaos of life. A place from where she could observe the world without getting involved. Smokey purred and wriggled himself close to her again.

'I haven't forgotten you, wee man,' she said as she pulled his biscuits from the cupboard.

With his face in his dish, Jessie could escape Smokey's attentions for a bit. Not that she complained, not really. She would be lost without him. She kicked off her boots and flopped onto the sofa. It had been a long day. Her ambition to rise to the rank of Detective Inspector was realistic, and with it came the long days and sleepless nights, but Jessie didn't mind.

Her first case as lead detective would never leave her, though. The sadness and pain of Shannon Ross's death oozed through every fibre of Inverlochty, and it would take a lifetime for the small Highland Perthshire community to come to terms with their loss, more accustomed as they were to welcoming tourists than the police. Not to mention the discovery that a convicted killer was living in their midst. She wondered if she would live her life differently if she didn't know Dan had been released. But she did know, and had to live her life accordingly.

Louise tucked the flowers under her arm and tightened her coat around her chin against the biting December chill, small flakes of snow tumbling around her. The unexpected blast of icy wind caused her to grasp her hat and yank it further down over her ears. She wiped the drips from her nose with the back of a glove and pushed open the huge steel gates of the churchyard. Reverend Malcolm offered a small nod before heading into the relative warmth of St Mark's. He had been so kind to Louise and Jason. His beautiful words had brought such comfort on the worst day of their lives.

Louise wiped the thin layer of powdery snow from the top of Shannon's gravestone, then kissed her fingers and placed them gently on her name. *Shannon Ross. Gone But Never Forgotten.* There were no four words in the universe that were truer. There were still some mornings that Louise lifted three mugs from the mug tree for breakfast. There were even times she'd gone as far as spooning coffee into all three before realising she'd done it. Setting the table for all four of them, too. Four of them. Louise hadn't just lost a daughter. She'd lost a brother.

Ben's name was never mentioned when Louise met people in the street. They asked how she was. How was Jason doing? Some even went as far as touching her arm gently and spouting words like 'time's a great healer'. Louise was grieving not just the loss of her baby, but the loss of the baby brother she thought she knew. It wasn't the fact that Ben had killed Shannon. It was his lies, and the fact that he had allowed her to go through the torment of not knowing.

Her relationship with their mother, Shannon's grandmother, was non-existent at the moment. Her own guilt that her son could do such a horrific thing kept her away from her grieving daughter, and that hurt. But it shouldn't have come as a surprise. Their mother did have a habit of putting herself before her children's needs. If history was anything to go by, that wouldn't change any time soon.

Ben had written four letters to Louise, none of which Louise had opened yet, but she had kept them, despite finding them in the bin. Jason's exasperation that she needed to keep them was an unspoken reality in the life they still shared. His struggle to understand her reasons he discussed only with Heather, his counsellor, for now.

Louise squeezed the pink roses she didn't recognise over to push the carnations into the vase after pouring the bottle of fresh water in. She knew who the roses were from. They weren't Eric's style. His family had provided the bronze elephant statue, which he explained was a private joke between them. Shannon would understand it and find it hilarious, apparently. Andrew Foster visited regularly, Louise knew that. She'd recognised his handwriting on a card.

'Eric came by today,' Louise began as she knelt on the frozen ground. 'We've got the place ready for Christmas, the way you would have liked. He said I'm not as good at it as you, but it'll do, apparently.' Louise laughed softly and pulled a tissue from her jacket pocket to blow her cold nose. 'He's going to Germany for Christmas. It will be nice for him to see his grandma, won't it? He says she makes gingerbread stars that are legendary in the street.'

Louise touched the headstone and closed her eyes.

'Oma,' a voice chirped from behind her. 'In Germany they call her Oma.'

Louise snapped her head round to see Andrew Foster standing over her. His body cast a long shadow in the dimming light. The white snow-filled sky illuminated the space above his head, making him almost angelic in appearance.

'Andrew, I didn't see you there, sorry.' Louise sighed. 'I thought I was alone.'

Louise stood to wipe powdery snow from her jeans.

'I talk to Shannon.' Andrew nodded. 'I miss her, too. She was a good girl.'

'Thank you,' Louise whispered. 'The roses are beautiful, thanks.'

Andrew stamped his feet against the cold. 'Roses were Mum's favourite.'

Louise removed her scarf and wrapped it around his neck, then held out her hand to him.

'Come on, I'll treat you to a coffee. Warm us up a bit.'

Andrew put his hand in hers as they walked through the churchyard and out towards Maria's cafe.

CHAPTER SEVENTY-SIX

Everything inside Dan Holland screamed that this was a bad idea, but he was compelled by an inner voice that would not let it go. He wondered if Jessie found Perth boring compared to the hustle and bustle of south London. His probation officer had explained that Dan had to stay away from her, but he couldn't leave things like this. They were married for just shy of ten years. That had to mean something. Yes, he'd made mistakes, but didn't everyone mess up sometimes? If he could just get Jessie to listen, she might understand how sorry he was. How much he was hurting. How the loss of his son affected him, too.

He watched the light blink off from his hiding place behind an overgrown beech hedge, then turned to walk in the opposite direction. He pulled the collar of his leather jacket further up his neck, then slipped his leg over his bike and revved the engine before disappearing into town. An increasing flurry of snowflakes followed him under a heavy, snow-laden sky. The moon was invisible behind a cloud.

A LETTER FROM KERRY

Thank you so much for investing your time in *Heartlands* and Detective Inspector Jessie Blake. If you would like to sign up for information on further books, then please subscribe to my newsletter. Your email address will never be shared and you can unsubscribe at any time.

www.bookouture.com/kerry-watts

Jessie and this story have been living inside my head for so long now that it has become part of me. Sharing her with the world was not easy. For a long time she was locked away, protected from the big bad world, but like all parents, I had to believe I had equipped her to the best of my abilities when the time arrived to let her go and make her own way in the world.

I hope you have enjoyed this book as much I have enjoyed writing it, and have come to love Jessie and Dylan as much as I do.

If you do, I would be grateful if you could leave me a review and perhaps recommend *Heartlands* to your friends and family. Writing can be a lonely business, so it would be lovely to hear your thoughts on Facebook or Twitter.

Thanks again for your support. I look forward to hearing from you soon.

Kerry

KerryWattsAuthor

@Denmanisfab

ACKNOWLEDGEMENTS

First, my heartfelt thanks go to Bookouture, and, in particular, to Helen Jenner for her initial enthusiasm and continued belief in Detective Inspector Jessie Blake. I still pinch myself on a regular basis to check I'm not dreaming this fantastic adventure.

It goes without saying that I couldn't do all this without the love and support of my husband Mark, alongside the copious amounts of tea he willingly provides without complaint.

Hannah and Flynn's excitement for my books inspires me every day, and pushes me when it might be easier to give up. They have shown me that I am so much stronger than I think I am.

To my sister Denise, for her words of encouragement and enthusiasm for the crime genre.

I think it's important to thank those others who have been with me every step of the way, too. Encouraging me to keep writing when I wondered whether my writing was good enough. Susan Hunter, Dee Williams, Craig Gillan, Norma Ormond, Carol Broadfoot, Irene Foster, Louise Mullins and, especially, Sarah Markbride. From the bottom of my heart, thank you, all.

A massive thank you to book lovers everywhere, because without you none of this would be possible.

Finally, a huge thank you to Richard Marx, whose music has kept me company for all the hours I have spent at the keyboard, as well as the past thirty-plus years of my life.

Printed in Great Britain
by Amazon